Black V

BRIAN ANDERSON

Copyright © 2018 Brian Anderson

All rights reserved. No part of this book may be reproduced or transmitted in any form or by any electronic or mechanical means, including information storage and retrieval systems, without permission in writing from the publisher, except by reviewers, who may quote brief passages in a review.

This novel is a work of fiction imagined by the author for entertainment purposes. Any persons living or dead referenced are fictitious or used in a fictitious way.

ISBN 978-1-7753785-2-5

Published by Force Publishing
forcepublishing@gmail.com

This novel is dedicated to my wife.

Acknowledgments

This novel was made possible by the contributions of Madame Justice of the Supreme Court of British Columbia, Canada and former British Columbia Human Rights Tribunal Judge Nitya Iyer; website host and Islamic authority Dr. Bill Warner of the website politicalislam.com; radio show host, author, and Islamic authority Mr. Tom Wallace of the website FortressofFaith.com; and Islamic expert Mr. Raymond Ibraham.

PROLOGUE

JANUARY 1944
BERLIN, GERMANY

A vicious, diabolical morphine-addicted Jew-killing butcher, Tank thought. *I should just slit his throat right now.*

He paused momentarily and then let the feeling pass. Goering would be held to account in due course.

Slit headlights approached out of the dark forest as the droning of bombers was heard coming down from the Berlin sky. Tank drove the black Maybach limousine along the forest floor to the airfield, parking near the huge waiting aircraft.

Field Marshal and second-in-command of Germany Hermann Goering was roused from his slumber and pulled out through the rear door and rolled onto his feet into the cold night air. He was unsteady from a raging morphine addiction.

His trusted assistant Lieutenant Karl Tank helped steady him amidst a stream of slurred curses directed at no one in particular, as the ground crew ran toward them to help Goering walk to the aircraft. A tall, athletic man of only twenty, Tank made sure the crew had a good hold of the 300-pound, morbidly obese Goering before standing back to oversee the proceedings.

The ground crew pushed Goering up the crew ladder as far as they could, groaning with the effort.

The Horten brothers, designers of the aircraft, shivered as they stood nearby.

Wiley Horten walked over to Tank and whispered in his ear, "There are two upper hatches, one for the passenger module and another for the cockpit. They are both a little larger than the belly hatches."

Tank saw the cargo crane ten meters away, profiled in the dim distant light of the fires and thumping bomb flashes in Berlin.

Tank barked orders while the crew secured Goering into a makeshift harness.

Tank watched Goering rise over the top of the plane, with the boom positioned to allow a straight drop down through the cargo hatch. Two crewmen uncoupled Goering and secured the hatch.

The Horten brothers huddled near the pilot, Hanna Fitch, who had one leg on the lower crew access ladder, on her way up into the cockpit.

"Don't worry; if it has wings, I can fly it," she said with a cocky smile.

As Germany's finest test pilot, she was confident in her abilities. Showing off to Hitler, she had even landed and taken off in a small Stork plane inside the Berlin Stadium at the 1936 Olympics.

"Frau Fitch, please take this in the cockpit with you," said Tank, as he handed her a sealed, locked leather satchel.

She pushed it ahead of her, up into the cockpit.

"What's this? Shouldn't it be in the rear compartment?" she asked.

"Please, take it in the cockpit with you, and keep your eyes on it," he insisted, his piercing blue eyes only inches from hers.

She nodded.

"This is payment for the artwork," he explained. "Give this satchel to the Gambian dealer. You can trust him implicitly. Don't show it to Goering."

Fitch nodded, albeit puzzled, and disappeared up the ladder, closing the hatch behind her.

The ultra-secret aircraft was an Amerikabomber prototype awaiting orders for mass production, which never came. With specifications unlike any other aircraft built, it could carry a massive atomic bomb to the USA and then fly back, all while not showing up on radar screens. It could be built with mostly non-strategic wood, assembled in sections from small furniture makers all around Germany, which made its large-scale production almost invulnerable to enemy bombers.

The Maybach limousine and various support vehicles were all moved to the far end of the runway.

The engines were throttled up and reached a shrieking roar, and the chocks were removed from the wheels, freeing the aircraft to charge away.

Before the end of the runway, Fitch pulled back on the stick and felt the plane's front wheels rise from the asphalt, followed by the pair of rear wheels, and then was forced back in her seat as the black V gained altitude like an upward elevator. The bat-like profile continued climbing toward its 55,000-foot cruising altitude, heading south at a speed beyond any aircraft of the day—or for decades to come.

Karl Tank paused and then sighed with relief. He watched as the experienced ground crew efficiently removed equipment from the site and towed a gargantuan rolled boom down the airstrip, hiding the asphalt under an effective camouflage screen. Landscape features mounted on rollers were moved over the tarp to complete the deception.

The secret airfield was nested well within the perimeter fence of Goering's private property, which was over two thousand acres in size and could not be noticed even in daytime by aircraft flying directly over at anything above a one-thousand-foot altitude.

Soon after the bustle of activity, everyone dispersed.

Driving the Maybach limousine back along the forest road toward Karin Hall, Tank pondered the Allies' reaction to his surprise gift.

JANUARY 1944
RURAL SPAIN

There had been scattered remnants of the Islamic 13th Waffen Mountain Division of the SS Handschar across Europe, fleeing the scene of their mass mutiny and murder of SS officers in France.

Originally attracted to Adolf Hitler's common hatred of Jews and desire to eliminate Christianity, the Islamic regiments had lost interest in fighting as the fortunes of war turned against Germany.

The two Islamic soldiers' provisions were running low, as they hunched behind a rock on a hillside with the sun to their back. Knowing they would be shot if captured, they were going to lie hidden for the day before resuming their trek to their Middle East homeland.

They were surprised to see two American P-38 Lightnings swoop down from behind them, beginning a strafing run with their heavy machine guns.

But the intended target was thankfully not them.

They watched in shock as a black SS train came barreling around the mountain base, the tracer bullets from the P-38 streaking across the valley floor to their target, bringing destruction in their wake.

CHAPTER ONE

TODAY

CANTERBURY, ENGLAND

Constable Robby Adams was in uniform, walking home down a lane from his shift for Scotland Yard in Canterbury, England when he heard a faint whimpering.

He stopped in his tracks and rotated his head, cocking his ear to find the direction of the sound.

Finally, he looked down and saw a small, barred window at foot level.

Crouching down, he could see the dirty face of a young girl, crying, with tears streaming down her face, looking dazed.

"What's that, then—why the tears? What's the matter?" he asked.

She looked up and was momentarily quiet.

He pushed his face right down to the window, resting on one knee. He peered inside, trying to see if it was a flat of some sort.

He could hear more whimpering coming from deeper in the structure.

"What's going on in there, then?" he asked with some urgency. "Where's your mommy and daddy?" he asked, pulling back slightly to look down the alley in both directions and up and down the building.

He spotted an ancient, unused door partly blocked by a broken down staircase.

"This is Adams, number 3342. I am on Diggin's Alley, just off the square. I am requesting immediate backup. I am entering a red doorway off the west side of the alley," he spoke into his radio.

He hung up the microphone onto his belt and looked down.

"What's your name?" he whispered, not wanting to frighten her further.

She stayed silent.

"You stay right there, sweetheart, okay? I will be there in a minute or two."

He walked over to the doorway and after repeatedly booting it with all his strength, it gave, the rotted frame tearing away.

He pried it open and entered. The air was dank and cold.

Making his way back toward the girl, he paused and could hear the whimpering more clearly.

He rounded a bend and peered into the dim light, seeing the little girl thirty feet away, perched upon the window, unmoving.

He reached down and picked her up, noticing that her pants were covered in dried blood. She couldn't have been much more than nine years old.

He carried her outside.

Four Bobbies walked toward him, looking concerned.

"What's this about?" one of them asked.

"Take her. Call an ambulance, a counselor, a family unit, and the major crimes unit," he said, passing her over.

"Come with me," he said to the other three.

They walked back into the doorway and followed the cries. Entering a room, they were shocked at the sight.

Ten children, young girls, were in various stages of undress and tied with ropes or chains to beds.

A loud shout was heard, a foreign tongue. Two dark-skinned men stood up from among the tangle of mattresses and sheets, half naked.

"Easy, white meat!" one of them shouted with a heavy accent, laughing, as they bolted out a back door and disappeared.

"Help us, help us," came the cry of a little girl, who was sitting on a filthy blood-stained mattress with take-out food wrappers scattered about.

The police officers stood, mouths open at the sight.

They had come across an Islamic grooming, rape, and prostitute operation for young girls.

Soon, there were ambulances and police and the area was cordoned off. The children were taken to hospital where some required reconstructive surgery after weeks of daily gang rapes.

Three committed suicide by jumping out the hospital windows. None would ever be the same; they were like walking corpses.

Constable Adams was debriefed and did not hear anything for weeks. Nothing was heard from any news source. It was as if it had never happened.

Adams began his own informal investigation and was shocked to learn he was probably the only police employee who had not known about it.

Hundreds of British girls were being manipulated, threatened, and tricked into drug addiction and then held captive for months while being raped by up to forty men a day. It had been going on for years. Over eighty percent of the groomers and rapists were Islamic.

The families' pleas were suppressed and not acted upon by police, politicians, or media. Apparently the same thing was going on all over Europe.

Adams had a fourteen-year-old niece. He started drinking heavily as he grappled with the shocking information.

Months later, at a black tie dinner in London honoring fallen police officers, he approached a man at the head of a table.

"Home Secretary Jack Traitor, Constable Robby Adams," he said, thrusting out his hand.

"Hello, Constable," came the hesitant reply from the Member of Parliament.

A security service man stood by.

"You must have seen my report by now," said Adams, the din of the social occasion fading away.

"I have."

"And are you aware that these grooming rape gangs are operating all over England and have been for years?" asked Adams, his anger starting to show.

He continued, his voice growing louder with each utterance, "There are thousands of victims a year, with over four hundred complaints a day. Why is this not in the news? Where are the court trials of the criminals? I have spoken to dozens of family members. This is a bloody conspiracy of silence!"

Adams was grabbed by the security man, and two more appeared out of nowhere.

He was being dragged away from the Home Secretary.

He broke free and rushed Traitor, grabbing him by his shirt.

"Why aren't you doing anything?" Adams asked in a desperate half-whisper, a tear leaving his eye.

"It's not so simple as that, Adams," replied Traitor, looking around as if checking that no others were listening.

"Remember, raping of non-Islamists is part of their religion, isn't it? We've already let them have their Sharia Law, haven't we? Do you know that over one hundred of our members have received death threats on this issue? And five politicians, including myself. I suppose the media has received threats as well."

"But then there isn't any law, sir, there's no law. What about the children?"

Traitor paused, looking into the distance.

The three security men had a firm grip on Adams.

Nearby, several of the guests had noticed the confrontation and were watching. Even the music had stopped, drawing more attention to the disturbance.

"It's too late, Adams. England is almost gone, and the EU is worse. They have us."

He glanced into Adam's eyes. "Our spies tell us they are expanding into the USA. Hopefully our American cousins won't be so…polite with the Islamic menace. Hopefully they can save the West again."

Traitor stood up and walked out of the room, his security detail trailing behind.

The musicians began playing again, and the hum of conversation resumed.

Adams sat down, stone-faced, ignored, staring into the distance.

CHAPTER TWO

Judge Epp sat at the front of an ad hoc meeting of about two hundred hastily convened between state prosecutors, senior government legal officials, and various lawyer's associations.

An impeccably dressed, heavyset man in his late sixties, he was presiding over a group of very frustrated and angry lawyers.

After he gave a short introductory spiel, a hand went up from a lawyer near the back of the large room, one of the meeting rooms in a luxury hotel in Washington, DC.

"Go ahead, sir."

"I have three Muslim clients—women—whose husbands won't let them leave the house, saying that it's the new law in the US. Their cases were brought to me by concerned friends or relatives," said the state prosecutor.

"When the defense started the rebuttal in court, a guy—I have no idea who he was—walked up to the judge and dropped some papers in front of him. The judge glanced at them, sat expressionless for a few minutes, and then called a recess. I heard shouts and screams coming from the chambers. He walked back in, sat down, and said that apparently forcible confinement in this case was not a crime. The court clerk passed out papers supposedly proving it—dozens of laws photocopied right from the government websites. He was right. We protested and created a fuss, as you would expect, and were escorted out of the courtroom," said the lawyer.

A chorus erupted as lawyers shouted out their own similar stories.

Epp rose to speak. "Okay, quiet please, quiet," he said into the microphone.

A quiet descended across the room.

"I can't explain it. And neither can anybody else I have talked to at the federal and state level. They don't even return calls. Meetings like this one are taking place across our land," he said with a shrug.

"The country's thousands of laws and regulations are rife with subtle wording changes that are having dramatic effects. For all intents and purposes, the courts have ceased to function in any normal way. And these unknown advisers dutifully passing out references to the changes—right in the middle of trials—are another mystery. I have no idea where they come from."

"What about all these advertisements? 'New Laws for New Times,'" came a shout from the front.

"It could be just a political party trying to capitalize on all these bizarre deaths and accidents. We've got every law professor, law student, and lawyer we can hire researching this. These laws were passed years ago, probably unnoticed by dumb or nefarious politicians as to their exact effect due to excessive legalese."

"Who and what is behind these changes? What lobby group would have any interest in changing so many fundamental laws?" The question came from a well-dressed lawyer, among the most respected in her field.

"That, my dear, is the question of the age."

The room exploded into chaos, with dozens of questions being shouted.

Epp scanned the room. He was aware of a report undertaken by a legal association documenting that there had been dozens of people, perhaps more, resisting these changes over the years, who had died under mysterious circumstances or simply disappeared.

All this was too much for his stage in life; he missed his grandkids.

They would have to hold more meetings to get to the bottom of this. The thought alone was daunting.

BLACK V

When he accepted the association's chair position, he expected it would comprise of little more than having cocktails every few months at a feel-good meeting of old pals.

He rose wearily to his feet, without anybody noticing or caring. His blood sugar felt out of balance.

He walked to the back of the room and disappeared through an exit onto the parking lot.

Seeing his parked car in the distance, he began walking toward it.

Hearing the shriek of tires, the judge glanced up just as a car jumped onto the sidewalk and struck him.

As he lay bleeding on the ground, his glazed eyes looked up at two young, dark-skinned men.

They had stopped their car and walked over to stand above him and were laughing, as the judge lay dying.

"Allah Akbar!" they both shouted in unison, as they ran back to their car and sped away.

CHAPTER THREE

Another innocent…

On a sunny spring day in North Carolina, a small red car was winding its way toward the town university's campus buildings. The driver, Chad Oster, was scanning the sports field for one cheerleader in particular, but he couldn't pick her out today.

Chad was the tall, clean-cut only child of an important Senator. Scarred by the death of his mother years earlier, he was soft-spoken and good-natured, honest to a fault, and had never caused his dad a whit of trouble.

The cell phone rang.

"Hey, what's up?" said Chad, holding the phone to his ear with his chin and keeping both hands on the wheel.

"Buddy, I'm lookin' and I'm lovin' the view," his friend Calvin, a sciences geek, joked.

Chad was aggravated. "Okay, what is it?"

"Buddy, relax. No guys are with her. At least, not now," said Calvin, grinning on the other end of the phone.

"I'm at the cafeteria," he continued. "She's sitting by herself, reading a book."

Chad suddenly felt tense. This was Jennifer Gill, his first serious love interest. "Wait there, I'm coming over."

The tires protested as he careened into the parking lot. He abandoned the car and ran toward the cafeteria, combing his hands through his hair.

He pushed open the double doors.

Spotting Calvin, he strolled over, sat across the table, and asked, "Where is she?"

Laughing, Calvin said, "Sorry, she walked out just after I called you. Guess she had things to do, or maybe she left because she knew you were coming," he teased, relishing his friend's discomfort.

Chad tried not to show his disappointment.

Both had no more classes for the day, and Calvin, seeing the tension in his friend's face, suggested they go for a cold beer at the campus pub.

They entered through large wooden doors with brass handles and surveyed the oversized varnished tables and cheap plastic and steel chairs.

Calvin walked over to the counter and ordered two beers.

Chad lifted his pint, nodded a thanks to Calvin, and drank the entire contents, feeling the pleasant effect of the alcohol.

After a pause, his eyebrows furrowed and his eyes winced. He asked, "Calvin, have you ever tried coke before?"

"What?" Calvin was shocked.

"What's it like?" asked Chad nervously, knowing Calvin was sort of a searching genius type.

"Your heart races, you talk too much," he replied. He was surprised to have his clean-living childhood friend ask him about drugs.

"Look, I want to try some; I'm really stressed," said Chad, persisting.

"Don't be crazy."

"Just a bit, a one-time deal."

"That's what they all say…"

"Come on, they used to put it in Coke; how bad can it be? Just a little, maybe fifty bucks' worth," pleaded Chad.

Calvin paused and turned away in frustration. Thinking, he decided to strike a bargain.

"Okay. One time only. And you didn't get it through me, remember? I'll call you later, I gotta go."

Calvin got up and walked away.

Oh well, he thought. *This would be the first and last time.*

Chad was watching TV; a news program was featuring a story about recent so-called "mysterious disasters," a rash of things gone wrong— shootings, car, boat, and plane crashes— all without explanation.

His cell phone rang.

"Hey," he answered.

"It's me," said Calvin. "I got some. I don't want to come to the front door…"

Two hours later, Chad heard the expected tap on the downstairs window and opened it.

Calvin held up the small bag, while grabbing the fifty from Chad's hand.

"That's it?"

"That's it," confirmed Calvin. "I know, hardly anything there, and it's brownish. The guy said it's some kind of new special stuff. I have a quiz tomorrow, I gotta go." He disappeared.

Chad pondered the tiny bag spot of powder.

He leaned over and clumsily inhaled a bit from a rolled bill from his wallet, just like he had seen in the movies.

He fumbled through his Day-Timer. There it was, Jennifer Gill. Her parents were very respectable, her father being a Judge.

With a calm confidence, he dialed the number on his cell phone and waited with sweaty palms while it rang.

"Hello," said the voice on the other end.

It's Jennifer, he thought.

Her smooth, feminine voice was unmistakable.

"Hi, Jennifer?" asked Chad.

He was still calm. The conversation would go well, he was sure. He would ask her out to a movie—nothing too heavy, as it would be their first date.

"Who is this?" the soft voice asked.

"It's Chad Oster," said Chad. "I was wondering if you would like to see a movie sometime?"

Chad waited. He became more uncomfortable as the seconds went by.

There was no reply.

She had hung up, he was sure. She probably had many guys calling her and had a policy of hanging up when it was a nobody like him.

He looked down and saw that the phone was blank. A dead cell phone battery.

Perfect timing.

He would charge his battery and call her in thirty minutes or so, as it was still early.

His mind racing, he slowly walked over to his favorite chair. He reached over and grabbed a root beer. He realized that he had accomplished more with Jennifer in the two minutes after taking cocaine than in the previous six months.

But the high was starting to decline.

This is unreal, Chad thought to himself. He noticed that the urge for more was not just an urge for the artificial pleasure, but was more like a direct screaming drive, penetrating deeply into his brain, bypassing his attempts to turn it off mentally.

Surely cocaine isn't this addictive, is it? he asked himself.

Panicking, he ran upstairs to the landline to call Calvin.

"Calvin?"

"Chad, I'm studying for the quiz."

"Where did you get this stuff? It's driving me crazy."

"What, the coke? What are you talking about?" asked Calvin.

"I need to get some more, like, right now," pleaded Chad.

"Are you kidding?" said a shocked Calvin.

Sensing his friend was not joking, he changed his tone. "When they say it's addictive, they don't mean like that. Look, if you need more after that little bit, you should never, ever touch any again."

"I need some now. It feels like I'm going to die. Come on, man. Get me some, get me some, do you hear me?"

Chad felt himself coming unwound, and the screaming was heard by his father.

"Chad, is that you, son, what's wrong?" his father called from upstairs, worried, as he turned on the hall light, illuminating the area around the phone on the floor below.

Chad could only hear a distant voice and was in no state for conversation. His entire internal circulation system was aflame with the urgent need for more cocaine, and it felt like he would explode.

"Chad, are you there?" asked Calvin. "Look, man, you should come over here. My old man's got some strong tranquilizers that should help."

Chad couldn't reply. He dropped the phone.

"Chad, where are you going?" called his father, the Senator Frank Oster, a tall, courtly southern gentleman with thick silver hair, blue eyes, and a perpetual suit, as he heard Chad fumbling to open the large front door.

He ran out of the house in his bare feet and started running down the street, wearing only light track pants and a t-shirt on a cold winter night.

His father ran to the front door after him, calling his name, confused at his son's out-of-character behavior.

He walked over to the phone, picked it up, and called the family doctor, a wise and trusted friend for the last thirty years.

"Henry." It was like he did not have the energy for even the slightest social nicety.

"Hi, Frank, how you been?" answered Dr. Henry Jones.

The Senator was almost numb with worry for his only child and skipped any pleasantries.

"Chad ran out of the house and down the street like a maniac. I didn't know who else to call."

"When did this happen?" asked Jones.

"About five minutes ago. He was on the phone and sounded very desperate. He was asking to get some more—it sounded like he wanted drugs."

Dr. Jones' mind instantaneously ran through several scenarios that could explain Chad's conduct. A high-IQ genius who had chosen a small-town career, he had developed an almost sixth sense over the years, able to seemingly deduce things from thin air.

Another long-time patient of his, fifty-five years old and overweight, had been heard by his wife, begging for more "stuff" to somebody on the other end of the phone. After he hung up, she had asked him what the call was about. The husband said nothing, but had walked outside with no jacket or shoes, got into the family car, and simply disappeared.

Two days later, he was found, having driven the car over a ravine into somebody's backyard. The coroner had said it was a heart attack that caused the death, since there was a coronary occlusion and the stock blood tests showed he did not have alcohol in his blood.

That diagnosis had been too easy, Dr. Jones had thought, and ignored the bizarre circumstances described by the wife.

Dr. Jones, thinking that it was a million to one chance that two people would leave their house under similarly bizarre circumstances within three days, tensed himself.

"Look, Frank, call an ambulance and the police. Tell them he is having an emotional episode and is not dangerous, but that he needs help," Henry said, using his years of wisdom on such matters.

If the police heard anything about drugs, they would assume a situation with possible violence and might rough Chad up unnecessarily.

"One last thing, Frank," said the Doctor.

"What?" asked the Senator.

"Pray," was the Doctor's last remark.

CHAPTER FOUR

Young and innocent, Chad Oster was running barefoot, frantically, with only a t-shirt and track pants. It was a cold winter night, wet and dark, and after running for fifteen minutes, his feet were bleeding, but he didn't notice and kept on running as fast as he ever had in his life.

Across the small town, through parking lots, not hearing the honking cars or astonished townsfolk, who thought it odd that a clean, respectable-looking boy would be running without regard for anything, with such a look of desperation.

As he ran across a 7-Eleven parking lot, a group of friends called out to him.

"Hey, Chad, what's up?" said a buddy he had known since his elementary school days.

"Chad, where you going, where's the fire?" the old friend persisted.

No reply came. Chad didn't even look in their direction; their voices didn't register in his brain.

Chad Oster ran blindly through the parking lot like an Olympic sprinter and disappeared down the street without saying a word.

Desperately, he scrambled over the top of the railroad embankment and ran along the tracks, easily matching the ties like he did as a boy.

Running across the trestle, the canyon floor was far below, and he couldn't hear the rush of the river, only the distant whistle, which was louder now. Chad was staring down at the ties and didn't notice that the train's light was shining from behind him against the mountain at the other side of the canyon in front of him, illuminating the aged steel bridge supports that arched high over his head.

Feeling the imminent rumble of the heavy train on the trestle, and for an instant braced with a sudden fear of the unknown, Chad called out, "Momma!" and briefly turned his head to see the oncoming bright light, as he was violently struck by the cow catcher of the freight train, which deflected him up ten feet across the locomotive engine's front window, then into the air, flailed against the steel bridge lattice like a rag doll, falling in silence to the rocks below.

His death kicked off a series of important events…

CHAPTER FIVE

Senator Frank Oster was crushed when two days after Chad had left the house running, the authorities found his son's dead body under the train trestle.

Soon Calvin's story about the cocaine was known.

However, blood tests confirmed that while there was an extremely minute amount of a substance in Chad's blood, it was unlike any type of cocaine known or classified.

He picked up the phone and dialed.

"Henry," the Senator said.

"Hi, Frank. Look, I just want to say again that I am so sorry," said a respectful Dr. Henry Jones.

"I know. My only child… I guess it hasn't fully hit me yet," said the Senator, lying, as tears streamed down his cheeks. "What was it you were saying about the toxicology report yesterday?"

"Frank, I wanted you to know that your son was an innocent," Jones started. "His friend Calvin says he tried only a tiny amount, and our reports confirm that. We are assuming it was a substance like cocaine, although the test does not actually confirm it. Normally, it was hardly enough to feel any effect. "

"So, why is my son dead?" asked the Senator solemnly.

"That's what we are trying to find out," said Henry. "I'm not a toxicologist. But I have been involved with a few cases in the past, where blood test investigations were involved. Apparently, the computer profiles tell us that the drug traces were unlike any tested before anywhere in the USA, until two weeks ago when similar cases started appearing. The lab experts are asking around the world and should know more soon."

"I don't get it," said the Senator. "What are you saying?"

"I don't exactly get it myself. Based on what we know so far, your son was sold a substance that only *looks* like cocaine but has never been classified. This could be a big deal. I'll call you when I know more," the Doctor told his grieving friend, before hanging up the phone.

CHAPTER SIX

The phone rang.

"Hello," said the Senator, picking up the handset.

"Henry here. How you holding up?" asked Dr. Jones.

"It's tough, Henry... real tough," he said, holding back tears.

"I know it is," empathized Dr. Jones, but he pressed on with the purpose of the phone call.

"The final results on Chad's blood have finally come back, and I thought you would like to know. There was no explanation for the compound in normally accessed medical records, so we cross-referenced the symptoms with only recently computerized federal archive data files accessed when all else fails, which gave us about seventy-five percent of the most likely chemical components in the mystery compound in Chad's blood," said the Doctor.

"What did you find out?" asked the Senator.

After decades in politics, he hadn't a hint of cynicism and only wanted to help each citizen whose problem he came across.

"Your boy didn't take his own life, and he wasn't so careless as to not know he never should have been walking on a busy train trestle. It's important you understand: Chad did nothing wrong beyond a little experimenting. In fact, because he took such a small amount of what he thought was cocaine—less than Coke used to spike their product with or doctors like me used to prescribe in so-called elixirs—it was very safe for him, and there was virtually no chance of any harm," said the Doctor as some kind of assurance.

Continuing, he explained, "But what he inhaled only looked like cocaine, as I said during our last call. In fact, it was a potent neuro-addictive toxin that has never been documented before."

"I am not sure I understand what you are saying," said the Senator.

"I am saying that anybody taking the small amount of cocaine that Chad did would get a slight sensation, but beyond that, would have their full capacities. In other words, Chad could simply not be 'out of his mind on drugs.' If in fact he had taken normal cocaine, the type that has been floating around the USA for the last hundred years, he would have never left your house the night he died," Dr. Jones explained.

"I am starting to get the picture but, Henry, if it's never been documented before, how do we even know what it is?" asked the Senator.

"We only know what it is because the computer searched data entered from notes taken from the Nazi's Albert Speer after the defeat of Hitler's Germany, which I was allowed privileged access to amongst the information in the government's special archives bunker, where the director of archives said he knows you very well."

The Doctor was referring to the nebbishly spectacled semi-recluse who ran the archives and appeared to live there, judging from his pale appearance.

"The Nazi chemists realized that, to stay working when the only programs that received money were those considered weaponized for the war effort, they had to 'modify' their research direction, and they came up with a great scheme. They isolated the addictive compound in cocaine and developed a way to manufacture that compound in a special process. By doing so, they claimed it was a weapons system, since they could infect the food and drinking supply of the Allies or even use it to create suicide soldiers of their own, who had no sense of risk to themselves," said the Doctor.

"Speer thought it was a great idea that could change the course of the war. He approved the budget, and the scientists refined the plans and tested them with a small-scale prototype factory, although after that, little is known. As with many things in the months prior to and after Hitler's suicide and the war's end, the country was in chaos, and the trail goes cold.

"The actual isolating and manufacturing formulas and processes were never found, and it's believed that the chemists involved were all killed while on a train. All the notes were thought destroyed. We can only confirm it is the same material from the notes Speer provided about the antics of the patients who tried the stuff."

"How do you know all this?" asked the Senator.

"The Head of Archives in Washington has been on the job for forty years. I guess he's a history buff, which would make sense given his career choice," responded the Doctor.

Dr. Jones continued, "Your son never made any mistake in judgment. He was murdered the same as if a person shot him with a gun. Whoever supplied that so-called cocaine is a murderer. But it's a real mystery… Who would have access to a WWII formula for a substance that Speer and others confirmed was lost for all time?"

CHAPTER SEVEN

Muhammed Assad, clean-cut, local born, and twenty-nine, sat on his yacht looking back toward the Los Angeles harbor and city beyond and the various multi-colored emergency lights along the shore highway.

It was as if the entire visible land area was one big emergency. Small plumes of smoke rose upward from across the city. Nearby, four jet skiers were racing crazed across the harbor, a police boat in hot pursuit. To the west, he saw a cruise ship, apparently at full speed, with a Coast Guard helicopter hovering over it and what looked like a crewman hanging from a cable in an attempt to board the vessel.

He looked at his laptop and scratched his head at the hundreds of emergencies being reported across the country and the explosion of small-time criminal activity robberies, assaults, and others.

Stranger still, hundreds of thousands of woman across the country were suddenly wearing full, body-covering, black Islamic dress, including the niqab feature—a slit opening for the eyes—appearing ominously like an alien invasion.

Owner of the largest advertising agency in the United States, he was pondering the recent years of business success.

Initially contacted by a mysterious businessman to undertake a small ad campaign that was arranged through emails and text messages, he now funneled billions of dollars from hundreds of firms into thousands of advertising contracts. He probably ran the world's biggest advertising and PR company.

The entire country was saturated with ads for judges, for politicians, and for particular political motions or amendments at the county, state, or federal level to satisfy his client, whom he had never met. Occasionally, checks and money orders were from the same account, although supposedly from different customers, which had always puzzled him.

He directly or indirectly employed thousands of people to develop the ads, using the latest focus groups and presentation techniques. The ads themselves were placed on billboards, computers, handheld electronic devices of all kinds, radio, TV, and all newspapers and magazines.

Last, the PR campaign had many times evolved into straight donations, horse trading, and outright bribes. He had realized early on that his clients were very determined to achieve whatever particular goal they had in mind.

In the last few months, they had just completed another phase of the ads that, strangely, were now all focused on the same thing. Those ads were now being featured across the land.

But one thing puzzled him.

The new ads, themed on the topic of "New Laws for New Times" and developed months ago, appeared to have predicted the very chaos flashing across the shoreline and his laptop.

They contrasted chaos and the fictional collapse of a lawful society with happy people living with a new and unknown legal system, always in peaceful settings. In the background of the ad were projected crime rates, which showed the fictional reductions under the proposed new legal system.

His clients had spent millions of dollars on ads, apparently, based on a prediction of the current collapse.

How could they have known?

The notion coming to his mind was so big, he could hardly contain it. He was trying to mentally organize the years of contracts, the topics of the various contracts, and what it all meant.

He was a billionaire now—but that mattered little if there was no USA to live in.

A dark and ominous feeling came across him as he realized he was the world's largest pawn.

BRIAN ANDERSON

CHAPTER EIGHT

"Senator, there's a call for you," his secretary, a pert brunette, announced.

"Frank here," answered the Senator.

"Frank. This is Vice President Smith. I am very sorry about your son; please accept my sympathies and those of the President. I am sorry to say, I have to ask you to come up to Washington."

"Of course, Mr. Vice President. Can I ask you what this is all about?"

"Sorry. I can't tell you anything at this point. Your Executive Assistant will supply you with the information you need," continued the Vice President.

"When do I have to be ready by?" asked the Senator.

"You are to leave immediately. The car should be pulling up right now. I will fill you in when you arrive. Have a good flight."

The Senator picked up the instructions for his trip, his briefcase, and an overnight bag while walking past his assistant and continued out to the waiting limousine, stepping in through the open back door.

The driver ran around to get in and sped off at full speed to the waiting government Lear Jet at the small regional airport, almost getting into two collisions on the way.

The Senator was hardly in his seat—the only passenger—when the jet roared down the runway like a fighter jet and accelerated to top speed in the direction of Washington, DC, where he heard the pilot cursing at the pilot of another off-course aircraft en route.

CHAPTER NINE

The flight landed at a secret government airfield on the outskirts of Washington, and after getting in another limousine, they drove rapidly along an off-limits country lane, finally arriving at a hidden garage entrance at the back of an underground bunker located under an old country inn.

Walking from the elevator, he was greeted by Vice President Smith, a gray-haired man considered by many to be the spitting image of Harry Truman.

"Sorry again about your son," said the Vice President while shaking the Senator's hand firmly.

"And sorry for all this cloak and dagger stuff," he continued. "When we have information coming in like we will tell you about shortly, we really have no choice. National Security rules and all that stuff."

They arrived at a juncture, where they turned left, and continued walking until coming to a door where, on the other side, were gathered ten of the most important United States political figures, all looking uncomfortable and without the flash of their trademark television-friendly smiles.

They were the important players that made the USA function at a much deeper level than the retail politics in the media. They ran the subcommittees and were the inevitable "go to" people of the United States government.

They were seated in black executive-style chairs in a large rectangular room, with various screens and projectors at one end and a large boardroom table, which had a simple imitation-wood finish.

There was a grimness that permeated the air, as if the meeting was a funeral wake. It reminded the Senator of the mood on the aircraft carriers during his military service, when they reviewed the loss of their flying comrades.

They all sat down.

"Gentleman, I give you the National Security Advisor," said Vice President Smith.

The National Security Advisor, Ian Taggert, stood to the side, his good reputation giving some comfort to the small audience.

A determined-looking man of medium height with gray hair visible at the temples, he began to talk.

"We are here today to agree on a course of action to save this country from descending into chaos. An unknown enemy is randomly injecting a difficult-to-trace compound into recreational cocaine, marijuana, and the food and drinking supplies of this country. It causes a violent withdrawal, which causes people to become so desperate for more of it that they lose their ability to function. We are working to fully understand the scope of this attack, as we have seen many misreported cases classified as drug overdoses, insanity, or other illnesses. It seems to be confirmed that a terrorist cell has developed a way to attack us from within, and if we don't take action, our entire society will—for lack of a better word—start to implode within days or even hours.

"The President has authorized the utilization of all available means to stop this threat," he continued. "However, the real problem is that another massive shipment of this stuff is apparently on its way from South America, and there is little we can do to stop it, since we have few assets in that region or partners willing and able to help us."

The Senator sat silently.

There was not a peep in the room. After a long pause, somebody spoke up.

"What about UNSB?" the short, ferocious-looking Military Chief of Staff Jack Ferret offered, referring to the United Nations Special Branch.

"UNSB is a myth; it doesn't exist. There has never been any confirmation of these conspiracy theories," Vice President Smith said abruptly.

The room was silent.

Senator Frank Oster had been watching quietly from the last seat near the door.

He spoke up, "I agree with the Chief. We need this to be done in hours or days, not months or years. The first shipment was probably just a trial. The next shipment could be a thousand times the size. I have heard about UNSB over the years, and I am not sure myself if they exist. But if there is any way we can get a message to them to help us, this is the time. Based on Mr. Ferret's comments, I think we can all agree that this is a problem outside the scope of our normal military, police, or civilian agencies to tackle quickly enough, despite what I am sure will be their best efforts."

The conversation moved back and forth.

Most present had heard of the unfolding disaster firsthand from their own districts. Cars crashing, people drowning, aircrafts in distress. The news was coming in at a higher frequency, and the media hadn't caught on to the fact that there was a pattern but government experts certainly had.

The group discussed the wording of the orders to the government agencies.

Most importantly, they decreed that there would be no public confirmation of the existence of the neurotoxins, since there was no defense to the introduction through food and water supplies. To avoid mass hysteria, if and when the media caught on, the public position would be that the government was "continuing to investigate," and they hoped this would buy them enough time to solve the problem.

Two hours later, Vice President Smith spoke out abruptly, quietening the room, "Okay, gentleman and ladies, we will meet again when we have information to report."

"God bless us all, and God bless the United States of America," Smith ended solemnly.

With that, they all left the bunker and joined up with their assistants to prepare lists of emergency agencies, and all agencies—whether federal, state, or country—urgently undertook all that they could to stop the spreading epidemic.

But it wouldn't be that easy.

CHAPTER TEN

Traveling across the capital with a police escort and through traffic lights that automatically turned green, Vice President Smith's car nonetheless almost crashed four times as other out-of-control cars careened over the road but eventually they arrived at the White House executive remote parking bunker, and he boarded the special underground monorail space train designed by NASA, to be whisked underneath the White House.

President Vance Virtue strode into the Situation Room. A tall man who walked erect as a flagpole, his sharp eyes and boundless energy belied his ninety years.

"Nice to see you, Joe," said the President, as he reached across the desk to shake the Vice President's hand. "How did the meeting go?"

"Well, we have everybody on board, and I think they are all getting reports from their constituencies confirming the urgency. Each of them will be doing all they can, I am sure."

"I know you are sworn to secrecy," he said, "but I simply can't approve this request for assistance without knowing the full story, or at least what you know."

Smith started, "Okay. I don't know much, but here it is. First, UNSB, or the United Nations Special Branch, is not their name; it's a name the media has made up, and these people are not connected to the UN in any way. No funding, no authorization."

"How do we know that?" asked the President.

"Because," said Smith, "there have been numerous investigations by the UN, and there has never been a trace of information found to connect it with the UN."

"They must be based somewhere…"

"Of course, but most developed countries have investigated independently and have never found a trace. No ex-staff, no money trail, no facilities, nothing," answered Smith.

"So what *do* we know?"

"I know nothing for sure, only what I have learned informally. They are thought to be real and to have intervened and averted problems for other countries. I have picked up what I know from different sources, informally, during my official duties, whether when traveling to other countries or when those dignitaries are in Washington. Over the years, I have heard about them from several sources, more than one time each in some cases," Smith said.

"Who pays them?"

"Nobody we can confirm. We think they are actually funded by rich, charitable citizens but have never been able to trace anything."

"Who runs it today?"

"Nobody I have ever spoken to has any idea," Smith replied.

Virtue sat silently, trying to process what he had heard.

After a few minutes, he could only muster, "Thank God they are on our side," and he walked out the door, where his handlers whisked him away to the Oval Office.

CHAPTER ELEVEN

Vice President Smith walked away from the subterranean meeting and crawled into his limousine. From a recessed compartment, he pulled out a black briefcase and opened it to press a large red button.

The phone rang.

"You called?" asked a muffled metallic voice.

"I don't know if you people know what is going on, but we have a big problem," said the Vice President.

"We know about the situation and have been waiting for your call," said the disguised voice. "Am I to consider this an official request for assistance?" the voice asked.

"Anything that you need, we have or will get for you. Report to me each day on this line," continued Smith.

"We don't report to anybody. You will be advised when we think it's necessary," the voice said, and then the line went dead.

CHAPTER TWELVE

"Hey!" yelled twenty-year-old biology professor and anonymous former Delta Force commando Kurt Tank into the mic. "Are you sleeping, or flying a plane?"

He released the button and waited for a reply.

He tried again. "Noddins, are you there?"

Again, after releasing the transmit button, no reply was heard.

Just as he was about to walk out of the field tent, he heard the crackly reply.

"Kurt, sorry, what's up?" came the reply from Will Noddins, the pudgy, bespectacled drone pilot, who was ten kilometers away at the base station located in a remote corner of the airport in Manaus, Brazil, deep in the Amazon Basin.

Stretching the radio transmitter cord, he leaned out of the tent and peered across the top of the jungle canopy where in the distance he saw the drone flying erratically.

"Noddins, it's happening again; can you reboot?" Tank yelled through the microphone.

"What's the problem?" came the crackly reply.

Tank pressed the transmit button. "Same as the other times," he yelled. "It's staying in the air all right, but the patterns have decayed—it's unstable. Sometimes it crosses over into the same path from a half hour earlier. We are spending half our time trying to analyze whether this is repeat data or new."

He went on to describe the on-ground printout data records from an aircraft that was supposed to be flying in neat rows, with only slight overlaps, like mowing a lawn, but was instead flying like it was out of control.

"We are using the plane within the wind parameters we were told, forty-knot winds or less, so we shouldn't be having this problem," he continued, exasperated. "If Rockland has loaned us this drone and it doesn't work, they have wasted a lot of people's time."

The state-of-the-art drone aircraft, about half the size of a small civilian aircraft like a Beechcraft Bonanza, had no pilot and an extensive array of sensors and navigational equipment. The information was transmitted and received via satellite or direct radio transmission as conditions permitted, so that the communications were always open, whether the plane was flying behind a hill or over the horizon.

"Okay, I'll reboot it. Hopefully it'll correct."

"Okay, we're waiting," replied Tank.

Grabbing the binoculars, he leaned out and peered over the jungle canopy from his small camp, located on a rise, and saw that the drone aircraft immediately increased throttle and climbed.

Hanging up the microphone, he turned to the miniature aluminum folding table. Taking the binoculars with his right hand, he peered in a different direction now, to another small science camp in the shallow valley below, picked up a walkie-talkie with his free hand, and said while holding the transmit button with his thumb, "How does it look?"

While he waited for a response, he saw a female figure in white jungle gear walk over to pick up the walkie-talkie and look up to wave at Tank as he waved back.

"It's okay," she yelled back. "The data stream has resumed. Tell Noddins to fix it for good this time."

"Okay," yelled Tank, pressing the transmit button, "I will, over and out."

He rested the walkie-talkie down on the table and walked back into the tent, picking up the microphone from the powerful radio set.

"Noddins, it seems all right again," transmitted Tank. "It's flying normally, and the data is accurate," he said, and then after a brief pause, he continued, "Look, Will, any chance of finding out what keeps causing these problems?"

"I'll keep looking," replied Noddins. "Over and out."

Will Noddins leaned over and grabbed a creamy donut to deal with the increased stress.

Back in the field, Tank sat his six-foot 205-pound muscular body down in his folding chair and continued to peer with his royal blue eyes at the jungle below. He raked his short dark hair with his hand, pondering what could be afflicting the drone. His mind drifted as it often did, full memories—enough to last a lifetime.

His aged father, a German engineer who witnessed evil up close during World War Two, imparted Tank with values of honesty and purity that made his decision to dedicate his life to saving others easy. He also homeschooled Tank to graduate from high school at age twelve, achieve his biology doctorate by age sixteen, and enter the military, where he soon became a legend in Delta Force.

Every motivation for Tank was sourced in caring for others; that's what drove the man.

CHAPTER THIRTEEN

With the drone aircraft buzzing in the distance and the field crew with Dr. Isabella Oliveira working to analyze the resumed incoming data from the drone's sensors, Kurt Tank decided to lie down on the folding aluminum lounge chair for a catnap.

He had been up since 3 a.m. and could no longer sleep in the oppressive Amazon heat and humidity. Catnapping was a custom he had learned during a stint in Delta Force—to grab sleep in small bites, whenever possible. With the bug screen holding the gigantic mosquitos at bay, he had slept in far worse situations. With his fine, thick dark hair cut short, broad shoulders, and manly build, he was conditioned for the tropics, but the sagging webbing on the fold-up lounge chair still caused minor aches and discomfort.

He rubbed a layer of Deep Woods Off over his exposed skin, turned the Motorola walkie-talkie and field radio to the lowest setting, and lay down, quickly falling into a deep sleep, with the relaxing sounds of the jungle. If an emergency arose, they could buzz him to wake up with a special radio set alarm feature.

He arose from his ninety-minute catnap in the late morning heat of the jungle and could hear the drone in the distance, coming from Manaus Airport toward their study area, under Will Noddins' expert control.

Dark clouds had rolled in, and the air had the heaviness and increased plant fragrance released during the first hours of a low pressure system that predicted rain would soon fall.

Noddins had pulled the craft back for an inspection at the end of a sensor run when it was nearest Manaus, and now it was returning.

With a few minutes to go before the drone resumed its low altitude runs, he turned to the lunch box and pulled out a pack marked, "bacon and eggs."

He poured the dehydrated powder onto a skillet and lit the synergistic heat pack, mixing the contents with bottled water. The resulting hot meal was scooped up and disappeared within seconds into a hungry stomach.

Tank was putting the meal mess into animal-proof containers when the drone's buzzing became erratic.

He grabbed the binoculars and ran outside to see the craft rolling over in spirals and violently pulling up and descending down, about to hit the topmost jungle canopy trees.

"Noddins, what's going on?" Tank screamed into the field radio, almost pulling the radio from its stand with the microphone cord.

Watching the craft spiraling, he saw the front of the drone start to point down, as the craft nosed over into a steep dive.

"Noddins, it's going to crash!"

"The controls aren't working. The sensors are blank. The digital readouts are flashing nonsense," Noddins matched his hysterical tone. "I don't have any control."

Peering with the binoculars, Tank could see the drone drop from view into an area without trees, over a lagoon, and the sound of its motor disappeared.

"I think it's gone," Tank told Noddins.

Neither spoke for several seconds, unsure of the drone's fate.

Suddenly, he could hear the craft's motor resume a steady buzz and then rev loudly at full throttle, rising back into view, smoothly arching toward Manaus, and then climbing steeply.

After a few minutes, it disappeared from sight into the clouds, and Tank casually noticed a black Robertson 44 helicopter loitering nearby.

"Hey, it just stabilized, and now it's heading toward you," said Tank, astonished. Minutes ago, it looked lost and about to crash. "I guess you rebooted the navigation computer and have control again."

"Nope. I am not in control. These controls are still dead and the console displays are dead. I tried to reboot, but nothing happened. It has a self-contained 'limp home to base' mode on board, for emergencies, and because this time its out-of-control maneuvers were extreme, the CPU sensed I could not intercede and that an actual crash was imminent, so the failsafe system kicked in to save it. I suppose my failed efforts to regain control, the g-forces, or some other parameters are all used to trigger the limp-home mode.

"A switch in the drone turns on a 'go home' mode, operated by a separate emergency battery pack and independent computer," he continued. "That CPU has the last forty-eight hours in its separate memory and simply retraces its route back to where it started, using a simple gyro-based mechanical guidance system, the same as the old German flying buzz bombs that menaced England in World War Two."

Tank said nothing, enjoying the technical explanation.

Noddins pressed the transmit button and continued, "The limp-home system is enough to get back to the approximate location but not enough to undertake the complex landing maneuver, at least not safely. The designers thought it best for the craft to fly at maximum altitude to avoid hitting any mountains, since the navigational system's hill profile avoidance ability is also inoperative. A secondary benefit of the high altitude is that the drone utilizes a simple power cut-off and explosive-activated parachute deployment system when above the base vicinity and can lose enough altitude safely to give time for the parachutes to inflate and slow the descent."

Noddins concluded, "We better hope it lands where I can get at it, either with the Zodiac or the Hummer. It has inflatable airbags which keep it from sinking or protect it from damage if it lands on land. The sensitive internal parts are water and shock resistant and should be fine."

Tank smiled as he reviewed his knowledge of his watery jungle home of the last few months, and the thought of Noddins, an out-of-shape computer geek, swimming in the jungle river to rescue the drone.

With Manaus airport located 1500 kilometers inland and west of South America's northeast Atlantic coastline, it was hard to fathom that they were in a primarily water environment. Manaus was located on the Niger, or "Black River," upriver or east of the confluence of the Niger and Amazon rivers, which combined to become the main Amazon. At certain times of the year, the river swelled to thirty kilometers wide, and, as the world's largest river, was the combined flow of the next nine largest rivers.

Perched on a low jungle hill, Kurt Tank could hear the drone faintly as it flew into the distance on its journey home to Will Noddins, who could hopefully retrieve and repair the sick craft so that they could resume their important research activities.

The black Robertson 44 helicopter, which had been loitering nearby, had disappeared.

The walkie-talkie lying on the table crackled. "What's going on?" asked Dr. Oliveira, with an indignation that only she could master. "We barely got started, the data flow came online for only a few minutes, and now the stupid drone is heading back?"

Picking it up, Tank transmitted, "Another technical glitch. Fortunately, it will fly back to Will and hopefully be back in business for Monday." He continued, "Come on, it's Friday; let's get back to town and relax. By the way, did you see that black helicopter?"

"Didn't see any helicopter from down here," Dr. Oliveira said, uninterested

"Would rather avoid the downpour that looks to be coming. We will meet you at the trail junction, over and out."

CHAPTER FOURTEEN

Tank packed the simple collapsible alloy field station into the large backpack, taking five minutes. With the clouds having released the first heavy rains that beckoned the start of the wet season, he wiped his face and looked back to the trail, impressed at how modern technology could provide an entire base camp that could be carried in a backpack.

His mind daydreamed about the weekend ahead and his ongoing efforts to charm Dr. Oliveira.

Walking down from the small hilltop radio field station, Tank hacked the jungle vines from his path.

"It's hard to imagine all this has grown over in only five days," he muttered to himself.

He watched where he put his feet carefully, as the exposed flesh could easily be bitten by a range of poisonous ants, spiders, or snakes.

Suddenly, Tank felt a familiar buzzing sensation coming from his neck.

"What a time for this," he said, as he shook his head at the inconvenience of the demanding satellite-activated subcutaneous signal device.

He immediately took off the backpack, pulled the radio antenna out, switched the set on, tuned to a secret channel, and pressed transmit on the microphone.

"Yeah, what's up?" yelled Tank, mildly annoyed at the rain, bugs, discomfort, and now demands from far away.

"We have traced a cocaine operation to a location near you," breathed the heavy voice.

"So what? That's no emergency. There are thousands of cocaine operations in South America; what else is new?" Tank groused, as his clothes were being drenched from the tropical downpour.

The heavy voice breathed a rasping reply, "At this very moment, the USA is collapsing. A cocaine baron has been boosting his exports with a lethal neurotoxin sourced to the Amazon Basin. Last I checked, that's where you are. Your orders are to neutralize the operation. A cache of tools has been dropped for you at the Emergency Drop Zone," the voice finished, referencing the exact coordinates.

"Okay, but I am in the jungle, and I—"

The line went dead.

Arriving at the Y junction where the trail from Dr. Oliveira's field data station and his own met, Tank paused for several minutes, waiting for her to arrive, and thought about the ominous message.

After a short while, sensing they were overdue, he took off his backpack and laid it down. When he arrived at her field station, she and her assistants were gone.

Tank carefully looked over the entire site and noticed something unusual.

All over the site—on the ground, the white tent, the folding table, the blankets, the cot—there was white spit. It was as if somebody had purposely spit on everything dozens of time with a heavy, white mucous spit, which was washing away in the rains.

"I've heard of spitting ants, but this is crazy," he said to himself.

In the distance, he heard the loud crack of thunder and looked up to see more black clouds roll over top.

Puzzled, Tank carefully followed the trail of white spit to the edge of the clearing, where he saw that a branch had been recently snapped off, leading him into the jungle. Peering at the soft forest floor, he could make out footprints of several people, some in shoes and some barefoot.

BLACK V

He laid down his backpack and began to traverse the jungle at a jog, dodging low branches and slogging through thick bog, peering ahead and trying to pick up the sounds of the Doctor's abductors, from the roar of the falling rain. The heavy jungle aroma changed almost with each meter travelled, reflecting the dense plant and animal species.

The rains had washed some of the white spittle from the jungle, but the overhead plants had protected enough in these early minutes of the downpour to allow him to see enough to form a trail to follow.

After briefly losing track of the trail, Tank paused and heard a muffled cry and looked up, where through the rain and mist and leaves he could barely make out a tiny speck of white on a platform 150 feet up, near the top of the jungle canopy.

Tank took small steps, walking backward, and wiped the rain from his eyes. He peered upward to get a better view, and then, from behind, was brutally clubbed over the head with a rock, and he collapsed on the jungle floor, unconscious.

CHAPTER FIFTEEN

He woke up slowly, slightly groggy and with a throbbing coming from his head. He heard the sounds of the jungle and regained his bearings.

Kurt Tank had formulated his plan. Hanging like a pig to be roasted, with his hands tightly bound, his captors had grossly underestimated him, thinking he was a limp-wristed field researcher.

Time to move, thought Tank.

He started grunting, just loud enough so the nearest captors could hear him.

The leader looked over at Tank, and the three of them approached him. Standing over him, they started to talk their gibberish and poke him aggressively with their spears. They laughed and grunted and were spitting the disgusting white drool onto his skin, which thankfully washed off in the rain.

BLACK V

In an instant, Tank arched his muscular body and, in one huge motion, used up the slack in the ropes, which had allowed his body to sag. Like a pro gymnast, the muscle contraction pulled him up above their heads, while their astonished looks turned to looks of fear. Arching his body like a cat away from the tree, the ropes grew taut, and he swung like a pendulum from behind his captors, pulling them toward the Malato tree they faced. With his long and rock-hard muscular body, they were smashed like bowling pins against the tree and knocked out cold, falling in a heap to the ground.

Two of their spears remained upright, with bases stuck in the jungle dirt, and Tank split the rope that secured his hands in one mighty motion. He leaned over and untied his feet.

He looked around and listened, crouching behind a stone statue. The camp sounded the same, and nobody had noticed his rapid escape from bondage.

He pulled the surprisingly light bodies of his captors down one of the strange trenches and let the bodies sink into the jungle mud.

Tank started running, retracing his trail, back to his jungle field station and the nearby backpack he had left behind.

He pondered this business of a drug operation in the jungle that was to be stopped. As he ran, Tank casually thought about how it shouldn't be a problem.

Arriving at the jungle field station area, he walked along the trail and found his backpack. He carried the pack up to the top of the low hill, where the reception was best, which was why he had been based there in the first place.

A feeling in his stomach made him concerned for Noddins. He wondered if the drone had been retrieved.

Within minutes, he had the radio set up and called Giant.

"Hello, this is Tank. Repeat, this is Tank," he said into the microphone.

He released the button and listened.

Nothing.

"Tank calling. Tank calling," he said, with a note of urgency in his voice.

"Where have you been?" came the haunting voice of Giant.

"I bumped my head on something, no worries. Did you make the equipment drop?"

"Everything you need, and more, is there," said Giant. "These drug operations may be well armed, so consider it Christmas when you open the container. By the way, we arranged a special gift to help you in your task. Good luck."

The line went dead—not a surprise, since Giant had never been one for manners.

Tank quickly entered the coordinates he was given earlier in the GPS, repacked the equipment, and was soon trekking in the direction of the drop zone, hoping nothing had been damaged or stolen.

Just as he was starting to break a sweat from the breakneck pace, he came upon the site of a large camouflage parachute draped in the trees.

Tank's eyes traced the cord down along the jungle floor to find the equipment crate, which was half the size of a shipping container.

He looked into the small retinal scanner and heard the container's seal break with a hiss. He would only need a few things to rescue Dr. Oliveira and her assistants.

"So, you look a little out of shape to topple a drug operation," came a voice from behind the crate. "Where are my welcoming dancing girls?"

"They were canceled on account of these torrential rains, sorry," said Tank.

Tank knew the voice: the voice of a familiar comrade, the voice of a man who suddenly caused him to relax a little. The weight of the world was not on just his shoulders, as Tank now had a capable companion who would increase his success rate immeasurably.

Manuel Bull was a huge round man, five feet tall, with heavy bones, blue eyes, a barrel chest, black wavy hair and mustache, and had been told by one old-timer that he looked like the Hollywood actor William Conrad.

An expert in all things technical, his intelligence and heart of compassion were only surpassed by his good humor. He was the heaviest man ever to be admitted to Delta Force and, at 280 pounds, most who met him were astonished that such a big man was not lethargic but actually had the fluid movements of a cat.

"Did the Giant include a meal in that big gift box? I'm starving," said Bull.

"I'm sure there is enough food to feed an army in here, since they knew you were coming on this picnic," said Tank, smiling. "I guess you were bored setting up the computer gun firing system on those new patrol boats for the Chileans."

"I had a beautiful lady with me on the cross city aerial tram in Santiago, and we were enjoying the view when this darn neck buzzer went off," said Bull, putting his hand on his neck and giving an expression of frustration. "I was hoping the view was about to get a lot better with her, and now here I am, stuck in a jungle with you and the bugs." Bull smiled. "How you been?"

"I was making plans on a nice lady too, but then I got told I had to topple a drug operation, and then I got clobbered on the head, and now I am stuck with you," said Tank. "I guess things could be better for both of us."

They both laughed, as they mixed their instant powdered food with bottles of water and gobbled down a helping.

Inside, they craved the excitement, the danger, and would have it no other way.

The type of work they specialized in, other than their "day jobs," was the world's most extreme mercenary work, and they were the best in the world at what they did. Working in an organization that helped save the bacon of any good nation that asked, they could do their work with a missionary sense of justice.

"You had enough to eat, you hog?" Tank eyed Bull, who was wolfing down his fourth ration pack of trail mix.

They both assembled the ropes, crossbows, and other equipment needed and put it all in two backpacks, setting off toward Dr. Oliveira and her assistant, with Bull running in front and smashing a route through the jungle underbrush with his rhino size legs, while Tank followed close behind, more stealth-like, watching and checking the route ahead and behind with the infrared heat-sensing binoculars.

CHAPTER SIXTEEN

Arriving in the vicinity of the jungle where Tank had been tied up, they both slowed their pace and adopted a low crouching crawl, as they moved from tree to tree, watching for poisonous snakes and spiders. They waited as they spotted the various guards, who were talking in their usual gibberish.

Reaching for the binoculars, Tank wiped the rain from the lenses and raised them to view the treetops to search for Dr. Oliveira and her assistants.

While a typical binocular might be blocked by leaf foliage, these could penetrate right through. They detected a heat signature and configured that signature into a human form for the user to see clearly. Tank could see three forms with normal heat signatures. He was relieved that they were in seemingly good health.

He reached into his backpack and took out what looked like a cigar tube. From it, he slid out what looked like a toy, a dragonfly. On its back was a small keypad and LED display.

He programmed a simple message: "Sit tight, free soon, Tank."

After, he changed the menu and programmed the altitude of approximately 150 feet, the approximate direction, and the approximate body heat reading of the Doctor, which the binoculars had shown.

Then he pressed another button, and the two sets of wings began fluttering, and he released the Flybot. It rose effortlessly, silently, toward the three captives tied to the tree on a platform in the sky. The Flybot would flutter just above them, and then the power to the wings would cut off, causing it to drop on them.

After a few minutes, watching with the binoculars, he could make out the waving arm of Dr. Oliveira. She had received the message from the modern-day carrier pigeon and was relieved, breaking into tears while hugging her assistants.

Each man took two packs of Crawlbots from his backpack, ten in each. Small eight-legged robots, they resembled large tarantulas but were microprocessor-directed, battery-driven killing machines. With a common set of programming buttons, the racks were pointed in the general direction of the captives, in order to set the gyroscopes.

The Crawlbots were originally developed by the Japanese, who were fascinated when their WWII Axis German partners introduced them to the Goliath, a remote control tracked vehicle, about the size of a wheelbarrow, that was loaded with explosives and used to kill enemy tanks, while the soldiers hid nearby and watched. In the years after the war, the Japanese Miracle of high technology electronics developed many devices with military applications, but as they were restricted to a "Home Defense" force in their Constitution, the public never learned of their weaponry.

Bull, being the tech expert, set the controls on the master robot, which in turn would transmit the same settings to the others.

The bots were set to crawl to within ten feet of the heat signature, breathing noise, and speech noise of a human. If a bot arrived and another bot was already there, it would try to find a human with no bot. Each bot would wait until a common signal between them indicated that all had targets. Instantaneously, a proximity charge would explode simultaneously in each bot, killing all within site range up to twenty feet away just from the blast and causing injuries farther away from the steel razor shrapnel.

Because Dr. Oliveira was 150 feet up and on a platform, she would remain safe even if they did sense the presence of her and her two assistants; the bots had altitude limiters and had been set by Bull to not climb that distance vertically.

The Crawlbot trays were lowered to the ground pointed in the general direction, and the "seek" button pressed, and they silently left their holder, moving over and under obstacles toward the voices of the savages, who had no idea they were now being hunted by something far more deadly than a jaguar or anaconda.

With the bots away, they had up to twenty minutes to kill.

Ignoring Bull, Tank pulled out a crossbow and loaded it with barbed arrows. He handed another crossbow to Bull.

"We aren't going to need these," said Bull. "The only thing we will need is a shovel to clean up the mess."

"No use taking chances. You want to be around to date my sisters, don't you?" said Tank, smiling.

"Okay, you win," answered Bull, taking a crossbow and loading it.

"Any leads on the drug operation?" he asked, skipping past the killing of the savages and the rescuing of Dr. Oliveira and her two assistants as though it were already done.

"Yeah," whispered Tank. "These savages are a strange lot and weren't interested in stealing expensive field equipment, which they threw aside. They have a boss somewhere because they are too stupid to be doing this on their own. Plus, I saw a Robertson 44 hovering around the field research area about the time the drone almost went down. They are an expensive chopper, too small to be of any use around here by any agency or government, as they can only carry a very light load. I would be interested in finding out who is running that machine... It looks like we are onto the drug operation already."

Without warning, there were twenty muffled explosions, almost all at once. Due to the delay in sound travelling through the jungle underbrush and past huge trees, the sound was ragged in reaching them.

"Presto," said Bull.

"Okay," said Tank. "You go make sure there are no survivors, while I ready the climbing gear."

"Why don't you just use the gear these savages used?" asked Bull.

"I told you, these guys are a little whacked in the head. Spitting, all drinking the same orange juice... They used vines, not ropes. A little too much 'back to nature' for my tastes, especially in this rain, which makes everything extra slippery. I will take good old-fashioned American high-test, anti-fray climbing rope any day," answered Tank.

Bull moved his bulk with considerable grace, as he ambled off to search the area for survivors.

Within a few minutes, he spotted a groaning savage with his arm blown off. Huge ants were already covering him, literally eating him alive, and more creatures would soon follow, as the smell of blood travelled across the jungle.

Bull took his crossbow, pointed the diamond-tipped arrow at the forehead of the savage, and pulled the trigger. The arrow sliced right through his skull and exited out the rear, and the savage slumped, dead.

Well, at least he didn't have to watch himself being eaten alive, thought Bull.

After a few more minutes, he deemed the area safe, as all were dead. He was surprised that there seemed to be no food or provisions, except a few packs of orange drink.

Must be some kind of orange juice, thought Bull. *It can even take the place of food. Maybe they were eating plants or animals directly from the forest.*

Looking around, Bull could see no campfire location or leftover food.

He gave two short whistles to Tank, indicating all was clear.

Tank readied his harness and the rope gun. He aimed at the tree trunk, about ten feet under Dr. Oliveira, and pulled the trigger. The explosive charge sent the arrow and line up into the canopy, where it firmly penetrated the tree, and the reverse barbs extended to ensure the arrow would not pull out unless the force exceeded 2,000 pounds, far beyond the strength needed.

Attaching an electric pulley to the rope, and after stepping into his harness, he pressed the button, and the rope wheel powerfully carried him up, so that after a minute, he was just below Dr. Oliveira.

"Funny seeing you here. Just because the drone was unreliable, it didn't mean I expected you to do the research from the trees," he said, smiling.

"Just get us down from here, please," she said, sounding as if she was in no mood for humor and just a little traumatized.

After checking the harnesses, Tank lowered the assistants and then Dr. Oliveira down to a waiting Bull, who gently directed them to the ground.

Tank followed, and soon they were trekking across the rain-drenched jungle to the river to catch a boat ride to Manaus, where each looked forward to a good meal and a hot shower.

Dr. Oliveira looked at Tank and asked, "Why does a group of natives harass people and not steal anything?"

Tank looked at her, pausing, and said, "That's what we are going to find out."

In the distance they heard whistles, which blended into the background noise of animals and the torrential rains on the leaves, but something roused Tank's suspicion. His intuition told him these calls were not the calls of animals but signals being used between people.

Grabbing a set of high-tech binoculars from his backpack, Tank scanned the jungle behind them,

"Well, it looks like we have company," said Tank, noting the heat signatures of a dozen natives. "I guess they were fond of you, Doctor, and miss you already."

"What's the plan?" said Bull, with urgency in his voice.

"Run," instructed Tank.

The group instantly started jogging at as fast a clip as the jungle would allow, ducking to the ground to go under huge branches or trunks or stretching to slide over the top of others. They had no time to be careful and avoid poisonous insects or snakes and prayed they would be lucky and not be bitten.

The downpour continued, and the rain striking the leaves masked the sounds of their pursuers, and they hoped it would also mask their own sounds.

Tank suddenly grabbed an overhead branch to prevent himself from falling down a steep bank where the earth fell away. Peering down, the earth disappeared from view, shrouded by leaves and vines.

"What's the holdup?" inquired Bull, puffing as he came up from the last in line position.

"It looks like we are going for a fast downhill ride," said Tank, as he rubbed his chin as if trying to determine if this was their only option.

"What, we can't run left or right?"

"Nope. We've run ourselves out onto a little peninsula of raised land. If we don't go over the bank here, we will be backtracking right onto the lap of our pursuers."

"Who elected you scout leader anyway?"

"Rainstorms in the jungle were not part of my Boy Scout bug lamp training," replied Tank.

Scanning with binoculars again to the rear, Tank said, "They are only a few hundred meters away and coming in this direction; I would say this is the only option. Making a stand with our weapons would work for a while, but for all we know, they have hundreds of reinforcements and could eventually block us from below, erasing even this option."

"One request," said Bull.

"What?" Tank humored him.

"Can we hold elections to see who will be the next scout leader?" asked Bull.

"Okay, I'm first. Since I got us into this mess, I should be the first to test our route," said Tank, who for once had no reply.

He jumped up so his legs were in front of him and, in an instant, disappeared from view.

Amidst the roar of the rainfall, they could hear nothing from below.

Bull looked at the Doctor and her assistants and said, "Okay, Doc, you three are next."

Dr. Oliveira moved delicately over to the edge and soon disappeared, followed by her assistants.

Bull moved a few branches and leaves to disguise the top of the chute from their pursuers and then heaved his bulk over the edge and couldn't help saying, "Geronimo," as he followed.

They all plunged down the chute, into the mud pool. Pulling themselves to firm ground by grabbing the overhead low branches, they emerged and huddled, hardly believing that they had escaped from their pursuers unharmed.

"What's that smell?" asked Tank, noticing the dank, foul odor.

"You don't want to know," replied the Doctor.

"Come on, I am strong enough to take it," said Bull.

"This pit is a sewage pool. The place where we got on the chute up above is the drop-off point, if you will, of an ancient sewage system. It was probably used for hundreds of years, and maybe the odd native still uses it, which is why it has a strange smell," she joked.

Bull thought it over and quickly lost interest, thankful that the downpour had already washed them clean.

"Hey, we are missing our backpacks," said Bull, noting that the packs had been ripped from them and were lost in the mud pool.

"Help me," replied Tank, motioning to a boulder which was off to the side a few meters, just above the mud pool at the bottom of the chute. "Let's give them a nice welcome in case anybody tries to follow."

They rolled the rock over a few meters and lodged it with branches so that whoever came after them would strike the rock.

"Do you think they will feel like following us after hitting this thing?" asked Bull.

"Nope, I think they will be dazed and confused and more interested in sinking to the bottom," replied Tank. "Let's get moving; the boat shouldn't be far off."

"What is 'Giant'?" asked the Doctor, who was starting to grow suspicious of these jungle researchers.

"Well, Giant's a he, not an it," replied Tank.

"You guys are more than researchers, aren't you?" asked Dr. Oliveira.

"What gives you that idea?" replied Tank, amused by her apt suspicions.

"I have been around academics all my life, and I have never seen anybody like you two. Did you both complete minors in university for heroics?" said the Doctor, looking at Bull. "And speaking of two," she continued, "where did your friend Mr. Bull come from anyway, and why do you two insult each other so much?"

Looking at Bull with a wry grin, Tank replied, "So many questions and so little time. It's best we get moving and find the Zodiac," doing his best to change the topic.

CHAPTER SEVENTEEN

Samir Hussan, owner of Excel Electronics, merged onto the Washington turnpike for the ten-minute drive to his gated mansion in an upscale neighborhood.

He pondered the many traffic accidents and chaos he saw across the city and an overhead sign saying the airports and train stations were closed.

Pulling into his driveway, he saw his wife Sasha walking up the front stairs.

He tensed and stared at her as she closed the door without noticing him.

Parking the car, he walked toward the house with building anger, entering the front door.

"Where have you been?" he shouted in the foyer. "Do you hear me? Where have you been?" he raised his voice further.

BLACK V

She came out from the bedroom door, upstairs, where she could see him through the banister.

"What, Samir?" she answered, unsure.

"Come down here," he commanded.

She said nothing and quietly came down the stairs, avoiding eye contact with him.

"I asked you where you have been."

She looked up to answer and was slapped violently, the force knocking her across the marble foyer floor.

According to the Muslim Sharia Law of his homeland, he had broken no law nor was the abuse a basis for divorce.

"Samir, please don't," she pleaded.

"A whore asking me for forgiveness. Only in America," he said. "Are you going to answer me?"

"I was nowhere," she whimpered, having simply been out to have her hair done.

He walked over to her and kicked her in the ribs, and she let out a crying shriek.

"Samir, please don't hurt me, please..."

She curled into a ball on the floor to protect herself, but the damage had been done; she was bleeding internally and needed medical care.

He grabbed her long hair and pulled her along the floor.

He dropped her head and walked around her and proceeded up the carpeted stairs to the bedroom, where he turned on the

Saudi Arabian satellite TV channel and lay back on the bed, closing his eyes after a stressful day.

He briefly remembered that his treatment of his wife may be a crime in America, as they didn't have Sharia Law here yet. He vaguely recalled that it was illegal to be polygamous, which is why he had only one wife here, not the four he was entitled to.

"Ridiculous," he said to himself. "What crime is it to make sure your property is not mistreating its master?"

His mind shifted briefly to a Hollywood movie he had seen in which a man who treated his wife like he did was looked down upon and eventually taken to jail.

"What a country," he said to himself in disgust. He couldn't wait for his brother in the Amazon jungle to lay down the final blow to America, to bring forth its collapse.

And then, introducing Sharia Law, absorbing America into the Muslim world, bringing forth the new Golden Age of Islam.

The American people had demonstrated such stupidity over the years, he was absolutely sure it would happen soon. As they were all infidels, or second rate nonbelievers in Islam, it was their own fault.

Awakening two hours later, Hussein walked down the stairs, to have Sasha prepare him a traditional Saudi meal but could not find her. She was not allowed to drive nor attend school, per Saudi Arabian custom.

He picked up the phone and called her brother, Jag, who worked for Hussan's company.

"Is she there?" he asked.

"Yes, I am holding her. She says she is hurt and needs to go to the hospital," said Jag.

"She has not been behaving," said Hussan.

"Do you want me to bring her over?" asked Jag.

"Yes, and tell her she better make me a good meal, for this trouble she has caused."

"I will have her there in a few minutes," said Jag.

Sasha was crying and looked to Jag's wife with pleading eyes. She had wanted out of the marriage for years, but while an Islamic man could divorce at the drop of a hat by simply telling his wife the marriage was over, it was near impossible for a woman.

Jag grabbed her arm and lifted her up, while she shrieked with pain. Her face had become pale, and she was weak.

Jag drove her over to his brother-in-law's and supported her and walked in with her. He looked around and called his brother-in-law's name.

With no reply, he left her alone in the foyer and drove home.

Sasha struggled to the formal chair in the foyer and sat. She felt her life ebbing from her.

She looked up and saw the deluxe security panel for the home alarm system. There were international symbols for fire, ambulance, and panic. She got up with difficulty and pressed the ambulance button and collapsed on the floor.

CHAPTER EIGHTEEN

They arrived at the riverbank and jumped into the Zodiac, whisking along the river at twenty knots, as Tank tried directing Bull on the route through the tributaries toward the main trunk of the Amazon River, which would lead them to the large city of Manaus.

But his internal compass was off.

The black clouds at treetop level darkened the jungle, and the torrential rains struck the water, splashing up eight inches, causing a white mist to shroud the river. Visibility was only ten meters or so. The massive flooding and water level rise had created hundreds of small new channels. Combined with the regrowth of the vegetation, the entire effect was disorienting and had Tank feeling like a new Boy Scout with a broken compass.

Tank could do little and hoped they would soon find the main Amazon.

There was a change in the engine sound, and Bull noticed that the boat was becoming sluggish.

He glanced over to Tank, who was enjoying sitting close to Dr. Oliveira, but had also noticed the slowing engine and glanced around the boat to check what could be to blame, such as a dragging jungle vine wound around the propeller, but he saw nothing.

He gave a kick to the inflatable Zodiac pontoon and noticed it was soft.

"Permission to jettison engine," said Bull, as they looked astern and could see that the deadweight of the engine dragging down the stern would soon cause the entire boat to sink.

Tank got up to join Bull as they both rapidly turned the hand-tightened fasteners which kept the outboard engine joined to the boat. With a mighty heave, they lifted the engine free, and it dropped into the river, disappearing from sight and yanking the fuel line loose.

Tank reached over and grabbed the heavy battery and tossed it overboard, along with an almost full portable, five-gallon reserve fuel tank.

"No need for a battery or gas on a boat with no engine," he said, as the boat noticeably rose in the water.

Dr. Oliveira and her young assistant looked frightened. The boat was now a lifeless hulk, drifting aimlessly through the jungle, and they huddled on the still-inflated portions up in the bow.

"Don't worry, Doctor, Manaus is downriver; we'll make our date yet," he said with a confidence she did not share.

"Okay, Genius, what's the plan?" asked Bull.

"Hey, Tubby, it's your chance to lose weight," said Tank, as he crawled over the half-submerged stern and sank into the water. "Here's your new job," Tank delegated, as he began kicking to propel the lifeless, deflated Zodiac.

"Hey, look at all the money I can save on Weight Watchers," said Bull, as his massive bulk easily belly-flopped into position, and his giant rhino legs began kicking and thrusting the raft forward like a small motor.

The deflated pontoons had appeared to stabilize without further air loss, and Dr. Oliveira and her assistants were kept just above the water, while Tank and Bull had their shoulders above water, kicking as hard as they could, holding on to the wood transom at the rear, where the engines had been.

As the hours went by, the torrential rains continued, and Dr. Oliveira began shivering uncontrollably, as all of them started to feel the delayed reaction to over twenty hours of being soaked and without rest.

"Doctor, are you okay?" asked Tank.

"No, I am not feeling well," said the Doctor.

"Don't worry, we will have you back to Manaus and a hot bath in a jiffy," said Tank, but she could tell he didn't believe it himself.

"I am worried about both of you. My assistant just reminded me there is a fish in these waters that may crawl into any orifice," said Dr. Oliveira, slightly embarrassed.

"What!" yelled Bull with all his might.

"It's true—and it has barbs that make it almost impossible to pull out," she continued ominously. "Make sure you keep your pants on tight."

"No problem," they said simultaneously.

In truth, it was like being in a garden maze, like those on large European estates. Except ten thousand times bigger and immersed in water.

There were now thousands of channels and small rivers in the vast territory outside of Manaus, and there was no way to know whether they were two kilometers or twenty kilometers from the main Amazon River.

And in this, the situation was desperate.

CHAPTER NINETEEN

The hours of being lost felt like weeks.

They were soaked to the bone with skin rubbed raw, and being without food for many hours had them growing weak.

Lack of sleep was catching up to them, and Tank and Bull slowed their kicking to a lazy sporadic pace.

Dr. Oliveira tried to keep her arm over her eyes to shield herself from the pelting raindrops, and her young assistants cowered at the bottom of the Zodiac.

Bull had been looking intently at the opposite side of the channel. "Hey, Tank," he said, "have you got a minute?"

"Well, let me have a look at my agenda," said Tank, without moving. "Nope, it looks like I'm all booked up for the afternoon. Please call back tomorrow."

"Do you notice anything about the shoreline over there?" asked Bull, pointing to the opposite shoreline.

Tank stared the shoreline. "Yeah," he said, craning his neck as far as he could see in either direction. "It looks smooth on that side. The other side is ragged like everywhere else."

"Smooth and circular. I swear we passed that vine two hours ago," said Bull, pointing to a vine that stood out, jutting over the water in an L shape.

"You are suggesting we have been going nowhere in our lives," said Tank.

"Something like that. At least we have probably been caught in this trench for hours viewing the same territory, and that's why we haven't had any luck orienting ourselves."

"I guess we flowed in by way of a small, partially hidden opening," replied Tank, not giving it much thought.

"I have no idea how things work in this dense jungle," admitted Bull, with a note of defeat in his voice. "We should have noticed this sooner."

"You got that right," said Tank, well aware that people who are lost have a finite number of hours they can survive, and wasting precious hours with mistakes can be deadly.

They were both silent for a few minutes.

Tank frowned. He was mildly annoyed at their situation and at himself. Minutes went by, and he rubbed his chin, as though he were Sherlock Holmes working on a puzzle.

Tank looked over to the Doctor, who was dozing off.

"Doctor, can you help us?" asked Tank.

"What is it?" she replied, pulling herself up.

"My good friend has noticed that we have probably been travelling in circles," said Tank.

"Interesting," said the Doctor, scanning the shoreline and peering up toward the clouds. "Those plants don't look to be growing naturally. They are too even. And it's odd the way they slope upward and inward. Can you bring the boat closer to the shoreline?"

Tank and Bull complied, and soon the Zodiac was bumping up against thick vines, which came up from the water and arched up and inward, away from the boat, until they disappeared from view in the mist.

She parted the leaves and peered into the thick branches of the vines. "Wow, this is interesting. Let me get a closer look." Doctor Oliveira pulled herself off the Zodiac and disappeared into the vines.

For ten minutes they waited and heard nothing.

Finally her head poked out from the leaves. "Hey, you guys want to get out of the rain?" she asked, inviting them in.

"What is this place?" asked Bull.

Dr. Oliveira was on her knees, scratching the dirt from the ground and uncovering a white smooth rock surface.

"It looks like an ancient public space made from rocks carried from hundreds of kilometers away, with the world's most natural roof keeping everything dry."

"You know where the rocks came from?" asked Tank.

"I know these types of rocks do not naturally exist near here," she finished, too tired to explain further.

They all gazed around in amazement at the huge, open, dry space. Fatigue weighed on them, and Bull was the first to give in.

"Well, that's all great to know, but what I notice is that this is relatively clean and dry, and there don't seem to be any poisonous animals nearby, all of which to me spells nap time."

Tank noticed a distant noise but was too tired to investigate further.

They all knelt down and lay on the ground close together. Soon they fell into a deep sleep, totally exposed on the floor of the massive, open space.

CHAPTER TWENTY

Tank woke up to the sound of strange music. It sounded like tubular bells being played softly, and the sound permeated the entire space.

He gave Bull a soft kick to wake him up.

Bull opened one eye and, still half asleep, said, "What's up?"

"Listen. Do you hear anything?" asked Tank.

Bull was silent for a moment, then pulled himself onto his feet and cupped his ear. "I hear music. Where's it coming from?"

They both walked around and then stopped, near the center of the space.

Tank turned his head and cupped his hand around his ear upward. "It's coming from up there," he said, pointing one hundred feet above their heads.

"That doesn't make any sense," said Bull.

"Be that as it may, the sound is coming from up there," insisted Tank.

Tank pulled himself up into the branches and was soon standing on a thick vine, looking down at Bull.

"I'm going to find out where that sound is coming from," decided Tank.

"If you fall and hurt yourself, you will probably die out here. We have enough problems as it is, in case you haven't noticed," said Bull.

"I will use all of my Boy Scout training," Tank assured him.

Tank disappeared up into the plant dome ceiling, walking carefully among the thick vines and watching for harmful animals. The inner vines were the perfect thickness for a handhold and since they were naked of leaves, he made good time toward the top of the plant dome—and the strange, haunting sounds of the tubular bells, which grew louder with every step.

Tank reached up and pulled himself up the side of the dense portion, and after about fifteen feet, reached the top and poked his head into the exterior air and pelting rain rains of the outside. He could see the giant green dome arch down toward the water with heavy leaves on the outside and the jungle view disappearing into the mist.

BLACK V

He pulled his head back inside the green leaf canopy and focused his eyes on the strangest seed pod he had ever seen.

CHAPTER TWENTY-ONE

A seed pod like no other…

Lying just beneath the leaves was a silver object that looked like a metallic space capsule.

Tank pulled himself over to it and saw that the vine branches formed a nest under the silver object, cradling it.

He lowered himself onto it and moved his hand over the smooth surface. There were several pieces of metal bars and runs of cables which extended horizontally from each side into the vines before disappearing from sight.

As the torrents of rain cascaded onto the leaves, they became heavy and drooped, with their ends striking the capsule with the buffeting winds. Over many years, the branch ends had formed knobs of wood, like calluses, from striking the metal.

"What on earth have we got here?" said Tank to himself, pulling a branch knob up and letting it go.

The knob hit the metal capsule and a haunting bell tone was struck. As many branches moved up and down with the rains and winds, they drummed the capsule with different tones depending on what part of the capsule they struck and the weight and force of the knob strike.

He pulled himself across to another large vine and moved along the stretched cables, soon coming to a massive stainless steel fuel tank shaped like a desert canteen, flat and round, which had its own chorus of knob end branches.

Shimmying back and around the capsule, Tank found an identical fuel tank on the other side, also with branch knob ends striking it. It was as if the skeleton of a gigantic bird had been left hanging among the vines, with cables and aluminum bars stretching far into the green dome's plant structure, hidden from view—except if you were crawling inside.

"I guess that explains the mysterious jungle orchestra," said Tank to himself.

Tank expertly made his way back down to the ground and said to Bull, "I bet you can't guess where the music is coming from."

"Okay, I can't guess—you win the bet," Bull conceded in jest. "What is it?"

"Come and see," said Tank, reaching up for a handhold and disappearing into the vines above.

Bull followed without saying anything. Having spent part of his youth in the Pacific Northwest, he climbed with the ease of a lemur, choosing limbs strong enough to hold his weight.

Within minutes, they arrived at the strange capsule and Bull said, "Well, I was right. I would never have guessed. Any theories on what this is and why it's here playing Raindrops Keep Falling on My Head in the middle of the jungle?"

"Obviously this is some type of plane that dropped on the dome in a slow, gentle flat spin, since none of the metal parts are damaged. The missing parts were originally wood and have long since rotted away. Beyond that, it's anybody's guess," replied Tank, more introspective than conversational.

Tank was already crawling over the object, feeling for a way to get in. Finally, he felt a handhold and pulled himself over to see a circular wheel, like on the bulkhead doors in submarines.

He heaved and tried to turn the wheel to open the hatch, but it wouldn't budge.

Bull shimmied over and pushed him aside. "Let a man do a man's job," he said and heaved, letting his mighty gut swing like a pendulum to easily break the wheel loose.

Tank reached over, and together they pulled, and the top hatch opened with the sound of a vacuum seal breaking.

"I am going in," announced Tank, letting himself drop through the hatch.

Inside, he was shocked at the sight.

The object's interior was like a huge aircraft cockpit, but had not only seats for the pilot and co-pilot but an extra ten seats situated in the rear, and everything looked to be in pristine condition.

"Talk about a time capsule," Tank said to himself. "This is the real deal."

He stood up to his full height and looked around.

The surfaces were smooth and looked like the interior of a spaceship in a 1950s science fiction movie.

In the pilot's seat sat a fully clothed mummified person.

Tank moved over and examined the pilot.

"I hope it was a good flight," he said, noting the body was that of a woman with long hair and a floral scarf. She was wearing leather flight gloves, a bomber jacket, and black knee-high boots.

A locked leather satchel was in the seat next to her.

Tank reached over and pushed it up through the hatch. "Here, hold onto her flight bag; we can examine it on the ground," he said to Bull, stretching as far as he could to pass the case over to his companion, who was outside and still balancing on a limb.

Bull grabbed it, and Tank sank back inside, sitting, rubbing his chin as he always did when puzzled.

"What's going on in there? What is this thing?" called Bull, curious about what he was missing out on.

"Give me a minute, will you? It's not like I see a UFO every day. Let me think a minute while I look it over," called Tank.

"Hey, let me know when you're done. You think your pretty Doctor Lady knows some plants or animals around here that we can eat? I'm starving. I am glad you solved the musical vines mystery, and I am sure this thing will look good in a museum somewhere, but in the meantime, we are still lost in the jungle," said Bull.

"Yeah, I know," said Tank. "But at least you're dry now. Why don't you see if the good lady can help us find something to eat? I will come down in a little while. I want to spend a few more minutes looking this contraption over."

"Okay, see you on the ground," said Bull, who had run out of patience and began to carefully retrace his steps to the ground.

Tank stuck his head back up to see his friend disappear from view, down into the vines. He dropped back inside and slumped on the floor.

There was natural light coming in from the hatch and faint light coming in from the windshield, which was covered in green slime.

Tank was staring at the inner surfaces and noticed a strange-looking area. He crawled over and rubbed the surface and saw that it was some type of technical information, written in raised letters in German on a metal panel, which had been covered over originally by a fabric of which only threads were still visible, the rest having disintegrated away. He studied the panel and continued cleaning more of it with his shirt bottom until it was all visible.

"EMERGENCY COCKPIT JETTISON" read the bold print. Underneath were pictures of various stages of what appeared to be an ejection sequence for the entire capsule. The instructions were exceedingly thorough.

Tank looked around and saw the main activation button located between the cockpit seats. Intrigued, he crawled out of the capsule and inspected the four corners, where, according to the instructions, RATO units where located.

Reaching down and pulling the vines back, he saw that they all appeared to be undamaged. Rocket Assisted Takeoff was normally used to attach to airplanes that were overloaded, or trying to take off from a runway that was too short, or both. After the plane was safely in the air, they were jettisoned to decrease weight and drag. Using RATO units for this capacity was a first, at least according Tank's knowledge of aircraft.

"Wow, saved from a crash and fed too," he said, pulling open a nearby panel behind which there was a metal case of emergency rations.

Tank was excited and wanted to tell the others. He put the emergency rations under his arm and climbed out and down the vines to the ground.

"Okay, here he comes," said Bull to the others ceremoniously. "The man who found the source of the jungle music."

They all sat together for a moment and listened to the thrumming of the vines on the capsule and fuel tanks.

"Your friend here described what you found up there. I would like to see the capsule, but I am too weak now," said Dr. Oliveira. "It won't be easy finding something to eat here, despite all the plants and animals. Obviously there is nothing growing on this bare rock surface, and the thrumming vibrations and sound of the plants striking the aircraft, or whatever it is, have kept this area completely free of wildlife during rainfall. That means we won't get eaten by anything but also that we probably won't find anything to eat."

"So that means we have to go back outside to Waterworld to find a meal?" Bull asked. "I was just starting to enjoy being dry."

"Outside in the rain, we won't be much better off," said the Doctor. "These torrential rains cause most of the animals to be displaced and on the move."

"How about a meal of schnitzel, authentically cooked in Germany?" asked Tank.

"Don't torture me," Dr. Oliveira said, looking defeated by the thought of the food.

"Would I torture you?" asked Tank, dropping the metallic rations case to the smooth rock floor in the middle of them.

Inside, the case and contents looked like they were packed yesterday. There were many shiny metal flasks with German labels on them and a variety of freeze-dried foods.

"Schnitzel, madam?" said Tank, as he unscrewed the lid and smelled the contents.

The Doctor grabbed the flask. "Hey, let me see."

"You aren't actually thinking of eating that stuff, are you?" asked Tank.

"Pathogens, in fact most types of bacteria, have a smell," she said, mostly to herself, as she peered closely at the food.

Bull was impatient and the hungriest he ever remembered being. "Does that mean we can eat it?" he asked.

"Since we are literally starving, it may be worth the chance to try it," she said.

"Okay, boss, I'll be the guinea pig," Bull offered, as he reached down and grabbed a piece of the freeze-dried schnitzel.

He placed it on his tongue, trying to notice if anything was wrong.

"Definitely stale," he said. "I wouldn't come back to this restaurant."

He finished eating the morsel.

Tank watched his friend and sat down nearby.

The small case of rations would not keep them for long in any event.

The torrential rains continued, and along with it, the haunting orchestral tubular bell music from above. Tank knew the surrounding area would be even more flooded as time went on, with the water from thousands of square kilometers filling the canals and covering any firm land.

He started rubbing his square jaw, deep in thought, with their prospects looking very dim indeed.

CHAPTER TWENTY-TWO

Tank suddenly stood up and asked, "Does anybody like to go on rides at Disneyland?"

Dr. Oliveira replied, "Of course, my father took us to Orlando when we were kids. What a strange question to ask."

Tank walked around, pacing and rubbing his chin. "Bull, let's go for a walk."

They walked away from the others, and Tank said, "Would you believe that thing has what appears to be an ejection seat type of arrangement but for all the seats at the same time, by way of ejecting the entire capsule?"

"You've got to be kidding," said Bull.

"I'm serious. There was an instruction plate on the inside that showed me where to find the ration case. There was another one that has detailed instructions about the ejection system. Its shows the location of RATO units at each corner, plus three parachutes for descent, and two inflatable pontoons to cushion a land landing or to keep it afloat if it lands on water," said Tank.

"Wow, it's really going to be a crowd pleaser at the Smithsonian, although it's looking more like we will never see it there. I know you have told me some stories from your father's time in the war. Does this relic ring a bell?" asked Bull.

"Whatever she was flying must have been very important, but how she ended up in South America is anybody's guess," said Tank of the pilot.

"But getting back to my Disneyland ride idea, what do you think of all of us jumping in that thing and taking our chances?" asked Tank.

"Are you nuts? It's over sixty years old and was damaged by a crash in the first place."

Tank looked at Bull, who he could tell was seriously considering his outrageous plan.

Bull looked over and asked, "How does a nice finish and edible rations translate into a working relic?"

"Usually the Germans were consistent with their quality," Tank posited.

"That's a lot of equipment that has to work," said Bull, with doubt in his voice.

"Yes, it is," admitted Tank, "but what are our options?"

Suddenly both men grabbed for their necks and the buzzing alerts by Giant. Without means to call him back, Giant had been concerned and was calling them more frequently.

They couldn't believe their predicament.

They were tasked with saving the United States, and it was looking likely they would not even be able to save themselves.

CHAPTER TWENTY-THREE

They were all desperately hungry, and as the hours dragged on, the WWII rations were soon consumed, and there was nothing else to eat.

Animals could be heard and occasionally seen, but there was no way to catch them.

They snoozed whenever they needed to, as there was really nothing to do, and in their weakened state, they had no strength to waste on talking, unless it was essential.

After the night had passed, Tank awoke and walked over to Bull, who was walking the perimeter.

"Maybe your idea to try that WWII contraption isn't that crazy after all. I've been going through the options. If we take to the Zodiac again, I, at least, have no strength to be the outboard, and you're probably the same. It's still pouring rain, and we will probably be just as disoriented as we were before. I still can't believe we are in the middle of the planet's most abundant wildlife area and there's not a thing to eat here. Just our luck," finished Bull.

Both of their neck buzzers activated, and they instinctively put their hands on their necks.

There was an uneasy silence as they became convinced that the old German escape capsule would be their only chance at survival.

They walked over to the big vine and grasped the branches and soon were back up on the roof of the green dome, clearing away the small branches and leaves that had spilled over the top of the capsule.

In the meantime, Tank was in the capsule, reading the German panels, memorizing the control sequence. At the same time, he sat in the two seats they would use. Amazingly, even the seat harnesses were in perfect condition.

Tank craned his neck out of the hatch and tossed Bull Hanna Fitch's scarf. "Hey, boss, how about a window clean? And check the tires for air," he called out.

Bull crawled over to the windshield and used his knife to start scraping away the layer of slime.

Inside, Tank was amazed at the appearance of their escape module, which glimmered like it was just off the assembly line.

Tank craned his neck out of the hatch and smiled at Bull, who was soaked again in the pouring rain. "Why don't you come inside and let's have a pre-flight discussion?"

"I guess I just pull the handle, and we pray it works," said Tank.

"Seems like that's all we can do. It's not like if the motor quits we can row."

"Okay, well, let's go down and talk to Dr. Oliveira and try to get her and her assistant on board for our escape plan."

As they climbed down to the ground, Tank had a change of heart. He called back to Bull, "What do you say we leave the metal and cable scraps in a way that they can do some good?"

CHAPTER TWENTY-FOUR

"What's that supposed to mean?" asked Bull.

"I figure the metal will show up on scanners if a large enough concentration of it is placed in one spot. Plus, we can arrange the metal to read 'SOS,' which will be tough to miss."

"But why bother with that since they are coming with us?"

"I changed my mind. I believe that contraption will work, but I don't think I should ask the nice lady and the boys to bet their lives on it."

"Actually, it's better than that. Did I tell you that thing up there has a working radio in it?" asked Tank.

"You are kidding me," replied Bull.

"Nope. I pushed on a spring-loaded panel and out popped a rescue radio, permanently tuned to only one frequency, since I suppose they thought whoever was saved by the capsule might not know much about operating a radio. It had a water-activated dry cell. I reached out, cupped my hand in the rain, and poured water into the cell, and the radio sprang to life. I pressed the single red button, marked 'Rescue,' which showed a depiction telling the story of the transmitter and then rescue forces finding the capsule by honing in on the radio beacon, which I am guessing is giving pulses even as we speak. The kraut who depicted all the instructions must have been a hieroglyphics fan."

"What about the regular radio in the plane?"

"It didn't work. I guess it was built to a lower standard than the rescue radio, which was made almost destruction-proof and for that reason still works."

"So why do you think the woman and boys will be rescued? Obviously, the rescue channel the radio was tuned to is long gone in World War Two, so it would be transmitting to nowhere."

"I initially thought the same thing, but then I remembered that all German rescues by any forces were processed through Goliath, which was the most powerful in the world and was engineered and built to be optimized to that frequency."

"I don't get it. If the radio base in Germany was destroyed, then all this doesn't matter," said Bull.

"But that's the point; it never was destroyed. When the Russians overran the world's most powerful radio transmitter and receiver before the end of World War Two in Germany, they recognized the outstanding engineering and quality and instructed their own engineers to carefully disassemble it, move it by train, and assemble it again in Russia," explained Tank. "Believe it or not, it's still the world's most powerful system and has stayed in use all these decades later by the Russian Submarine Fleet. Desperation is the mother of invention.

"What do you say we carry out this pilot's body and try to leave it with some protection on the ground? Next, let's arrange the metal, inform the Doctor and the boys, and get this show on the road!"

CHAPTER TWENTY-FIVE

Tank felt his way along the wing's metal substructure and was amazed at the massive size of the plane and that there did not seem to be any fuselage or tail assembly. It appeared to have four engines made of an advanced corrosion-proof material and metal attachment points for an extra two engines that were missing.

After arranging the metal parts into a large SOS—lying on top of the leaves of the green dome so they could be seen from the air but not from the water in case the natives were still looking for them—they then stripped any final useful items off the Zodiac and sank it, so that if any of the violent natives were still searching, they would not be alerted to the Doctor's location.

They told the Doctor to move to the edge of the clearing so that the downward exhaust from the RATO units during takeoff would not harm them.

They said farewell to the Doctor and her young assistants and crawled up to the capsule.

They each felt their neck buzzers activate.

"Looks like the world needs us," said Tank.

"Well, I guess us getting lost in the jungle wasn't in Giant's plans," replied Bull.

"I think running into trouble with those natives is a little too coincidental to not be in some way related to our mission, so you could say we started the mission yesterday."

They attached their safety harnesses, and Tank looked over to his friend and said, "Okay, one free Disneyland ride coming up—hang on to your hat!"

With that, he reached over and pressed the large red button on the panel, and before he could pull back his arm, there was a tremendous explosion of sound and vibration as the four RATO solid rocket booster units simultaneously ignited with a fury from their seventy-year sleep, and they were both pinned to their seats with the g-forces, as the craft rose into the sky with smoke first filling the green dome and then trailing the capsule into the sky.

For the first few seconds, the rain ran across the windshield, and as they broke through the clouds, this was followed by bright sunlight and a blue sky.

Just then, the engines cut, and there was no sound.

"Hey Tank, I have a great idea: let's deploy the parachutes!" said Bull.

They both felt like they were just going over the top of the hill on a roller coaster, and the capsule soon started dropping like a runaway elevator.

"Really, I am not so sure; let me think about it for a while," deadpanned Tank with the hint of a smirk.

Tank reached over to the panel, pushing against his safety harness, and pressed the big red button with the pictograph of the capsule landing with three parachutes deployed.

Immediately, there were three explosions, and seconds later, they felt the jerk of a parachute inflating and slowing their descent.

They looked out the window and with the capsule's swinging motion could only see one parachute, not the three that were supposed to be working.

The capsule was falling too fast and would hit the ground so hard they would be injured or killed.

"Do you mind if I go outside for a stroll?" said Tank.

With that, he quickly unlatched his harness and nimbly jumped across the cockpit and reached up to open the hatch. He pulled himself up and through the hatch and was outside the capsule, hanging onto the grab handles, using them to move down the side of the capsule toward the opened parachute compartments.

The capsule was swinging wildly as it reacted to the unusual braking of a single parachute, where the design was for three to be functioning.

Tank's legs and torso were pulled out from the capsule sides by the centrifugal force, as he struggled to hold on.

Within seconds, he reached down to the first parachute compartment, which was open because the cover had been blown off by the explosive charges, and pulled the chute out a little. Then the wind grabbed it and pulled it all the way out, and it rose up and inflated.

The spinning stopped and the descent slowed, and Tank was glad to have his legs planted on the capsule sides.

He reached down the other side and pulled out the third chute and with this, the capsule's descent slowed to a leisurely rate.

Rocking gently back and forth, they swayed with the winds like a giant pendulum and descended down into the clouds, and soon they heard the familiar ping of rain against the capsule hull.

"Looks like our mysterious orchestra has set up shop in a new location," said Bull.

"They can play anywhere they want," said Tank, who was still lost in admiration that a seventy-year-old airplane escape pod had just worked almost like it was brand new.

"You better hope we land on land," said Bull. "I haven't heard any air hissing, which means the flotation devices aren't working."

Within a few minutes, they abruptly plunged into the jungle marsh with a splash, and then an upward surge, as the capsule rose to float on the surface.

All was silent as they saw the parachutes through the windshield settle over the capsule so they were blinded by the bright white of the chute over the windshield. A quiet hissing sound could be heard, as the flotation pontoons finally inflated and the capsule rose to sit like an oddball boat.

"What now, boss?" asked Bull.

CHAPTER TWENTY-SIX

"Did you hear that?" asked Tank.

"What?" replied Bull.

"I thought I heard something just before the noise of our splashdown."

"Can't help ya. Only heard the rain on the sides."

"Sounded like a damaged turbine shrieking as if a plane had just gone by."

Tank was the first to loosen his safety harness and crawl up to open the hatch and pull himself through.

He felt the familiar pelting rain and heard the sound of rain on the leaves of the lush jungle canopy and the birds and monkeys and looked down to see that the capsule was resting in a swamp, which accounted for their soft landing.

The torrential rains were certainly the same, and looking around, he could see the low white mist over the water and large, black-as-ink clouds hanging at the treetops.

Could we be just as lost now as before we left the Doctor and her assistant behind? thought Tank.

Tank noticed something different. He crunched up his nose and sniffed the air. There was a distinct burning smell.

Intrigued, he leapt down from the capsule and landed waist-deep in the water and started moving in the direction of the smoky smell.

As he moved away, Bull squeezed himself up like an eel and popped up from the capsule hatch and asked, "Hey where are you going?"

"Toward a weenie roast, I hope," said Tank, as he waded through the water, which was becoming shallower. He soon found himself pushing through the jungle on firm ground.

Bull decided to stay put, to at least think about their next move, and watched the wildlife, including shouting monkeys and a large anaconda that was swimming by.

"Funny," said Tank to himself. "That sure doesn't smell like farmers clearing the land."

He was trying to place the smell.

What was it?

As he pushed a thick layer of jungle leaves from in front of him, they opened to reveal an open, flooded field of short grass about the size of a football field, cleared from the jungle for agricultural use.

At one end was the source of the smoke. A battered aircraft sat with thick black smoke pouring out of one engine. The entire surface had hundreds of dents and looked like it had been pummeled with rocks.

An emergency exit popped open, and the slide inflated. Several men poured out and landed in the gumbo.

As Tank approached them, two men with the white shirts and ties of a flight crew leapt at one of the others and started yelling in Russian.

"Hey, guys, take it easy," shouted Tank, walking toward them.

With his towering presence and sonorous voice, he commanded attention and respect.

The three men looked up from the ground and immediately fell under the spell of Kurt Tank and stopped their quarreling.

"This guy, he destroyed our plane," they said in coarse English.

"Hey, you guys are the pilots; don't blame me," said a mid-fifties man with thick gray hair and dressed in civilian clothes—Frank Lugar.

Tanks neck buzzer activated, and he instinctively moved his hand to the spot until it stopped seconds later.

"What's that, a mosquito bite?" said the Russian.

Tank ignored the comment and walked closer and peered inside the aircraft, where he saw several groggy, young people in technician suits and a very interesting payload.

"You guys must be from Rockwell Aerospace," said Tank.

"And the only person who would know that would be Kurt Tank. Nice to finally meet you; Noddins has mentioned you numerous times. I guess you noticed that this drone looks just like the one you were having trouble with," said Lugar, Operations Head at Rockwell.

"So this is our replacement drone. It looks to be undamaged, which is the only spot of luck in this mess," said Tank.

"Service with a smile," said Lugar.

"Well, it's no good to us mired in this swamp. By the way, where exactly are we anyway? Is Manaus Airport nearby?"

"I hope so. I was heading for it, but with the navigational radar knocked out, I couldn't see a thing. This may sound nuts, but there was a flash, and when I looked toward it expecting lightening, it looked like a laser coming from a black helicopter. Anyway, right after that, the engine exploded," said Lugar, with a puzzled look on his face.

"Any food inside?" asked Tank hopefully.

"Yep. Lots of food and lots of vodka, if that's your flavor."

"I don't drink, but I have a friend just through the jungle at the end of the opening who will be interested in your food supply," said Tank.

"I realize we seem a little foolish crawling out of this beat-up plane in the middle of a swamp," said Lugar.

"Agreed," said Tank.

"But can I ask you a question?" said Lugar, who continued and didn't wait for an answer. "What's a field scientist doing walking around in a swamp, hungry for a meal, and looking like you crashed yourself?" said Lugar.

"First things first," said Tank, evading the question. "I have a friend who would be very angry if he found out there is food and I never told him."

He walked off to get Bull.

"Back in a moment," he said and ambled off across the clearing toward where he had come from.

CHAPTER TWENTY-SEVEN

Tank, Bull, Lugar, the Russians, and the Rockland employees all sat around eating. The Russians had started drinking vodka and soon began to look drowsy.

Tank had told their story quickly, or at least, the portions not related to their drug interception mission or alternate occupations.

"Well, I must say, I feel more than a little concerned for your Doctor friend and her assistants," said Lugar.

"Great!" said Bull. "Manaus could be twenty kilometers away. And there's not a thing we can do to help them, since this plane could never take off in this short field even with two engines, let alone one."

"You are wrong, my good friend," said Tank, rubbing his square jaw. "We have a large speedboat with an excellent state-of-the-art navigation and scanning system, which is going to take us right to our favorite restaurant in Manaus—after we rescue the Doctor and her young assistants, of course."

"Are you sure he doesn't drink?" asked Lugar, looking at Bull.

Tank walked over and crawled inside the Beriev, which stank of vodka.

After a few seconds, they heard the high-RPM whirring of a powerful electric motor. The shocked Russians looked on as the exposed wheels retracted from the swampy mire and were covered by smooth metal clamshell doors, which squeezed out the soft mud as they closed.

The Russians, now drunk on vodka, started screaming amongst themselves.

Tank heard the commotion and crawled out of the plane with a message he had scrawled on the inside cover of a flight manual he had torn off: "IOU $20 million for 1 damaged Beriev 200 aircraft."

"Here, this is your first export sale; congratulations. We will pay you when we get to Manaus," said Tank.

With that, he walked around to the front of the plane and surveyed the jungle.

After a few minutes, he crawled back into the plane and yelled for Bull to come in.

They both could be heard banging and crashing inside, with the occasional sound of an electric drill.

Bull came outside and mounted a piece of wire across the top of the windshield, with the connection coming in through the open pilot's window.

Tank crawled out and yelled, "Everybody in; we are leaving!"

Looking slightly fearful and confused, the group entered the plane to the sound of the remaining engine being spooled up.

The door closed and Tank rammed the throttle to wide open. The smooth-bellied Beriev 200 amphibian soon inched forward and pushed across the gumbo mud, gathering speed and heading straight toward the small trail opening, where Tank had emerged from the swamp earlier.

"Hey, Tank, I hope you can see that you are going to crash straight into those huge trees," warned Bull.

"That's what I was hoping for," said Tank.

They could see the lush jungle approaching in the windshield, and it looked as if the plane would crash and they would all be killed.

From the rear of the plane they could hear the Russians screaming and the sound of Lugar yelling to the cockpit to stop the plane but being too afraid to loosen his safety harness and grab the controls, as he was sure they would crash in seconds.

With a screeching crash, the giant Beriev left the open field and penetrated the jungle, and the wings struck two giant Malato trees on either side of the trail and were torn off cleanly from the fuselage. The forward fuselage exited on the other side of the jungle, hurtling forward and just missing the capsule and splashing down into the water.

Tank pulled back on the throttle and cut the engine.

The plane settled in the water, and the open holes torn in the fuselage when the wings were ripped away were well above the water line, due to the amphibious design.

Lugar came from the rear and grabbed Tank by the neck and yelled, "Are you a lunatic!"

"Sorry. I sized it up and this was our best option. Mr. Bull and I have something urgent to do, and the Doctor must be rescued. I have bought the plane, and we don't have time for long discussions."

Looking over at the Rockwell drone and the obvious parts that had been removed, Lugar exclaimed, "That's not your drone!"

Tank reached over to the service manual and ripped off the rear cover.

He scrawled, "IOU $5 million for drone," and handed it to Lugar.

Bull had been adjusting an electronic screen and said to Tank, "Okay, Kurt, let's get this show on the road."

With that, Tank started the right-side turbine again and rammed the throttle wide open.

Soon they were skimming across the water in the giant Beriev.

"Okay, turn a little to the left and head for that canal opening over there," said Bull.

Bull stared down at a small screen on his lap that had wires running back to the drone and to the wire across the windshield.

Tank smiled. "Nothing like a state-of-the-art integrated radar and sonar to help us in our hour of need."

The high-definition specialized scanning software and hardware from the drone was being put to good use.

"Hey, what do you know," said Bull. "Would you believe I see the edges of the SOS straight ahead?"

"That's what I want to hear," said Tank, who was concentrating on controlling the strange craft.

"Okay, we are coming up on the green dome—let's cut the throttle," said Bull.

The great white whale of a craft soon slowed, and the hull started to plow the water, as Tank turned the wheel to direct the nose to nudge up to the huge vines.

Tank killed the engine and crawled out from the cockpit and walked to the rear to push open the fuselage door.

Sticking his head out, he heard the heavy rains coming down. He leapt into the water and swam the few strokes to take him to the vines and then crawled out of the water and inside the green dome. Looking across the smooth rock surface, in the distance, he could see the Doctor and her assistants lying huddled together.

"Hey, Doctor!" he yelled.

She looked up as if to see her savior and weakly got up and pulled her assistants up, speaking to them in Portuguese.

Tank walked over and gave them all a hug of assurance. He guided them across the giant open area toward the edge of the green dome, helping them through the vines, until they reached the plane waiting outside.

Tank put each of them on his powerful shoulders and swam across the expanse to the plane's door and lifted them up to Bull's waiting arms.

The Doctor still carried the sealed leather satchel brought down from the capsule by Bull, and Tank retrieved the pilot's body.

"I see you are still with this bad luck guy, and a few others have joined you," she said to Bull.

"Well, I figured his luck had to change."

Looking at the openings straight through to the water, where the wings used to be, the Doctor said, "If this plane is any indication, his luck has gotten worse."

Tank fired up the turbine, which was soon screaming, while he pulled the engine braking deflectors, intended just for landing on runways and not for use when the plane was in the water.

Suddenly, the huge clamshell doors closed over the rear of the engine, and the thrust was deflected to the front. Huge gushes of water washed over the plane as it inched backward and away from the edge of the jungle.

Tank cut the engine to an idle, and the Beriev swung around, and then he pushed the throttle wide open, and the mighty craft was soon skimming across the water like a giant jet ski.

Settling back into his co-pilot seat, Bull said, "I adjusted the scanner to home in on Manaus airport radar. We now have a direct heading for Manaus. Just look out for the trees."

Bull began using hand signals to direct Tank as he steered the craft through the canals, and soon they burst out from a canal onto the main Amazon River and could see the river traffic and the city in the misty distance.

"Thank God," said Doctor Oliveira, who had been gorging on rye bread and caviar along with her assistants.

Tank kept the throttle wide open, and they avoided a small craft, where the crew and passengers stared with mouths wide open at the strange sight.

The Beriev cruised effortlessly across the twenty-five-kilometer expanse of the river, and Tank headed to the remote, unused portion of the airport where Noddins was located.

As he approached the shoreline, he yanked on the lever that deployed the wheels and drove the strange craft right up the beach, over the raised lip of the asphalt, scraping the belly but not doing any serious damage. Within seconds, they came up to Noddins' control shack, and Tank cut the engine.

They all poured out and walked around in the rain, disoriented but thankful that they had all survived a situation that could have turned out far worse.

They looked to Tank, and he smiled. "Yeah, I know. You're all welcome."

Lugar walked over to the original drone, which was still on its catapult launch truck.

Tank walked over and looked inside the control shack.

Seeing the blood and Noddins on the floor, he pulled him up but could not wake him, although he was able to find a pulse.

Tank called the airport medical team, and the emergency vehicles arrived minutes later and soon had Noddins on a gurney and headed toward proper hospital care. The pilot's mummified remains were also taken.

He could answer all the questions later.

He felt his neck buzzer.

Tank walked over to join Lugar, who was still inspecting the original drone.

"Heck of a service call," said Tank.

"As I said, we aim to please. It looks like this thing has been blasted with a laser," he said, pointing to the plastic cover of the navigation unit, which was slightly distorted. "Only a laser could cause this."

Just then, Tank looked up and could see a black Robertson 44 helicopter hovering a few hundred meters away, over the jungle.

"That's it. I have had enough of that guy; he's the one who did this," said Tank with gritted teeth.

The Doctor and her assistants were loaded into another emergency vehicle and taken to hospital for monitoring and to check for exposure.

The Russian pilots were taken mainly because they were so drunk they couldn't answer the normal evaluative questions.

Tank could hear the Russians calling back to him to pay them for the wrecked Beriev.

"Well, I guess I might as well get my money's worth from this hulk, since the Russians seem to think I can't return it without the wings."

"What, you don't think you got your money's worth already?" asked Bull.

"Nope. We have a cache of toys sitting in the jungle that we definitely don't want any nutty natives to stumble across. We can remove the drone, and I figured if we pull out the brain of the old drone, our jury-rigged sonars and radar will keep working and help us find the cache quicker, right?"

"You got it, boss," answered Bull.

"Then we can use these Rockwell people to unload our nifty, new drone and leave it here on the tarmac."

"After that, we are going to take the Beriev and go pick up our tech stuff?" Bull surmised.

"You're a smart man," said Tank.

Within minutes, the Rockwell crew—under Bull's directions and Lugar's advice—had removed the drone's brain to make sure the scanning systems integrated into the Beriev earlier would continue working and then took the disassembled drone out of the Beriev.

"Lugar, can you help me with something with this drone?" asked Tank, scanning the hundreds of parts and tools scattered on the tarmac.

"Sure, you're the customer—what can we do for you?"

"Put it together and get it launch ready."

Looking at the pouring rain and knowing his crew was exhausted from the harrowing trip from Miami, Lugar then thought of the potential for a massive order of new drones if the Brazilian experience was positive.

"No problem. I guess your science program can't wait, eh?" said Lugar.

"Yeah, right, scanning the jungle canopy for the Brazilian government is job one," said Tank to Lugar, with a wry smile to Bull, who was standing nearby.

"What's this about picking up tech equipment?" asked Lugar, who had overheard the conversation between Tank and Bull.

Tank grew tense. "In the jungle? You've got to be kidding. Actually, I am thinking of recommending your drone to my association. And since the scanning hardware is all set up in the Beriev, I wanted to give it another try. After all, I don't think this plane without its wings will be ever used for more than scrap—don't you agree?" Tank bluffed, to cover his true identity and their true mission to stop the cocaine operation as ordered by Giant.

Looking back at the Beriev, which although almost brand new, looked like it had survived a war in Afghanistan, Lugar nodded his head in agreement, though still a little puzzled.

Minutes later, the Rockwell crew had removed the drone and associated equipment from the Beriev.

"Hey, guys, do any of you know how to fill up a tank?" yelled Tank.

In a bustle of activity, he and Bull and one of the technicians were soon topping up the Beriev's long range belly tanks with jet fuel liberated from a parked jet refueling truck.

Bull and Tank crawled back into the Beriev and looked back at the Rockwell crew starting the intricate job of assembling the drone.

Tank lit the turbine and didn't wait for it to warm up before jamming the throttle to wide open.

The right-side engine screamed in protest as the huge plane rolled along, gathering speed toward the edge of the remote runway and tumbling over the asphalt's edge in a shallow dive through mid-air and making a huge splash into the water of the Amazon River.

Tank pulled on the lever to retract the landing gear.

Bull waited as the engine stabilized and was pushed back in his seat as the jet engine thrust the huge speedboat forward, now much faster, as they had lost thousands of pounds of people and equipment.

Within seconds, they were travelling at one hundred kilometers per hour across the mighty Amazon toward the equipment cache, with Tank smiling at the refreshing rain coming in from the smashed cockpit window.

After thirty minutes of high-speed cruising among the canals, while letting the scanners guide them, Bull yelled out, "Bingo, straight ahead. Slow to idle."

Tank yanked back on the throttle, and the huge Beriev came off a plane and settled down in the water and slowly passed the shoreline of thick jungle, until Bull motioned to nudge it against the shore.

Tank gunned the throttle, and the Beriev nosed up snuggly into the thick jungle vines, so there was no need to moor it.

"Okay, let's do our packhorse routine," said Bull.

"Just like President Theodore Roosevelt in 1912. He came down here for a holiday and never recovered his health and died five years later," he explained.

For the next two hours, they packed the crates of tech toys from the still well-hidden drop location back to the Beriev. The K rations were of special interest and were the last to be removed.

"Don't ever want to be starving in the jungle again," Bull said darkly.

They both pulled the giant camouflage tarp back over the empty, unmarked crate.

Walking back to the fully loaded Beriev, Bull asked, "So, what's next?"

Above the sound of the downpour on the jungle leaves, Tank heard a familiar sound.

"I can't believe it," he said.

"What?" wondered Bull, who was wiping his face of heavy rain and settling down into the co-pilot's seat.

"Look over there," said Tank, pointing through the broken windshield at a tiny black speck hovering just within seeing distance.

"You've got to be kidding," said Bull. "Is that the same Robertson you've been talking about?"

"That's him," said Tank, as he quickly set the controls to start and pushed the rear thrust deflector into place to back them out of the jungle mooring spot.

"You're not going to try to do what I think you are, are you?"

"Yep. Okay, navigator, keep me on the tail of that pesky mosquito," yelled Tank.

With all the rain, most of the Amazon Basin was now filled with water and was a labyrinth of canals and shallow lakes.

The Beriev gathered speed as Bull called out directions for Tank to alter course and close in on the helicopter.

It would all depend on Tank's helmsmanship as he maneuvered the ungainly Beriev with flight controls in a way never envisioned by the designers.

The rain pelted their eyes through the smashed windshield as the Beriev kept accelerating in hot pursuit of the black chopper, which was still in sight.

They seemed to be staying with the chopper—maybe even catching it—but that would all change if the pilot noticed them and flew over land. As it was, in the storm conditions, the pilot was probably concentrating on finding his way to his base, wherever that was.

Suddenly a strong gust of wind came from the side, and the Beriev began rolling over, and Tank's excellent reflexes responded to counter the roll.

Bull looked over. "Thanks. This heap makes a nice speedboat, but a submarine I am not so sure about."

"Hey," responded Tank, "if we both believe that guy in the black chopper is a bad guy—and I think we do—why don't we slow him down and at the same time lighten our load?"

"What, you want to shoot at him?"

"Why not? We probably have enough firepower back there to bring down a squadron of fighters."

"Sure, but how is he going to lead us anywhere when he is crashed in the jungle?"

The Beriev was flat out and making eighty knots and was catching up on the chopper to the extent that Tank actually pulled back on the throttle a little, to avoid the pilot noticing them.

"What, have you stopped the torture test of that engine?" said Bull.

"Don't worry, the torture will resume later," said Tank, as he expertly steered the huge Beriev along the large canals in hot pursuit of the little black chopper.

"Why don't you go back there and start unpacking some weaponry, so at least we have guns at the ready if we need them?" said Tank.

"Are you saying you think we are getting close to the chopper's base?" asked Bull. "I don't see anything on the scanning equipment."

"Best to be ready. We can't scan over hills, remember," said Tank.

"There have been hundreds—maybe even thousands— of cocaine smuggling operations over the years. I am starting to think that we might be underestimating what we are up against, at least judging by the incessant buzzing in my neck," he said, with a look of frustration and his hand held to his neck.

Bull's face became serious, and as he crawled out from the co-pilot's seat to go and ready their weapons, he said, "Okay, one drug operation about to go down."

CHAPTER TWENTY-EIGHT

After being advised of his daughter's ordeal, Admiral Oliveira had ridden in his personal car over to the hospital and entered through the rear.

His chauffeur was a little perplexed, but it was a small price to pay to keep the media and any others off the trail of an explosive story.

The Admiral leaned over and gave his daughter a hug as she lay in the hospital bed.

"How are you feeling, my dear?" he asked. "I understand you have been through quite an ordeal. The doctors tell me you are in perfect shape except for a little dehydration. Thank God. Perhaps this will teach you not to go into the jungle and get lost with your crazy hobbies. Don't you think it's time to get married and move down to Brasilia and start a family?"

"I was not lost!" she shouted. "Who said I got lost? We were only ten kilometers from Manaus airport. I was kidnapped by crazed natives and held in a tree. These guys—they were like secret agents or something—they rescued me, and we were stranded in a rock plaza, but we kept dry because it was covered by a plant roof, and then they took off in an old spaceship or something…"

"I know, dear, I have been talking to the doctors and have heard the whole story that you told them. It seems you have been bitten by a parasite that affects your thoughts, or perhaps the lack of proper rest and food has caused this delusion."

"Delusion? Let me speak to the doctor. I am not delusional. I was rescued by a plane without wings. When have I ever been delusional?" she added, more than a little affronted.

"Honey, look at me. For now, your stories of supermen rescuing you will have to wait to be confirmed. Doctor, can you help here?" asked the Admiral, as a doctor in a white lab coat approached with a large hypodermic needle in his hand.

"No problem, Admiral. This will help her sleep it off."

The young doctor proceeded to inject a strong dose of sleeping agent into her veins, and she immediately closed her eyes and fell asleep.

As he walked out the back of the hospital, the Admiral got in his car and raced to the secure military base located along the Amazon River.

Once there, he turned on CNN and then BBC and was shocked to see so many scenes of carnage and chaos in the USA.

It appeared to be the War of the Worlds.

All modes of transportation were experiencing difficulties. There were so many air crashes that the FAA was holding an emergency meeting to consider grounding all aircraft. Car crashes across the country were so numerous that CNN had simply taken to showing numbers of reported accidents along the bottom of the screen. The numbers were rising by the hundreds every minute.

After a few minutes, the reporter started to talk about incidents of domestic abuse, shootings, and other violent acts. The reporter said that officials across the country were sure it was some kind of coordinated attack but had no idea what it was, where to start looking, or how to solve it or defend against it.

As employees were affected by their own actions or those of others, businesses and government offices were disrupted and closing. The owners were in despair as the losses were mounting, and they could not pay their suppliers.

Government offices supplying critical aid to parents and children and others in need could not open their doors because so many were absent that there were no staff to deal with people, even if they let them in. Computer servicing was in short supply, so that desk work stations were closed, even in the event that staff showed up.

The Admiral sat silent. He thought of his daughter and her two assistants being held in a drugged state at the hospital. One day, when all this was over, after she understood the need for absolute silence about her new imaginary heroes, Tank and Bull, she would realize she could not possibly be allowed to inadvertently blow the cover of the world's best hope for salvation, just as they were in the middle of their mission.

CHAPTER TWENTY-NINE

Nastin flew low and slow over the treetops and could only see the canal in front, as the sky was black with low-hanging clouds and the rain continued to obscure his visibility.

About half a kilometer back and in hot pursuit, the Beriev was cruising at forty kilometers as it maneuvered through the twists and turns of the canal leading to Gran Hussan's compound.

"Hey, look," said Bull.

"Look at what?" asked Tank, whose eyes were stinging from hours of pelting rain.

"It looks like our boy has arrived. He's slowing down. Wait, it looks like he's spinning toward our direction."

"Take him out; we don't want him to radio his base when he sees us."

"But won't a crashed helicopter seem a little suspicious?"

"I don't have time to explain—shoot!" yelled Tank, setting the throttle to idle, as the Beriev settled low in the water.

Bull, who had been holding a mini-zook in his hand for the last thirty minutes, reached through the cockpit window. It was a bazooka but handheld like a Magnum 44 for easy-to-damage targets, like a helicopter.

Bull pulled the trigger and the rocket-propelled grenade silently left the gun's upper surface, which was configured like a catapult ramp, with a guide in the center and a thick foil hand, arm, and face heat shield.

The grenade only took about three seconds to bridge the distance between the Beriev and the helicopter and struck the tail rotor, which only took a slight hit to critically damage.

Out of balance, the rotor wobbled violently and soon broke off, cartwheeling into the jungle, leaving the pilot frantically trying to regain control of the rotating copter. His efforts were futile, as the helicopter spun out of control and struck a giant Malato tree and crashed in a burning hulk on the wet jungle floor.

"Man, do I love toys," said Tank.

"Me too," replied Bull.

"Do you think he survived?"

"Nope."

"Let's duck into that little canal off to the side," said Tank, as he gunned the engine like an outboard and steered the air rudder hard over and waited for the Beriev to slowly make the turn.

He yanked back on the throttle and then killed the engine, so the plane floated forward silently with just momentum and nudged into the jungle at the water's edge.

They waited as the whine of the turbine slowed and the engine became silent.

They cocked their ears and tried to hear what was going on at the helicopter crash site but could only hear water, the torrential rains on the leaves, and the Beriev's fuselage.

"Well, I don't hear anything," said Bull.

"It may be that nobody else even heard the crash, for all we know," replied Tank.

"So, what's the plan?"

"Let's grab a backpack of toys and go see what trouble we can get into."

They simultaneously reached for their necks as the buzzers went off.

"When do you think we will get back to Giant?" asked Bull.

"Maybe never," said Tank with a smile, as they both finished loading their small backpacks and opened the Beriev's fuselage door.

"Before we walk into a nest of trouble, why don't we use a Flybot first?" suggested Bull, as Tank reached into his friend's backpack and removed a small case, which he opened.

Inside was what looked like a larger version of the dragonfly-sized Flybot used to alert Dr. Oliveira during her rescue.

This one had a full sensor package and could be controlled in flight. It also came with a small video screen on the control handset, which showed information, including what the little craft could see.

"I don't think that thing's going to work very well in these conditions, the way you have the sensors configured," said Bull.

"Why not?" said Tank, as he powered up the half-meter-sized dragonfly. "With dual sets of wings, dragonflies are the best fliers of the natural world."

"I am not worried about the flying. I am worried about the camera seeing anything in this rain. There will be raindrops all over the lens."

"Okay, you are the boss; set it up your own way."

Bull set to work on the big dragonfly, setting up the sensors to identify movement, noise, and infrared heat signatures.

When he was finished, Tank powered up the wings and tossed it in the air, and it soon began fluttering in the direction of the helicopter crash.

Within a minute or two, there was a large image on the screen which identified the hot heat signature of the engine of the crashed helicopter. Nearby, strapped in a wrecked portion of the cockpit, was the much cooler heat signature of the pilot. There were no other heat signatures nearby.

"Okay, that's the pilot. And nobody is on the crash site now, so his friends may not have even noticed. But how do we know if he's dead?"

"Take it to within two meters of the body, and set it to hover mode. Within ten seconds, it will process the body motions and his exhaled breath to determine breathing or not, and presto, we will know if he's dead."

"Good to have you along," said Tank, who did as Bull said.

"Okay, he's dead all right. Now let's have this little bug do a bit more looking around," said Bull. "We can let it do the legwork for a change."

"What is the range of that thing?" asked Tank.

"Five kilometers or so, depending on conditions. The heavy rain will definitely cut that down," answered Bull.

"You mean, the wings will have to work extra hard to flick off the raindrops?"

"Not just that, that little microprocessor is working extra hard in these winds trying to separate what it is looking for from the complex and changing background conditions," said Bull.

"Sounds like it will be lucky to fly twenty meters and report back," said Tank, who appeared to have lost confidence in the gadget.

"Don't worry; it should work just fine. Now hand the controls to me to program or we will be here all day," said Bull, who quickly and expertly set the controls.

Bull set to work on the control panel while the Flybot hovered harmlessly thirty feet above the crashed helicopter, out of their sight, fifty meters off in the jungle.

"Okay, now what are we looking for?" asked Tank.

Bull finished programming the new parameters and pressed the Enter button, and then turned to Tank.

"We are looking for humans and man-made structures. Sound good enough?"

"Okay, let's do it."

To avoid the continuing downpour, they both sat inside the Beriev's side fuselage door, and Bull held the control panel out in the rain to ensure good reception while operating the controls, while Tank focused more on the screen and commented to Bull about what he was seeing.

They decided to break into the caviar and Russian black rye bread, as they had no idea when they would next have the opportunity to eat.

CHAPTER THIRTY

Gran Hussan walked to his communications room, looking out at the violent Amazonian downpour and hearing the cracking thunder.

He picked up the microphone and pressed the transmit button.

"Nastin, this is Hussan. Are you there?" He waited.

"Nastin, this is Hussan. Are you there?" he repeated.

From the speaker came a response with a lot of static, "This is Nastin, over."

"When will you be back at base?" asked Hussan.

"Fifteen minutes," replied Nastin.

"Is the coast clear for our launch?"

"I have been trying to reach Carlos, but the reception is too poor in these conditions. It seems the troublesome scientists survived, or at least some of them. They were joined by a wrecked aircraft in Manaus, and the last I saw they were heading back into the jungle."

"Heading into the jungle where?" asked Hussan.

"Back near where we thought we had dealt with them."

"What were they doing?"

"It looked like they were packing crates from the jungle into the airplane."

"And what direction did they fly off in?"

"They didn't fly anywhere. The plane looks like it has crashed; it's pretty rough."

"You are not making any sense. If it can't fly, how did it get them to the jungle to pick up cargo?"

The line crackled with poor reception. "It's a big speedboat," said Nastin, slightly exasperated at not knowing what to call the wingless Beriev.

"You are not making any sense," said Hussan again, his temper rising. "Get back to base and we will talk then."

He would have a chat with Carlos about this assistant who talked in circles.

Hussan walked across the open area with the tennis courts, using his arm to shield his face from the pouring rain, and arrived at what looked like an innocent guest house. He strode across the foyer and pressed a wall panel button and waited while a huge painting slid out of the way, revealing an elevator door.

The elevator took him down twenty feet to a bunker that was still above the high water level of the nearby river canal.

Seeing Carlos talking to a group of Ukrainian engineers, he interrupted and said, "Okay, when can we launch?"

"The vessel is filled to the brim. The red radar masking soil has been swept from the top, and with these rains, the dry-dock has been filled with water, raising it to launching level," replied Carlos.

"So, can we say the ekranoplan is full of cargo and fuel and is ready to do its delivery?"

"Yes, sir, I am told the vessel is ready to go."

Had Carlos answered differently, he would have been shot on the spot.

"What should I tell the crew?" asked Carlos.

"Tell them to have their bags packed and be ready to launch at a moment's notice. For the other seven sites too," replied Hussan.

Carlos repeated the order, and the crew talked urgently amongst themselves and then walked toward the door.

"And, Carlos, have you told them about the bonus?"

"Yes, I told them what you told me: if the mission is a success, each will receive a one million dollar bonus."

Hussan looked at the crew, and they all smiled and laughed at the prospect of the money and then turned to get their bags and walk over to where the vessel was floating in its lock, ready to be launched.

Gran Hussan smiled to himself at the prospect of giving out the bonuses as he walked back to the radio room. He picked up a satellite phone and called his brother Samir Hussan in the United States.

The line buzzed and crackled, and then Samir picked up the line.

"Hello," he said in Arabic.

"My brother, the time has come."

"The vessel is ready for launch?"

"Yes, we will be leaving in an hour."

"You will be aboard? Why? You should stay safe in the compound and keep well away from this."

"My brother, these people are worse infidels than the Americans that we are going to destroy. They continually make mistakes, and I will be required on board to ensure we are successful."

"Your dedication will be rewarded," said Samir, while relaxing in his soft leather chair. "Call me later when you are underway."

The Americans, Samir thought to himself, *would be caught so flat-footed by what would occur over the next few days, it would be almost pitiful to watch.*

Already, with just the sample quantities shipped, the TV channels were swamped with stories of accidents and odd occurrences that caused Samir to smile, since he had caused them, and they knew nothing about him or the drugs or the master plan.

If not already, then very soon, they would start to realize they were under attack. In the hours and days after, they would realize that the most important part of the attack, the part that would ensure their defeat in their own land, had been waged and won years earlier, right under their noses.

While the media had mentioned many times that it was odd that in the hours after 9/11 dozens of Saudi Arabian nationals had casually flown out of the country in their private jets, while every other aircraft, including all US military planes, had been grounded, this revelation of gross and blatant preferential status only gave a small glimpse at the influence of that time—and it had grown immensely since.

Many of the most toxic Muslims were now fully integrated in the county, state, and federal governments and agencies, and few of them had an ounce of loyalty to the United States but would lie to their death denying that was true.

Americans did not know that their national identity had been dismantled right before their eyes by the same groups behind 9/11 that burned with more hatred than ever. Far from letting up in the face of increased national security steps and the so-called war on terror, these Muslims had been fighting on a second front in what they called a cultural jihad, within USA borders and in plain sight.

Built on the lies permitted within the Qur'ān to further Islam, the Saudi Arabian government had been pouring billions of dollars into colleges and universities across the USA to establish and support Islamic student associations and to influence weak and stupid politicians or candidates who supported their causes, lobby groups, and the Muslim Advocates and its hundreds of affiliated groups.

Samir had been stressed when some years ago, an FBI intercept had actually discovered their Advocates USA Manifesto, which stated their plans and goals in plain type, and alarmed agents had gone public.

As with so many things in the United States, the public, concerned with their own problems and inundated with thousands of sources of information from TV, internet, and newspapers, viewed the story as just more meaningless information.

Other than the initial run from one news organization, the story had been effectively buried by the well-financed Muslim lobbyists funded by the Saudis, who mailed out thousands of threatening legal letters and who complained it was hate mongering and breached their constitutional rights. The letters were not only sent to the actual TV stations and newspaper companies, but also to the homes of the journalist employees and were officially registered. They were being sued privately. Although it was a corporate matter, they knew that left-leaning judges had started a trend of personal liability years before, in apparent ignorance of the longstanding traditions and concept of the corporate veil which insulated staff, and that was enough to strike fear into the hearts of the reporters and editors, who had families to support and who wanted to avoid the controversy.

With each audacious and aggressive move, which was met with little or no response—and in essence, capitulation—the Muslims grew more confident in their adopted lands.

Over the years, the Muslims had found that America was more interested in promoting freedom of religion than protecting its own founding religion, Christianity. The country retained images and symbols of the Christianity that had formed the foundation, but they were hollow and meaningless. More importantly, nobody was defending Christianity or its importance because they bought into the sophisticated attacks, funded by the Saudis, that were packaged in arguments proposing that the United States' historical linkage to Christianity was wrong. It was too much work to sort out a correct position during a news flash because they didn't care anyway, since stuff about church was boring.

The lies increased.

This allowed Muslims to move in and increase the rhetoric along several fronts. First, they made sure that it was understood that Islam would not tolerate offensive comments. That meant that any speech, articles, or television shows that were deemed offensive—which they single-handedly and outrageously defined as anything that was not complimentary—would be protested. Next, they developed a proposal in the United Nations that would define it as hate speech, worldwide, to comment in a non-complimentary manner about Islam. That this was contrary to the United States constitutional right of free speech did not matter to them; it was the dumb Americans' loss.

Due to Islamic influence, new bibles, called Chrislam, had been written and were in print. They had removed words and sentences that were absolutely fundamental to Christianity but were offensive to Islamic people, to further confuse new, casual, or less attentive Christians that were not fully up to date on these activities, which was difficult even for the most devout. They had paid off so many thousands of government officials and press throughout the country that a clear and full accounting of their activities over the years would be next to impossible to assemble.

Samir smiled. When the infidel Americans tried to solve the crisis that was about to unfold, they would find it very frustrating to put the solution into action.

While the Americans often said that nobody was sure how many hardworking Mexicans were in the country illegally—and the numbers ranged from ten to twenty million—what they also did not know was how many devout Muslims were already in the USA.

The official census said that there were seven million. But it had been the fastest growing global religion for forty years, and with the impetus to lie to spread the Muslim faith written right in the Qur'ān, the immigration papers, student visas, working visas, and all other related documentation had routinely been falsified, assisted by the new employees' Islamic loyalties. Loyal federal government employees were in short supply and had never verified the information and didn't keep track. There were actually thirty million practicing Muslims in the USA. The names and contact information were all in Samir's secret offshore databases.

And they were all ready to start a massive and overwhelming campaign of rallying and writing letters and appearing on TV and internet to adopt Sharia Law to deal with the coming law and order crisis, which the drug importation scheme would foment. Of course, they would call Sharia another name to confuse and overwhelm resistance. To those that discovered the truth, they would accuse them of racism in opposing Islam.

The call to arms would be made at the worst point of the crisis. The inability to strictly and swiftly convict the hundreds of thousands of drug abusers, who had collapsed the economy and almost all of which who were falsely implicated by the spiked neurotoxin and were in truth innocent, would be blamed on the lax courts, the lawyers, the cops, and on the Christian-based American legal system, which still included such outrages as swearing on the Bible and due process.

But, behind the scenes, using every liberal law available amongst their Islam dictate to lie, would be the promoters of Sharia Law.

It would be sold with intonations of love and caring as a gift of law and order from the people of Islam to the people of the United States. Other countries had been convinced to adopt Sharia Law, so why not the USA?

However, the truth was that the Qur'ān did not differentiate between church and state; they are one, and Sharia Law in any form whatsoever if adopted would be nothing less than the adoption of a key facet of Islam by the American government.

Thereafter, through lobbying and bribes, Christianity would be suppressed and opposed at every opportunity, all while the public face of Muslims would be loving and caring and would grow dominant.

Unseen billion-dollar funding from Saudi Arabia and other Gulf Muslim states tainted all political discourse and media coverage because most elected officials over the last ten years had been funded by Islamic dollars or had had elections with tampered Excel Electronics voting machines.

Christianity would be cast as unreasonable and extreme in its views and holidays such as Christmas falsely portrayed as commercialized frauds. Christian leaders and politicians and citizens who spoke against the Islam steamroller would be blackballed as ignorant, bigoted zealots.

There would be no turning back, and the United Sates would become the symbol for the world of Islam, and the founding principles of the Christian God as intended by the creators of the United States Constitution would be lost to the dustbin of history, all without a gun having been fired.

CHAPTER THIRTY-ONE

Thirty minutes went by, and they only heard the sound of the torrential downpour.

The monitor screen was blank, and they started wondering if the helicopter pilot had only paused to hover and turn to see if he was being tailed, before continuing on his journey. Maybe there was no jungle compound there.

The seagull-sized dragonfly drone fluttered amidst the thick trunks of the Malato trees and the huge leaves of the underbrush and continued to compare the sensor information it was receiving with the memory log of the typical parameters of those things it was searching for, such as dimensional wood, cement, glass, or metal.

The buffeting winds, rain, and many jungle obstacles caused the flight CPU to use up a lot of its battery reserves just keeping airborne at its programmed six-meter search mode altitude. The search CPU was also using maximum battery power to separate many false targets—including abundant wildlife— from the programmed search targets.

"Hey, Tank, can you believe this thing has already used fifty percent of its flight endurance time?" asked Bull, glancing down at the flashing screen warning, intended to alert pilots that if they wanted to ensure the return of the drone, they should start heading back when they saw the warning.

"Are you kidding? I am enjoying this caviar too much to start stomping through the jungle."

"Well, if we don't find anything soon, we may have to," said Bull.

Tank turned to grab another tin of caviar and left the screen with Bull.

"Hey, you better have seconds later. Take a look at this," said Bull.

Tank crawled back from the crate of caviar and looked to the monitor in Bull's hand, which was flashing with numbers and lights and emitting a quiet beeping sound.

"What does that mean, the battery's dead and we have to retrieve it?" cracked Tank.

"It means you better get behind the controls and crank up that turbine," said Bull, with a seriousness in his voice that Tank recognized from their long association.

"Do you hear that?" asked Tank, who thought he heard a muffled roar coming from deep in the jungle.

Bull was too preoccupied to answer.

Tank quickly ran forward and sat himself down, while Bull closed up the Beriev's front side fuselage door, while the starting groans of the jet turbine engine could be heard coming from the rear.

"How bad?" asked Tank.

"Bad. There's a massive compound back there, with one section stretching 1500 feet. There's at least seventy guys running in this direction, and some are firing weapons," said Bull.

"That little screen told you all that? How far away are they?" asked Tank, as his question was answered by the telltale pinging sound of bullets hitting the fuselage. "It sounds like they don't like my Beriev."

Within seconds, there was a hail of bullets ricocheting in the cockpit and smashing what was left of the windshield.

The sound of dozens of AK-47s firing could be heard coming from the jungle. Hundreds of rounds could be heard striking the craft, and the cockpit instruments exploded in a shower of glass, plastic, and sparks.

Bull and Tank ducked toward the cockpit floor and hoped they would be spared.

"Can I ask you a question?" said Tank.

"Sure, I love answering your questions when I am about to die," replied Bull.

"Did the Flybot happen to tell you the position of these guys that are now shooting us?"

Bull grabbed the monitor from the floor and looked at the screen.

"Well, this is a saved image, which means they shot down the Flybot. But before it died, its last report was that these guys are actually straight in front of us."

Two men suddenly landed on the fuselage just below the windshield and were trying to pull themselves up with their hands, holding the shards of glass in the open window frames.

As they peeked over the edge, they were met by strong kicks to the face by Tank and Bull, and both men tumbled to the ground in front of the plane.

"Okay," said Tank, over the scream of the abused single jet turbine of the Beriev, "let's see how they like 20,000 pounds of thrust in the face."

Tank reached for the engine reverse thrust deflectors and yanked on the control.

The deflectors activated and moved in front of the rearward jet blast, and immediately the hurricane-force jet engine thrust was redirected frontward past the cockpit and directly on the gunmen approaching from the jungle, lifting them up and tossing them fifty feet back into the jungle, as the giant Beriev started to slide from the jungle, where it was beached backward into the canal.

With the jet still moving rearward, Tank reached down and retracted the deflectors to arrest the plane's rearward motion. He turned the control rudder hard over and again and jammed the engine to wide open, and the engines thrust against the rear air rudder, turning the plane's tail toward the confused gunmen and spraying them with tons of water and muck from the canal.

Bull was flat on the floor trying to avoid the occasional bullets, which could be heard ricocheting in the interior.

"I'll have to remember that trick: jet engine as assault weapon," he said with a grin.

Tank sat hunched in the cockpit seat and looked over to Bull. "You better hold that thought. Have you got a piece of Ton O Gum?" asked Tank.

"Sorry, I haven't had any since I was ten years old," replied Bull.

"Well then, how about a pair of gumboots?"

"Can I ask what you are driving at?"

The jet engine was screaming at maximum revs, as the massive wingless plane shuddered as it plowed its way down the canal and away from the hail of bullets, which were still striking the fuselage and leaving hundreds of holes.

"Look down," said Tank in reply.

At their feet there was a flood of water coming from around the cockpit foot wells.

"They have turned the front end of this bus into a perforated sugar scoop with all those bullet holes in the hull. It looks like we can't even get this thing above ten knots, let alone the high planing speed that got us here."

"Okay, so we chug off into the sunset and arrive downriver in Manaus a few hours later than planned. I can handle that," replied Bull.

"You don't get it. Those guys have surely got a flotilla of small boats they are running to as we speak and will soon be in hot pursuit. And with the holes below the water line, since they were shooting at us when the lower bow was lifted up onto the jungle beach and fully exposed, this bus is going to keep shipping water—and far more than the bilge pumps can handle. And I can't find the bilge pump switch anyway," said Tank.

"So, you're saying it's going to sink with those holes, no matter what. Okay, you're the boss; any bright ideas?" asked Bull, who was now looking worried.

"I think we have a solution, and in part we can thank the volumes of rye bread and caviar you have consumed."

The plane continued to shudder as the weakened fuselage and the tons of water sloshing around in the lower hold took their toll, and the continued abuse had caused massive stress cracks in the fuselage.

The hail of bullets suddenly resumed, as the gunmen had retrieved small boats and were in hot pursuit.

"Get onto the tail," instructed Tank.

"What?"

"Crawl out the access hatch at the base of the rear vertical stabilizer and use the handholds to crawl up and onto the top of the horizontal T-tail," ordered Tank.

"Are you nuts? It's thirty feet above the water, not to mention the jet engine. Plus, I will be a sitting target for those guys—they will kill me in five seconds. What an earth would you ask me to go there for anyway?"

"With your weight, if you hang on top of the tail which extends ten feet over the water at the back of the plane, the leverage will raise the nose, pulling the holes up out of the water and stopping the leaks, so we can get this bus up to a high speed plane like a ski boat and get out of here. And don't worry about getting shot; the jet stream will deflect any bullets. You can take my word for it."

"What about the hot jet blast? I'll be fried," said Bull.

"Remember, only the engine on one side is running. The other engine is cold, and it's twelve feet below you to boot," replied Tank.

Looking at the water streaming across the cockpit floor, Bull knew the amphibious aircraft would soon sink and that their options were somewhere between nil and none. He remembered that Tank was a ballistics expert and would be basing his comments about the jet blast deflecting bullets on facts.

"Why don't you pull back hard on the stick to lift the nose with the horizontal T stabilizer, just like trim tabs on a boat?" asked Bull, without conviction.

"In case you haven't noticed, I am already pulling back on the stick, and we are at full throttle, so this is as good as it gets without you taking a ride on the tail. Remember, these air controls work best when the thing is flying, and we're not flying."

"Okay, but what about the water that's already in this pig? There are thousands of pounds of water around our feet, in case you hadn't noticed. That's going to keep slowing us down and won't be helped by my deflecting bullets on the tail," asked Bull, who was still looking for flaws in the plan.

"I've already thought of that," replied Tank. "Before you climb up, use the Glock machine gun to blast a few holes behind the fuel tanks, at the rear part of the fuselage floor, so that as the front lifts when the hull rotates, all that water will rush to the back, and it has somewhere to drain out."

"You are telling me to put holes in the plane to let out the water from other holes in the plane?"

"Something like that," said Tank.

"What about when we slow down? Won't we have water coming in from both ends then? How are you going to solve that?" asked Bull.

"I haven't thought that far ahead yet. Hopefully I can beach it. You better get moving or we won't be alive anyway," said Tank, who gave his big friend a strong shove to the rear.

Tank could feel the plane's nose rise a little, just from Bull walking to the rear.

Seconds later, Tank heard Bull firing the machine gun down into the plane's rear fuselage floor, turning the aluminum into Swiss cheese.

Tank heard the increase in noise from the engine as the rear access hatch was opened and Bull crawled out to carry out their risky plan.

Tank wagged the rudder back and forth to increase the spray that the engine was pushing back to the gunmen, who were getting closer in their small boats and firing with increased intensity.

Bull leaned over and grabbed a crate of mini grenades and then pulled his massive bulk up and out of the hatch and cringed as the engine screamed at maximum RPM and the bullets could be heard striking the fuselage.

He pulled himself up the rear vertical rudder footholds and could feel the massive Beriev rotating backward, the same as when he used to go to the back of a canoe as a youth and the entire length would rise. The nose was rising and the speed was increasing.

He looked to the rear and saw four gunboats gaining on them.

Wedging the small crate of mini grenades between his leg and the vertical stabilizer, he quickly pulled the pin on all ten of them, two at a time, and tossed them into the jet blast, which carried them hundreds of feet back to the boats chasing them.

Like a row of firecrackers, they exploded, and three of the boats were blasted out of the river.

Bull could see the spray from the hull being deflected to the sides as the aircraft became a planing hull once again, and the accumulated water flooded out the improvised drains he had shot in the floor at the rear.

High above the water, Bull looked forward, and the massive Beriev looked like a white whale stretching out in front, as Tank maneuvered the plane to follow the canal and re-enter the Amazon River to make their way down to Manaus.

With the wind making it difficult to hang on and the remaining gunmen having given up and fallen far to the rear, Bull crawled back down and in through the hatch and soon joined Tank in the co-pilot's seat, having noticed on the way that the water was swirling as it left through the holes in the rear floor, like in a bathtub drain.

"Not bad, not bad," said Bull with a smile, as he complimented his friend's successful plan to save their lives, as he had so many times in the past.

"I heard the explosions. Your idea was great too, but we're not saved yet. I think the turbine is finally fried," said Tank, as he pointed out the engine temperature gauge, which showed that the engine was overheating and should be shut down immediately.

Bull went to the back and opened the hatch to have a look and then closed it and crawled forward to Tank.

"I hate to tell you this, but that engine is smoking a little, and more gunmen are going to notice and come after us again."

The engine began making grinding sounds, and the Beriev was slowing again.

Immediately, they both noticed water coming from the cockpit and also from the rear where Bull had shot up the floor.

"Okay, genius, what's plan B?" asked Bull.

"Let's break open a few boxes and see if we can give them a few gifts," said Tank, locking the controls and walking back to the crates of gear from Giant they had taken with them after dropping the rest near Manaus.

"Decisions, decisions," said Tank, as he surveyed the selection of high-tech weaponry spread over the cargo floor.

The first bullets could be heard zinging by from the gunmen, who were still well out of range for accuracy.

"Can I help? We want long-range and multiple targeting," said Bull. "That narrows the choice for us."

Bull leaned over and picked up a case the size of a briefcase and opened it. Inside were five recesses with miniaturized torpedoes in them.

"This is too easy," he said, adjusting them one by one.

"If they work. What are they supposed to do?" asked Tank, who didn't really care, since they had no other options anyway.

"Torpedoes take out ships. We don't need that kind of power for these little boats. These are short-range mini torpedoes with more than enough TNT to take out those fourteen-foot skiffs."

Without fanfare, he tossed the lot of them out the side door into the Amazon, which they had just merged with from the canal.

Immediately, the mini torpedoes sensed water and the propellers started screaming as the tiny CPUs activated and started homing in on the skiffs' propeller signatures using acoustic sensors.

Tank walked back to the cockpit and sat down, shutting down the turbine before it caught fire or broke up and sent parts flying in all directions.

Water was flooding the floor and had risen past their ankles.

"I give us five minutes before the water reaches the huge holes where the wings were torn out and we go to Davy Jones' locker in a hurry," said Bull.

"Davy Jones never came up the Amazon, so it's no locker for you," said Tank.

"No worries; he never kept anything good in there anyway."

They both were sitting and watching the water rise, while listening for the explosions that would put a stop to the machine gun fire that was perforating the plane and would otherwise be shredding their flesh.

"We are a big target. I guess they have no problem hitting us, no matter how far back they are," said Tank.

Suddenly they heard five explosions, and the gunfire stopped.

"I guess we won't get shot to death after all," said Bull.

"Nope," said Tank, as the water started spilling in from the large wing-root holes.

"Question for you," said Bull, who was rummaging around in the rear of the plane.

"Shoot," said Tank.

"Do you think a plane that is designed to act as a boat would have a life raft?"

"That's a good question, and the salesperson who sold me this thing never covered that in his sales pitch," said Tank, who was now starting to partially float from the rising water level.

"Ah, I guess those Russian designers couldn't get around the life raft requirement, since this plane was intended for international sales," said Bull.

"Are you saying you found a raft?" asked Tank.

"Bingo," said Bull, who pulled the large, square rubber package from a side locker and pushed it along the now waist-deep water and out the door.

"What about the rest of this equipment?" asked Tank. "It's a shame to send it all to the bottom."

"Well, you can come back and retrieve it if it means that much to you. Let's grab a Glock each and let the rest go. As you can recall, these rubber life rafts have enough problems keeping afloat without a thousand pounds of armaments."

"Agreed," said Tank, as they both pushed out the door and swam away before pulling the ripcord and watching the huge life raft inflate within seconds.

They pulled themselves up and over the sides and fell into the cavernous interior and watched as the hardworking Beriev filled with water and sank lower with each moment.

"Seems a shame," said Tank. "That plane is probably only a few months old and, I bet, costs millions to replace. I mean, it only had one engine out and a few scratches when I took delivery."

"You are forgetting one thing," replied Bull. "You are hard on things."

They both looked on as the Beriev 200 Amphibian sank by the front first, then slowly along the long fuselage, and finally only the tall T-tail could be seen, and then it too disappeared.

CHAPTER THIRTY-TWO

The massive ekranoplan rolled over the jungle floor, squeezing the plants down as the air supporting it was compressed.

On the bridge, Gran Hussan was impressed and had called his brother to hail the aircraft as a masterful creation of the Muslim world that would ensure the mission's success. The gargantuan mystery craft was invisible to radar and almost completely silent. Except for the huge imprint on the jungle floor, they would be all but invisible—only a massive rolling mist.

Peering ahead, he could see the endless green jungle and low-hanging black clouds above.

"How long until we reach the rendezvous point?" asked Gran Hussan, staring at Carlos.

"About four hours. As we approach the east coast, the weather will lift, but the white sea mist will shroud our presence. To ensure we are not spotted, we will settle onto the waters of the estuary and let the craft sink to just below the surface, alongside the ship."

"A plane that floats underwater? This had better work," said Hussan with a threatening tone.

"I have been checking over the vessel for hours, and every single detail is as the chief engineer said it would be. I have no reason to believe it is not able to stand a shallow water immersion; after all, even amateur drug smugglers are using home-built subs."

Hurtling over the jungle floor, the juggernaut rolled toward its destination through the pelting rain, unseen by anyone.

CHAPTER THIRTY-THREE

Tank and Bull were lazily paddling the raft toward the south side of the river when a chicken boat spotted them, after almost running them over, and altered course slightly to pick them up. An old-fashioned double decker boat seventy feet long with a narrow stern and a bow that tapered like a canoe and hammocks with people sleeping, chicken boats were usually loaded with people and livestock headed to market in Manaus and could be seen plying the river all year long, their ancient diesel engines making a distinctive chugging sound like the African Queen.

The boat did not come to a full stop, as the captain expected even rescued survivors to do a little work for the ride. Tank and Bull quickly knifed the raft and jumped over and pulled themselves aboard, hearing the hissing air and watching as it crumpled and sank.

"I guess we are just a couple of typical gringos like the captain picks up on the river each day," said Bull.

"I suppose would-be adventurers are not unusual on this river, since all manner of explorers have been coming here for the last four hundred years," replied Tank. "I bet he figures that if there were other survivors to pick up, or anything drastic that couldn't wait till we reach Manus, we would tell him. We might as well enjoy the ride."

They both found a little space and lay out under the deck cover and tried to get some rest, watching the goats and chickens and their owners who were sleeping in hammocks.

"Any ideas about that 1500-foot structure the Flybot spotted?" asked Tank.

"Not sure. I know it wasn't made from concrete or steel or, for that matter, any normal building materials."

"So, what did the Flybot suggest?"

"Nothing. It just gave the dimensions but otherwise drew a blank."

"Was that all there was?"

"Nope. The Flybot listed fifteen other structures that extended a little above ground, of all different shapes. Some were typical jungle palace type structures, such as the large house, tennis courts, and a dock structure with a good size yacht… The rest impossible to tell."

"Yeah, but the gunmen rule out a legal operation, and only cocaine could drive the type of firepower those guys have. Something big was going on there," said Bull.

"Getting back to all those structures, any ideas?" asked Tank.

"Kurt, I only got a glance at the screen before we came under gunfire and I had other things to do. Normally, with a few adjustments, it's possible to get much better data from those Flybots, but as you recall, we were running for our lives."

"Agreed. But I'm going to tell Giant that this is very likely our candidate and proceed on that basis, okay?"

"Hey, you're the boss," replied Bull.

"We better let him know first thing, or this buzzer is going to vibrate right out of my neck," said Bull, holding his neck.

"We will check on Noddins and the Doctor and see how Lugar is coming along with assembling my new drone."

The chicken boat pulled up on the red beach in downtown Manaus, and after walking ashore, Tank hailed a cab to get them to his apartment suite located on a hill overlooking the Amazon.

Once there, they each got cleaned up, grabbed a bite to eat, and contacted Giant with Tank's spare satellite phone.

The line hissed, and finally the haunting voice of Giant could be heard echoing from the phone. "Did Bull find you?"

"Affirmative."

"Where have you been?"

"We found what we believe is the cocaine operation," said Tank, skipping to the main point.

"Have you stopped the shipment?"

"Not so simple," said Tank. "They are extremely well armed and we were unsuccessful. But we know what we are up against and will be heading back to neutralize it in the morning."

"Do you have enough firepower?" asked Giant.

"We lost some along the way but have enough left to do the job."

"Tank," said Giant.

"Yes, I am here."

"It seems this mission is not about cocaine after all."

"No. Then what is it about?"

"It's about the fall of the United States of America as we know it," replied Giant.

"Are we not attacking a cocaine operation?"

"Yes, but the cocaine is actually different from normal cocaine. Already, the entire United States has been disrupted, and authorities are scrambling to find out what is going on and stop it."

"So, if they don't know what is going on, how do we know this cocaine operation is the problem?"

"I can confirm it's linked to much larger forces at play, and we have substantial proof of this."

"Can you send in the cavalry to help us?"

"We can't be advising the US government, or any government for that matter, about issues that they officially don't know about yet. If we do, we will debase our own existence."

"Are you saying we are on our own?" asked Tank.

"Yes," said Giant, who then hung up.

Bull had been listening in the background.

"Let me guess. No help, and it's urgent?"

"Yep," replied Tank, as he sank into his couch and watched the rain and mist-shrouded river.

"Nothing ever changes in this business, does it?" he asked Tank.

"Nope," replied Tank, as he closed his eyes and drifted off into a deep sleep.

Doctor Oliveira and the others would have to wait.

CHAPTER THIRTY-FOUR

Gran Hussan hung up the phone after talking to his brother Samir in Washington. His adrenaline was spiking, and he was as excited as he had ever been in his life.

The master plan they had first talked about while sitting cross-legged on the floor in a village in Saudi Arabia fifteen year ago was now going to happen. The plan had been massively altered, but the effect was the same. The evil USA would finally be collapsed into the dustbin of history as a blip, an aberration, with its oddball democracy and freedoms and fallen Christian society that only served to enslave the people to the wishes of the corrupt and blasphemous leaders, who were intent on suppressing the teachings of Muhammad and criticizing the Qur'ān.

He closed his eyes and could see the future.

The groundwork of the Saudis to strip the Christian faith from the entire country had worked. It was not in colleges, schools, or universities. It was gone from pledges of allegiance, from the military, from the city halls, and from the federal and state governments and all their arms. And it had all happened with the billions of dollars of money from the secretive Saudi, who bankrolled the hundreds of lawsuits from "secular" residents who were falsely acting offended at the traditional inclusion of a small amount of Christianity, although hypocritically being Muslim themselves, a faith which advocated a thousand times the integration of church and state as that in the West.

Hussan smiled as he recalled that his brother had told him last year that they were successful in getting the Federal Broadcasting Licensing Board to make it illegal to play Christmas carols on the radio.

He was amazed. Nobody seemed to be catching on.

The actions funded by Muslims to eradicate Christianity from life in the USA had nothing to do with the separation of church and state; that was all hogwash. Muslims believed that the church and state were inseparable anyway. All they were doing was sweeping the floors of the Christian faith—to which they were diametrically opposed—to set the stage to fill the vacuum with the Muslim faith.

BLACK V

The idiots, he smiled to himself. *Did they think the blood lost in fighting Christians in the Crusades was forgotten or forgiven? Hardly.*

Scholars confirmed that the mainly Catholics of the Crusades had been responding to the calls for help from people under the heel of the Muslims, but it was not to be believed.

Muslims had butchered 380 million Christians so far. The memory was burned into the brains of devout Muslims and the resumption of the Crusades had already commenced, which against soft democracies would be far easier than any of their Muslim historical military leaders could have dreamt.

The country was in chaos, and there was nothing anybody could do. Their master plan was to cause a continuous flow of international crises to bleed the US treasury with military expenditures and simultaneously attack the US from within, which would cause it to rely on its ineffectual police, courts, and politicians, who could not even balance the budget, let alone identify and defend against a fifteen-years-in-the-planning Muslim stroke of genius. As for Homeland Security, they would continue to bleed the US treasury as their Muslim brothers continued the worldwide terrorism and obvious attacks that caught the headlines, which in essence provided cover for Hussan's cultural attack that was far deadlier.

Most of the involved politicians were in a conflict of interest. They had been receiving money for years to fund their campaigns and keep them living the plush lifestyle they did not deserve. Along the way, many incriminating phone calls and meetings had been recorded. There were party girls who had found eager new male friends in the married politicians with families. There were the unexplained and undisclosed gifts and trips. And finally, there were the long lists of anti-American votes that they had undertaken, usually that was directly or indirectly disassembling the structure of the very country they were supposed to be serving. Keeping records of politicians for potential extortion had kept J. Edgar Hoover of the FBI in power for decades, when his bizarre position that organized crime did not exist in America was obvious bunk, Hussan had read in a magazine in an airport.

The same strategy was now working for Muslims, meaning that no matter how obvious the Islamification of America was, there would be official denial across the board from the compromised or the stupid.

Hussan stood up from the chair in the small room just off the bridge that he had started using for his calls to ensure privacy. After all, while the rest of the people on board believed various stories as to what the vessel had been built for—from a secret Brazilian military vessel to the more realistic story of a drug-running vessel—not one person on board knew the true purpose of the vessel.

Carlos walked over to Hussan and said, "We are approaching the estuary. Are we still to slow and stop at the small island you indicated should be entered on the GPS weeks ago?"

"Yes, we are to approach the small bay on the east-facing side of the island. You will approach at as close to full speed as possible and then slow down and submerge at the coordinates immediately. There must be no delay."

"Exactly as I have instructed the chief engineer. We will descend to thirty feet below the surface, and the vessel will be stabilized and secured at that spot. Then, the cargo column will extend up to the surface and open to the side to form a seal with the cargo-carrying ship's side opening," Carlos explained from memory.

Hussan looked over and could not help but smile, showing his blackened bean teeth and releasing his fetid breath. "Make sure it goes as I directed. I want the cargo to start being offloaded within minutes of the engines being turned off."

"As you wish, sir," said Carlos, who walked over to the chief engineer and conveyed the message.

The engineer immediately began shouting in Russian, and the group of other engineers started frantically making adjustments, as the forty-eight mighty jet engines slowed. The massive vessel sank down to the water's surface and crept up alongside the cruise ship and then sank into the water alongside it.

The positioning was completed, and the column rose silently with electric and hydraulic pressure, lifting up from the water and extending twenty feet into the air. A door opened on the side, and a surrounding seal compressed onto the side of the ship, ensuring no moisture or even wind entered past the seal.

Hundreds of men began carrying the cocaine in backpacks up and down the dual ladders and handing the packages to the crew on the cruise ship, who dropped the packages down a chute they had fabricated right at the opening. It allowed the cocaine to pass all the way to the bottom of the ship, where awaiting crews packed it into the crevices among the ship's inner keel, where the lead ballast had once been removed.

Hussan looked out from the bridge windows and was amazed to see fish swimming by and the looming hull of the cruise ship only a few meters away.

He walked down to the section at the base of the raised column, and it was a beehive of activity, as hundreds of men passed the cargo packages to each other and crawled up the ladder to be offloaded.

He walked back to Carlos and asked, "How much longer? My brother wants to know."

"At this pace, two more hours."

Hussan could feel the rush of sheer joy inside himself as he knew without any doubt that their plan would work and America would soon be a Muslim nation.

"Okay, let me know when we are ready to head back to the processing area to park this vessel," said Hussan.

He said it with a sense of deceit. He knew that while the impression was that the vessel would be used on an ongoing basis and thus the entire operation would continue perhaps for years, in truth with the massive breakdown in American society underway, there would likely be no need for further journeys. Although the vessel, which had cost close to a billion dollars to construct, would be safely hidden and stored with its sister ship.

Carlos walked off to supervise the offloading.

On the cruise ship, the manic crew was filling every nook and cranny and welding the original panels back into place and repainting the entire lower decks, all for the cover story in case of a Coast Guard search: the vessel needed to be spotlessly clean, since it had just been fumigated and the paying customer wouldn't tolerate any smell of the poisons used. Of course, they would tell the Miami travel agent whatever excuse came to mind for the cancelled Manaus run.

Hussan smiled.

No Coast Guard of any nation, and certainly not the US Coast Guard, would catch onto their clever ruse. The most massive and destructive cargo ever to reach the harbor of any nation would soon be pulling into the cruise ship berth in Miami and would be unloaded by the same motley gangsters successfully plying their drug trade with bribes and coercion and impunity as they had been for decades.

Up above, the happy tourists would be smiling as they boarded the ship to embark on the cruise of a lifetime.

Hussan was assured by his brother that the hijacked cruise ship had already been booked out by a shady agent in Miami, who had advertised cut rates to fill his own pockets and who didn't know or care why the vessel was unexpectedly available for rent. Apparently the Dutch owners had ordered the vessel to be fumigated and repainted and, due to logistics, were happy to receive at least some revenue for that time slot, or so the story went.

CHAPTER THIRTY-FIVE

"Hey, Tank," shouted Bull, as he jabbed Tank in the ribs.

Tank awoke from his deep sleep and rolled off the couch and was on his feet in less than a second.

He rubbed his face and stretched like a cat, while listening to Bull's update.

"I called the hospital, and Noddins is resting comfortably and is going to be okay. The Doctor and her assistants are staying in for observation, but it appears they will be okay too."

"In that case, what do you say we grab a cab and see how Lugar is coming on assembling my new drone?"

"Sounds like a plan," said Bull.

They hailed a Brazilian-made Fiat Sierra cab that was driving at a relaxed pace, with the driver on the last leg of his all-night shift, and, in the early morning traffic, within twenty minutes they had arrived through a seldom small, seldom used dirt road through the jungle at the far back portion of Manaus International Airport.

Walking toward the control trailer, Tank looked over at the launch truck and could see that the new drone had been assembled and fully prepped on the catapult ramp, ready for its mission.

CHAPTER THIRTY-SIX

Tank redirected his attention back to the large screen and started exploring the sub boxes to confirm the various options Lugar's team had installed in the drone.

"Hey, this may help," said Tank, sounding like he had just found a valuable gem.

"This drone has a soil density sonar device. It looks like there is a beacon under the front belly that transmits shock waves that determine the solidity of the soil, by determining the time it takes for the sound to bounce back to a listening device near the tail," Tank mentioned, as he entered the file and adjusted the controls to start the testing.

Soon a stream of data started appearing on the screens in numeric and graph form so that the differences in soil compactness could be clearly seen.

"It looks like a steamroller has just rolled over the same forest sections where the trees have a different signature. The soil is compacted."

Tank looked over to Bull. "Why don't you take our eyes down to the forest bottom to see for yourself what is going on?"

Bull reached over to the control panel and dialed in a low-altitude flight pattern and, minutes later, the familiar warning flashed over the screen.

"Our little flying friend is nervous again about flying across the forest floor. Too bad it can't be helped."

"Hey, it's really scraping the forest floor this time. Look, it's down to twenty feet," said Bull.

"Okay," said Tank, adjusting the viewing camera, "let's see what's going on."

In full-screen images, they saw the forest floor darkened by the low-hanging black clouds and streams of water from the driving rain running down the lens surface. The image was poor and difficult to make out.

Tank pressed the focus button, and there was a flash on the screen as the image was interrupted and the drone's CPU automatically selected an alternate lens.

After a few seconds, the image became clearer. The forest floor looked flattened, as though a giant had stomped the trees and plants down.

"Wow. This is bizarre," said Tank.

"I have viewed thousands of square hectares of Amazon Basin forests and nothing like this exists."

Bull was also in shock. "The felled trees remind me of the blast radius of a bomb, but that's the only similarity. I don't see any damage or craters. It looks like an unseen force has gently pushed everything down, but there seems to be no trace of human activity."

Bull adjusted the camera to a pan view. "It looks like the world's biggest bowling ball has been rolled over the jungle floor," he said, pointing to the image on the screen.

Tank looked and then squinted and looked closer. "Can you get me an image of the edge of the swath?"

Bull adjusted the flight profile and, after a brief lag time, the drone moved over to the edge of the wide swath and focused in on the trees.

Tank rubbed his chin. "This was caused by air."

"Explain?"

"There is no true edge to the compressed area. It looks like it gradually lessens and then the forest looks normal again a few meters away, with trees standing to their full height."

"I see that. So, how does that help us?"

"This compressed forest has not been caused by something with direct mechanical force but with air pressure," explained Tank.

"I guess your months of working here in the Amazon have educated you in the unique weather patterns. I have never heard of any micro storms or other weather systems that would cause this oddball effect. Educate me, oh master," said Bull with a smile.

CHAPTER THIRTY-SEVEN

The large drone control monitoring screens flashed confirmation that the drone had initiated the return-to-base and landing cycles, and Bull pondered Tank's comment.

"What, may I ask, are you referring to?"

"I am sorry, my good friend, but we have to follow the trail while it's hot, and there are no other means available," replied Tank.

"If you are referring to doing further investigation along that flattened forest trail—if you want to call it that—the drone is doing a fine job and still has a full tank of gas, so you should be letting it continue on its job."

"We can do better," said Tank.

"No," replied Bull. "The drone is the most sophisticated in the world and has already identified the trail we want to follow, so there is no way we can do better."

"Yes, there is," replied Tank. "The drone will fly along the trail and likely find something, I agree. But that may take hours, and then we will want to go and spend more hours to actually see what it finds with our own eyes because we can't really take any action without firsthand knowledge—as we found out when we went over to the cocaine operation in person."

"Okay, that makes a certain amount of sense. But if we want to investigate along the trail with our own eyes, why don't we borrow a helicopter from over across the tarmac there?" said Bull, pointing to the Manaus Airport buildings and many aircrafts of all types parked nearby.

"Because it won't have the sensor ability; plus, as I will remind you, we are not here in the capacity you assume," said Tank with a smile and a shrug.

"Right now the air traffic controllers and any military people in the area only believe we are some biodiversity scientists investigating the forest. They have seen people and craft come and go but they are respecting their government's instructions to leave us alone with our comings and goings in this vacant portion of Manaus International Airport. If we steal an aircraft, it may set off a series of events, including the media's involvement. The media in Brazil, as in all parts of the world, pays massive amounts of money for tips on anything newsworthy, and the five o'clock news with our activities and possibly identities will certainly tip off whoever is behind the disappearing 1500-foot building and the gunmen who tried to kill us. Giant would have a fit, since anonymity is the most important aspect of our organization, and our cover may be blown permanently, and I certainly don't want to undergo any plastic surgery to design a new face, do you?"

Bull was reeling from his friend's comments and trying to process where he was going with all this.

"Okay, I understand there are problems with potentially blowing our covers by pinching a copter or plane, but there's no other way to do it," said Bull.

"Yes, there is a way, and it will be landing outside the door in a few minutes."

"It's a ridiculous idea," said Bull, wondering why he had to point out the obvious. "Nobody can hang onto a slippery flying aircraft, particularly in a downpour like this. I remind you, this is a drone, and there are no seats or places for passengers. And how would you control the thing even if you could hang on? There are no controls, which means we would have to simply hang on—if we could, which I doubt—for the entire programmed flight duration, which would be of zero help in taking action against any drug bandits."

Tank leaned over to the control console and highlighted a sub box titled, "Manual Onboard Flight Package."

Bull looked at Tank and said, "Are you kidding? This must be some kind of a joke."

"I thought it was at first too. However, Rockwell has engineers working to try to devise every possible option to appeal to the various governments around the world. It's called line extension, or, getting more product variants or uses from the main product—in this case, the drone. I guess somebody came up with the idea that the aircraft could be used to fly passengers, maybe in an emergency as a medevac or to escape a dangerous situation. I have no idea. Maybe Lugar thought it might be useful to fly a biologist with a bug bite to safety. I do know that conversions are not unheard of since the WWII Harvard trainer was converted by the Australians into a fighter plane—and not a bad one at that," said Tank.

"No, only you would know what the Australians were doing back then, and I bet both versions had seats!" he said, his voice rising in alarm. "You are telling me you are actually thinking of riding on a drone across the untamed jungle without seats, controls, or parachutes, which we will surely need. Tank, the heat and bugs have affected your thinking."

"Take it easy, my rotund friend," said Tank. "Let me explain; it's not as nuts as it sounds."

He pressed the buttons that brought up the components: self-flight manuals and instructions, each pictured as though on a shopping website.

"First, we will have modest but nonetheless workable seats, which clip into place, and we will each have a clip-on wind deflector at our feet near the leading edge of the wing, so we won't have the wind pelting us with rain and bugs. It will create a relatively windless pocket for each of us. The seats are like the bucket seats in a small aluminum boat and have sturdy safety harnesses to keep us in place. Next, we will have leather headgear, including goggles and radios to communicate, since we will be seated on opposite sides of the fuselage and would have difficulty shouting back and forth. This weather-proof wireless laptop, with wrist strap, will handle the control function, since the inputs will continue to be by radio control. We won't have to control it manually in the traditional sense, since we will only be making adjustments that the autopilot will follow, and therefore there will be a lag time between our flight profile program inputs and the drone's response. You could sort of say that we will in fact have parachutes, since the drone has parachutes, and we can ride it down to the ground like a feather. Heck, we will even have a life raft for any flight portions that go over the Amazon River, since it has inflatable pontoons to support it in case of a water crash."

"How are we supposed to stay in place during the catapult launch?" asked Bull. "I remind you that there is a huge propeller that will be a few feet behind us, ready to chop us to pieces if we slide back from our places. In my experience, safety harnesses can stretch," he added, patting his bulk for emphasis.

Bull sat and stared at his friend, and then a huge smile spread across his face, as if he had just been dared to ride on a roller coaster at the amusement park.

Bull was never one to turn down a challenge if there was a sliver of sanity to it, which Tank had just provided.

"Okay, let's do it," said Bull.

CHAPTER THIRTY-EIGHT

As per the custom in Brazil, the beer was ice cold, and if it were even half of a degree colder, it would have been frozen.

Bull leaned over and pulled a Brazilian Gol beer from the fridge and fumbled with the tiny pull tab on the can until he heard the loud click.

Tank selected a Guarana, the national soda, and they both leaned back to gulp down the contents.

"I thought computer geeks fly these things. I guess even they need ice cold beer in the Amazon jungle," said Bull, who was surprised a US Air Force flight officer would have cold beer in the control room, which broke every rule in the book and would be comparable to having a six-pack in the cockpit of a jet fighter.

"Noddins is a man of many mysteries," replied Tank.

"I feel like I am about to jump off the high diving board for the first time," said Bull. "Have we lost our minds?"

"Nah," replied Tank. "Flying uncertified experimental drones over the jungle is the latest craze; everybody's doing it."

"I think one beer should be enough. I should have a clear head," said Bull.

"Yeah, being clear-headed definitely won't hurt," Tank replied, rising from his seat.

"Our ride should be arriving any minute, now that the rain has eased a bit. Why don't we search through that stack of items Lugar left along the trailer side?" Bull suggested.

They walked outside into the rain and pulled back a tarp that Lugar had left in place, covering tools and support equipment for the drone.

"Here we are," said Tank, as he pulled a small crate marked "Manual Flight Kit" from the pile and opened it up.

"Two plastic seats with attachment clips and harnesses to hold even you in place and two plastic wind deflectors," said Tank in a mock official tone. "One weather-proof laptop with downloaded drone programs for all operational systems. Two leather headsets complete with goggles and two-way radios so we can talk to each other, and I even grabbed a sat phone in case we need to talk to Giant."

"One question," said Bull. "Do I get a set of earplugs so I can at least have some peace and quiet during my cross-jungle cruise?"

"I'll have to answer that later; it appears our ride has arrived," said Tank, who wiped the rain from his face and pointed up at a tiny speck that was approaching the airport, descending automatically on a perfect flight path that allowed it to touch down and effortlessly glide toward the control trailer and silently roll to a stop.

"Shall we ready our ride?" asked Tank, as they walked over to the drone and quickly attached the seats and wind deflectors, grabbed the laptop control, and pulled on their headgear.

With the fuel tank still ninety percent full, Tank carried over two jerry cans to top it up, as he had no appetite for being marooned yet again in the jungle.

After sitting in his own seat and watching Bull squeeze into his, Tank said, "Okay, what do you say we get this ride underway?"

"I'm ready when you are. Say, how long does my ticket give me to ride this thing on my sightseeing tour?" asked Bull, as they both grinned at their newest thrill-seeking adventure.

"You will get your money's worth, sir," said Tank, who pressed the laptop screen, engaging the runway takeoff cycle. "There're thirty-five hours of flight time available."

The wind and rain buffeted both men, but it was warm, and their goggles protected their eyes. The ride was exhilarating as the vast, misty, dark Amazon jungle unfolded below them. With the drone engine set to silent mode by Tank—a feature included for military applications so they could sneak up on terrorists—the pusher propeller engine to their rear could hardly be heard above the whistling wind rushing by their leather helmets.

They both looked at each other with rain streaming down their faces.

"Yahoo! What a ride," they screamed at the surprisingly well sorted out arrangement.

CHAPTER THIRTY-NINE

The hours passed, and both men could smell the change in the air as they approached the South Atlantic where the Amazon River emptied into the ocean.

The air now contained a salty aroma that gave them concern, as an airborne jungle inspection to find a drug operation could soon turn into a journey over the open ocean.

The skies started to clear, and the wind was stronger as the cooler ocean air was swept inland and rose over the vast sand islands of the complex Amazon River estuary.

Bull looked over at Tank and said, "I thought this was a jungle tour. Nobody said anything about cruising over the South Atlantic Ocean."

They both looked ahead and could see that the trail of flattened trees disappeared into the ocean water that surrounded the hundreds of islands of the estuary.

Tank looked at the ocean below and then glanced at Bull. "Agreed. Neither of our tickets included running out of gas over the Atlantic."

Suddenly they felt the heat as two streaks of white tracer smoke ran past the drone, and they both looked back to see a black helicopter with missile launchers attached to each landing skid.

"Can it be?" asked Bull.

"I guess the little drone was a bit hasty in concluding that guy was dead," said Tank, watching as the rockets arched downward to an island's desert sand below, exploding with a muffled impact that sent sand shooting upward.

"So would you, if you saw gunmen walking toward you, and you were trying to stay in the air in a torrential downpour," said Bull, craning his neck to look backward at the black Robertson 44 helicopter. "But why don't we discuss it later? It looks like he has more rockets in those launchers, and even after having survived a crash, he may be smart enough to hit us with one."

Another two rockets sped past the drone, missing by inches and arching downward to the desert sands to explode.

"That was close. If he keeps adjusting after each round, the next round should hit us. Any ideas?" shouted Bull into the headset microphone.

Tank fumbled with the laptop controls, frantically struggling to press the touch screen and alter their course to avoid the next round of incoming rockets.

"Hey, the autopilot has no provision to avoid incoming fire. I am not actually flying, remember? I am only selecting or modifying programs for the computer to automatically follow," he said, expecting death at any moment.

Coming from the rear, they could hear the helicopter's engine roaring at full throttle, approaching at its top speed of 125 knots.

"He's got us beat on maneuverability, not to mention weaponry and speed, with us fumbling along at sixty knots. Why don't you come up with a good idea this time?" said Tank, who was staring down at the keypad and frantically pressing the screen display to try to find a way to avoid death.

"Would it help if I told you I have a bag of weapons tied to the landing gear?" said Bull.

"Hiding a bag of food wasn't enough?" replied Tank.

"I had to even out the load," came the flat response.

"We can't get our hands on them for now. I might have found something."

"What?" shouted Bull.

"I think I will make a toll-free call to California," yelled Tank.

"Are you nuts? Don't make your last calls before dying yet," said Bull.

"This guy is somebody we need to talk to," said Tank.

Bull looked back through the spinning propeller and said, "I think I am going to die with a madman."

Tank pressed a large screen button and heard the ring tone on his headset and heard a man say, "Hello?"

"Hi, can you help us?" yelled Tank.

"I don't know. Where you are calling from?"

"From a thousand feet over the ocean in the Amazon River estuary."

"What seems to be the problem with the drone?" asked the voice.

"We are using the passenger option and are being chased by a helicopter that is shooting what look like Sidewinder missiles at us," screamed Tank.

Two more rockets left the Robertson and came hurtling at the drone, closely missing Tank—who felt the scalding exhaust—and deflecting off the tapered front fuselage, falling to explode in the hot sands below.

"So, you want to increase speed," said the good-natured voice. "Well, you want to cancel the current manual flight mode, which was intended for human passengers on a temporary basis because you can't get around the limiters unless you completely cancel the program," replied the voice, which had a distinct Israeli accent.

"Right. Done," said Tank, who then heard the call connection cut off with a click.

Immediately the drone's Rotax engine revved, as it was no longer governed by the sixty-knot speed limit intended to reduce wind buffeting for the two exposed passengers.

The drone accelerated strongly toward its 125-knot top speed.

Tank increased the altitude to the maximum of 25,000 feet, far above the helicopter's 14,000-foot ceiling.

The drone angled upward sharply, pressing the men back in their seats and was soon far above and in front of the copter.

The men could see the white mist obscuring the South Atlantic below to the front, and to each side, they saw the vague outlines of islands of which half were lush green and the other half were harsh dry, white sand dunes.

Each man craned his neck back and could see the Robertson as a tiny black speck, far below and to the rear.

"Looks like he's turning back," said Bull.

"I don't blame him; running out of gas over shark-infested waters is not a great way to go," replied Tank.

"Not for him or us," said Bull. "Why don't we turn back now? Remember, cruising over the South Atlantic won't help us capture an inland drug runner."

"Maybe. But since we're already at this high altitude, why don't I run some quick scans to see what's below?"

"Okay, but the operative word is 'quick.' I don't feel too comfortable being buffeted at twice the speed and twenty-five times the altitude, and by the way, that arrow wound is still bleeding; you should probably get it looked at," said Bull.

Tank was busy with the keyboard and ignored the comment, as the blood running down his calf was of no concern to him while his leg still worked, although there was a numb throbbing.

The new search parameters he entered directed the scanning equipment to take advantage of the high altitude.

"Okay, it looks like there's an 800-foot ship, and its current direction shows that it is leaving the same island coordinates that the last compressed jungle trail was aiming toward before it disappeared into the water."

Tank peered down and couldn't make out anything definite, as the heavy sea mist kicked up by the wind completely obscured the ocean.

"Well, we have no need to be flying at 25,000 feet. I am going to take it down for a look."

He adjusted the laptop controls for a steep descent toward the ship.

The nose sank as the drone began to dive and the speed increased. The wind buffeted them, and they clutched their seats and pulled against the straps as the wind deformed their faces and they approached the maximum drone speed of 250 miles per hour, at which point the dive automatically shallowed to reduce the speed so that the long wings wouldn't rip off.

After a few minutes, they were skimming the waves, approaching the massive mystery ship from three kilometers behind.

Suddenly, the landing gear touched the water, and the drone's engine revved furiously to increase the speed and avoid a crash.

The two men hung on, waiting for the drone to crash in the water, but the strong headwinds allowed it to easily increase the altitude between massive ocean rollers and miss the next one, stabilizing at an altitude higher than the highest roller top.

"That was a little close," said Tank, breathing a sigh of relief.

"What went wrong? Is this thing okay to continue, or has the salt air fried its brain, and we should head back to Manaus while we can?" asked Bull.

"No, we are okay. It's my fault," replied Tank. "I dialed in a twenty-foot cruising altitude, since we don't want anybody on the ship to spot us, at least unless it's unavoidable. But I didn't notice these massive rollers from 25,000 feet, and the little drone's CPU—which was running its terrain following program—simply couldn't keep up with the adjustments needed to clear the alternating wave tops and keep us dry too."

The drone was again flying at sixty knots, and the ship's mist-shrouded stern was slowly coming into view.

"That's funny. That looks like a guy hanging by a rope from the stern, poor chap," said Tank as the drone approached, so they could clearly see the blood-soaked man hanging above the waves with a petrified look in his eyes, as his feet were dipped in the waves when the ship took its massive plunges at the bow, causing the stern to rise and fall.

The man looked up at the strange aviators and weakly raised an arm to wave for help, as the drone silently flew by just atop the waves and circled the ship.

"What have they done to a nice cruise ship?" asked Bull, scanning the massive ship, which was rolling heavily from side to side.

"That's strange," said Tank. "They must be running out of seasickness bags. That thing is heaving like an old herring trawler on the west coast."

"West coast of where?" asked Bull.

"Anywhere," replied Tank. "Either the stabilizers are broken or turned off, or the ballast is removed. In either case, they are running that ship in an emergency mode, and if there is no genuine emergency, then they are breaking maritime law, as it's a hazard to shipping."

The drone was circling, and Tank and Bull were scanning the sides and the deck to see if it was a drug running vessel.

It was an older Danish-built cruise ship of eight hundred feet, painted the usual white to avoid attracting the sun's heat but looking a little haggard.

On one side, there was an area where the metal had been cut in the shape of a large rectangle and re-welded and poorly repainted.

"Well, what do you think?" asked Bull.

"With the bloodied guy tied up hanging as shark food, the rolling of the ship, and the fact that I think I have seen a character or two through the windows that certainly don't look like typical cruise ship crewman, I would say this ship is mighty suspicious."

"I was afraid of that. But mighty suspicious is not confirmation. We can press the drone's return-to-base mode and be back in Manaus for a hot shower and let the Brazilian Coast Guard or armed forces take over," said Bull.

"That guy will die for sure," said Tank. "And this ship carries a flag of convenience and is making twenty-eight knots flat-out with no load, up the coast toward the Caribbean and, let's see, how about Miami? Plus, it will be cruising by several countries on its port side as it heads north and could start unloading its cocaine cargo the minute we turn to fly back, for all we know, or it could make it to the States by other means.

Remember, Giant said that the drug operation we were originally to stop is now a USA national emergency."

Bull looked across the Predator's fuselage and said, "Okay, indulge me. That ship has no landing deck, in case you hadn't noticed, and I bet those guys in there have got the same guns that made Swiss cheese out of your Beriev and almost out of us. We can't swim for long in these waters. With the blood trail from our friend hanging at the rear, there are probably three hundred sharks following, and they won't even need to smell the blood from your open calf wound to give you a nice big bite and swallow you whole."

"So, you are saying you don't want to swim to the ship and then board somehow?" asked Tank.

"Let's say I prefer to eat and not to be eaten."

"What if I told you we can simply walk onto the ship from this plane?" asked Tank.

"Impossible," replied Bull.

Tank was making adjustments on the computer screen.

They circled further out and flew past the stern, disappearing into the white mist toward land.

"I guess you agree with me, eh?" said Bull. "It would have been great, but there's no way to get on board."

The drone had slowed to the slowest speed it would fly at, forty-five knots, just above the speed when its wings stopped generating lift and would drop.

Bull noticed the change in engine RPM and looked down and could see the ocean waves moving by at a walking pace.

"Hey, Tank, we are hardly moving. You better give it gas."

The long wings entered a gentle bank as the drone aligned, pointing at the hazy outline of the giant ship's stern in the distance.

The winds buffeted the plane as the autopilot's CPU frantically tried to adjust the flaps and remain airborne. The slow speed and unpredictable buffeting of the wind at water level made the drone almost impossible to fly, and the engine RPM fluctuated as it struggled to obey its instructions of low speed and low altitude and also to save itself from crashing.

The ship was looking larger as they approached from the stern. The bloodied man hanging on a rope wiped his eye to make sure he was not seeing a mirage, as the tiny drone approached from five kilometers away and rose and fell with the wave tops, quietly.

It seemed to hang like a dot in the white mist, as the man on the rope had not seen a plane fly at so slow a speed.

With the African headwinds bucking at fifty kilometers per hour, and the drone only needing forty-five knots of air passing over the wings, the drone was approaching the ship from the stern at only five knots true ground speed—the pace of a brisk walk—and seemed to hang in the air for an eternity without getting large or smaller.

Bull looked down and asked, "What are you trying to do? If this thing misfires on even one of its four cylinders, we are in the drink," as the drone bobbed and weaved, flying at a speed so low it was a miracle it was even hanging in the air.

"The CPU's range profile flying program couldn't keep up with the changing sea swells when we first approached, and that's why we almost ditched."

"I know; I was there," said Bull.

"But we know it has the land profile program, or in this case, sea wave profile program, right? And I told you before that it has a learning computer."

"Okay, I am with you," said Bull.

"By flying dead slow, I am giving the CPU time to learn the wave rhythm, and that allows it to keep us flying at a lower altitude because it has learned to predict the next massive roller and when it's time to slightly descend or ascend."

"Unless you want to take over Noddins' job, how does it help us with our mission?" asked Bull, as he tasted salt water in his mouth from the spray on his face, whipped up by the wind from the cresting whitecaps on the massive rollers.

"You'll see," replied Tank, as they flew to within one kilometer of the ship. He looked over and asked Bull, "How high would you say that stern is?"

Bull peered ahead at the ship's stern, still shrouded in mist, then to Tank, "It's about forty feet up, if you are talking about the first level that is open to the sky, since I already know your devious plan that will probably get us killed, as usual."

"Yes, the open sky is right. I don't want to land between decks, since there's no way we can be that precise, and we'll probably smack into the stern and fall to the ocean below and that will be the end of us after the sharks have their way, or be squashed between the drone and the underside of the deck above," said Tank, who sounded tense.

The lowest deck level open to the sky was coming into clear view from the sea mist, with several decks rising above it, tapered in toward the ship's middle, with climbing walls, golf ranges with nets, tennis courts, or pools.

Tank was busy dialing in a fifty-foot altitude to the plane's computer, and the Rotax engine increased its speed, and the drone rose higher above the waves.

The massive ship loomed larger as they approached, and the stern could be seen moving through a wide range, up and down, as the vessel's bow plowed into the huge rollers.

The drone's long albatross-like wings were flapping up and down in the strong headwinds, and the wing flaps could be seen moving rapidly through their entire motion range as the CPU tried to keep the drone moving on the path set by Tank's direction entered with the laptop.

As the drone approached the rear of the massive ship, the waves were smoother from the ship having passed over, while the surface was whipped up with bubbles from the propeller's wash.

Thankfully, no people could be seen on the open decks, and it had remained that way over the entire time.

"The air conditioning must be working well, or they are exhausted. In either case, we are lucky they don't like wandering around on deck," said Tank.

"Hey, why don't you keep doing what you're doing and let's talk about air conditioning later, okay?"

The massive ship was looming ahead, closer and closer, moving up and down, and the man hanging from the stern on the end of a rope had fright in his eyes, as he knew that the plane could easily hit him.

The starboard side of the ship was over an acre in size and acted like a huge wind guide, deflecting the easterly winds along the hull toward the stern.

The drone was almost out of control as the ship affected the headwinds with its bulk, and in the area to the rear of the stern, there were wild gusts of one hundred kilometers per hour, which threatened to tear the wings off the drone, as first the left wing, then the right were yanked by the wind blast, and the wingtips came within inches of striking the water, making it like riding a wild bronco for Tank and Bull.

The drone approached the stern, and Tank clutched the handheld control pad and pressed the large, red engine kill button.

The Rotax fell silent.

For the first time, they were flying without power, gliding, and the noise of the ship's foaming propeller wash forty feet below and the flapping stern flag ahead of them could be heard. They smelled the ship's diesel fumes, mixed in with the strong gusts and carried from the high exhaust stack.

With the long wings of a glider, the drone had an excellent glide rate, losing little altitude with each meter of forward motion.

They were a few meters from the white railing at the stern, and Tank and Bull clutched their seats, as they were now just onlookers without any way of controlling the flight.

They both braced themselves with their feet against the wind deflectors at the wing's forward top edge, as the drone snapped off the flag pole with its bulbous nose and flew across the steel railing, sheering off its single front landing gear strut and then the two rears.

The drone's belly scraped across the railing, and the long thin wings dipped down with the momentum of the crash onto the railing and struck two large white lockers on each side, which were attached to the deck, slightly raised on steel bracket mounts. The wings became wedged between the lockers and the deck. The drone's fuselage was halted by the wings as though it had grabbed an arrestor cable on a carrier flight deck. The railing struck the rigid, rear downward-V vertical stabilizers just as the ships stern rose sharply from the huge rollers, pulling against the long flexible wings like a slingshot, launching Tank and Bull up, as their seats broke loose from the wing attachment points.

Bull and Tank flew through the air, up toward the top of the ship, passing several shorter decks that tapered inward.

They finally struck a golf driving range net twenty meters over the top deck, which stretched with their combined 500-pound weight, snapping the poles holding it up.

The men fell, landing on a phony snowcapped Matterhorn climbing mountain before tumbling down the mountain into a pool decorated like an Alpine lake with a mighty splash, with their harnesses still holding the seats to their bodies.

They scanned around the area, and there wasn't a soul.

The ship's swaying motion was magnified, as they were now higher up in the superstructure.

Stunned, they looked at each other and smiled.

The water in the pool was rushing from side to side and washing over the edge and onto the deck, leaving it half empty.

"You promised me I would walk onto the ship."

"Okay, swim on. I float corrected," replied Tank. "What do you say we pull that poor character up from his rope over the stern? I think he's had his fill of the cheap cabin arrangements. Next time he won't be so eager to take the sale price accommodations from his buxom travel agent."

"Okay, I guess the all-I-will-eat buffet will have to wait, but the next time we miss our cruise, no more desperate measures; let's just catch the next ship, okay?"

After removing their harnesses and seats, which they tossed up into a snowy mountain crevice, they crept along the inside pool edge until they were up against the base of the Matterhorn mountain, where a gnome stood. They pulled themselves out and crept over the deck, walking toward the outdoor deck stairwell that would take them down to the next level.

Both neck buzzers activated, and the men ignored them.

Pausing at the top to peer down, they could see that the ship's decks were as deserted on board as they appeared from the drone.

Looking at the water several stories down, they could see that the ship was faring poorly in the heavy seas, with the bow plunging into the massive rollers, causing the stern to rise and fall, while the upper decks swayed from side to side.

The ship's flare cut the heavy seas, throwing water thirty feet to the sides, and the wind caused a heavy white mist to carry up to the top decks, and they could both taste the salt water spray across their faces.

They made their way down the three flights of stairs and then reached the lowest level open to the sky, where the drone hung silently partly over the stern, with its wings wedged, solidly holding it in place.

Tank walked over to an emergency equipment locker and opened it to find a 100-foot manila line complete with a blunt treble grappling hook.

"Looks like this is where they keep their rescue equipment," whispered Tank, as he uncoiled the line and walked back to the ship's rear.

Looking down, he swung the hook over like a pendulum, until it grabbed the rope from which the man hung, blood-soaked and inches above the shark-infested waters.

They thought the man was perhaps hours from death.

The ship's stern rose and sank with each wave trough.

Pulling the line over to his other hand, Tank grabbed the line, and they pulled the man up onto the deck.

He was a small man with a sea-weathered face and thick, graying hair covered in disgusting spit and was almost skin and bone. Dried blood covered his shirt, tie, and pants, and they could now see that he was wearing a ship officer's uniform.

Laying there, looking up, the man could only whisper, "Water, water."

CHAPTER FORTY

Walking back to the locker, Tank grabbed a white emergency provisions case with a big red cross on it and opened it to find two bottles of water.

He twisted off the cap of one and held it to the man's mouth, who gulped the entire contents without stopping.

Tank poured water from the other bottle to flush the head wound and filthy hair and dabbed it with cotton bandages and then applied red mecuriform liberally.

The man paused and looked at his rescuers.

"If you can talk, tell us who you are," said Tank.

"My name is Manoa," he said with a weak, raspy voice, "and I am the Captain of the Good Times Express."

"Nice to meet you, Captain. Sorry we came aboard without a boarding pass," said Tank.

Captain Manoa smiled weakly. "It's okay; this time I will authorize it."

"Captain, we are on our way to the bridge, and you're in no shape to come along. Do you mind if we let you rest a while and come for you in a bit?"

The Captain nodded weakly and then closed his eyes and passed out.

"I guess adrenaline kept him awake," said Bull.

"It would you too, if you had sharks nipping at your heels. Helps to keep a man alert."

They picked up the Captain and placed him comfortably in a huge deck cupboard on clean, white towels and put an open package of emergency rations near his head along with the other bottle of water.

They closed the cupboard and turned to each other.

"Well, I guess it's finally time to work for our pay," said Tank.

"If what I've been through since meeting you isn't work, I don't know what is," said Bull.

"A swim in a river, a scenic plane ride, and now a bit of exercise on a cruise ship—what could be wrong with any of it?"

"Yeah, it's a real life adventure, that's for sure," scowled Bull.

Tank had walked back across the rear deck and picked up the grappling hook used to bring up Captain Manoa.

He swung the hook under the drone to hook at the point where the wing joined the fuselage and then tied the rope to the railing to make sure the drone didn't take a death dive to the water below. The wind on board at the stern was calm, as the ship's structure caused a vacuum by design for the comfort of the guests.

Then, crawling across the top of the drone's fuselage, he wrapped his arm around the rear propeller hub and reached down to the rear landing gear and felt only air.

Looking down, he could see that the landing gear had snapped off and become wedged between the steel railings, and the duffel bag placed there by Bull in Manaus was dangling over the ocean, with the rope shredded by the crash and ready to break at any moment.

Tank crawled back off the drone and walked over to get another grappling hook from the rescue locker. He coiled the rope and made a perfect pass, and the hook grabbed the bag, which he pulled onto the deck.

"What goodies did you place in here?" asked Tank, as he opened the bag.

"Nothing special," replied Bull.

They made their way into the lower deck cabin door and entered and felt the cool of the air conditioning. They crept along the aisle, using the railing to brace themselves from losing their footing from the massive ship's sway.

"Enough to take over a ship this size?" asked Tank.

"Tough to say; never done it before," said Bull, as they were going down the aisle, peering in each compartment.

Pausing, Tank reached into the bag and handed Bull a collection of weapons, each small, and Bull placed them in his front open shirt, forming an even bigger belly.

The vessel was quiet, with low lighting in the aisle, and the only sound was the distant hum of machinery.

They followed the signs to the bridge, bracing themselves with the railings, as the ship's sway was much stronger high up in the vessel, and found empty compartments all along the way.

"I've always wanted to know what it would be like after the explosion of a neutron bomb. People gone, but all else unharmed," said Tank.

Bull looked over, but they were becoming too tense for idle talk, as the bridge was around the corner.

Tank peered around the center rear bridge wall supports and could see the extensive charts and electronic viewing equipment on the bridge and the spectacular, white misty ocean views spreading out in front of the panoramic windows.

"What's the plan?" whispered Bull.

"There are only three guys, and their guns are on the table over there," said Tank, motioning to a chart table twenty feet away.

"Okay, what are we waiting for?" said Bull.

Tank nodded, and they both crept over to the men.

At the last second, the ship's sway caused a pen to roll across the map table, and the man, standing with his hands on the ship's massive brass and wooden wheel, looked up to see Tank. He reached to grab a knife on his belt.

Tank lunged from the side in a flash and wrapped his long muscular arm around the man's neck. He rapped his skull with a set of Zeiss binoculars at hand, causing him to slump unconscious, with his hands in a death grip on the spoked ship's wheel, dragging it down and causing an electronic beeping to warn that the autopilot had disengaged and the ship was now under manual control.

Bull was not yet at the other two, when one looked up to see what the beeping was. He ran toward Bull who was already charging toward him like a rogue bull rhino.

Just before meeting the front runner, Bull pushed out his mighty belly, and the cannon blow sent the man crashing backward into the third man, who also had the wind knocked out of him, and they both smashed across a map table, landing below in a heap on the deck, unconscious.

"Let's tie them up and put them in a locker," said Tank.

"Have you noticed the disgusting white spit all over the place? Seems these guys learned their manners at the same place as the guys we met in the jungle," said Bull.

They both dropped the unconscious men in a corner and crept down the hall, leaving the bridge abandoned.

"Do you think we should reset the autopilot?" asked Bull.

"Why?" said Tank. "If it's running in circles or hits another ship or attracts attention, that will make our jobs easier."

A black man was sitting on a swivel chair in the communications room, listening to a headset, with his back to the door.

"Do your thing," whispered Tank.

Bull walked over and sat on the man, who exhaled and was unconscious within seconds.

"Where do you think everybody is? It's impossible to run a ship this size with less than ten people, not to mention the drug operation aspect, which needs a lot of additional manpower."

"Maybe they're all sleeping?" suggested Tank.

"Sure, but where? We can't have them waking up whenever they want. It could be hazardous to our health, wouldn't you think?" replied Bull.

"I know where they are," came a voice from behind.

Tank turned his head and said, "Captain Manoa, shouldn't you still be resting?"

The Captain was sitting in an electric scooter with toggle controls that were left in key locations throughout the ship for those in need.

"I couldn't leave you to wander the ship alone. These guys are vicious; you wouldn't stand a chance," he said weakly.

"Who are they?" asked Tank.

"I have no idea. I returned to the ship in Jamaica from leave in Miami, and my regular crew was gone. They said they were a replacement crew there to move the ship to the next port while decontaminating it, as directed by headquarters, but I thought that was a lie after watching them working with welding torches instead of disinfectant. I was unable to contact headquarters for confirmation. After confronting them, they attacked me and left me for dead, hanging off the stern. Last night, another strange vessel moved alongside in a cove on an island in the Amazon Estuary, and that's all I know, until I saw you guys flying around the ship."

"How many of them are there?" asked Tank.

"At least two hundred," replied the Captain.

"And where are they now?" asked Bull.

"Probably sleeping in the rooms nearest the food and beverages, on the Plaza level."

"How do you figure that?" asked Tank.

"Work crews always sleep nearest to the food and drinks. They're mooches."

"Are they smart?" asked Tank.

"I wouldn't hire them to clean the latrines, although they got lucky taking it through the reefs hours ago," said the Captain.

"I guess I should have asked: where's the Plaza level?" said Tank.

"Next level down," said the Captain.

Just then, there were voices coming from down the companionway.

"The stairwell," said the Captain, pointing twenty meters down the companionway, where hanging ceiling signs indicated the stairs.

The Captain pointed across at an open door, and Tank darted over followed by Bull pushing the Captain in his scooter, and they ducked in and closed it behind them, just as a group of forty men poured out of the stairwell and started making their way toward the bridge in the direction of Tank.

"Well, I would say if there are two hundred men here, we best be on our way," said Tank.

Both men nodded in agreement.

"There's no way to get off," rasped the Captain. "The lifeboats are wired to set off safety alarms if they are tampered with. It's difficult anyway, since we are moving at flank speed.

The minute the boat touches the water, it will flip over. The high seas and the ship's rolling would make it impossible."

Tank paused and rubbed his square jaw.

"Captain, can you explain to me the quickest way to permanently shut down these engines?" asked Tank.

"Easy," replied the Captain. "Shunt fresh water into the main diesel fuel tanks. Those tanks feed all fours engines simultaneously. The second that water hits the combustion chambers, the engines will explode and the ship will stop dead in its tracks. The water tap is connected to the fuel line to facilitate flushing the tanks during maintenance, but it's always been a dangerous design they were too cheap to fix."

"Is there any way they could get the vessel underway again?" asked Tank.

"No. The only way in is to be towed as a salvage operation," said Manoa, slowly realizing his ship of ten years was soon to be sacrificed.

"And water to the engine... How complicated is that process?" asked Tank.

"Can you turn one marked, yellow knob?" replied the Captain.

"I think so. Can you give me directions to the knob?"

The Captain was too weak to come along, as it meant descending ten levels, so he described the engine room and where the knob was. He paused between sentences for so long that they thought he was going to pass out.

Bull gently picked him up and placed him in a linen closet.

"What, in with the towels again?" said the Captain.

"There must be hundreds of linen lockers on this tub. It's the last place they'll look. Have a nice rest; we'll be back for you as quickly as we can," replied Tank.

"Wait," the Captain said with urgency. "If you damage the engines, how does that help anything? As you can feel, the boat is swaying excessively since they disconnected the stabilizers. This vessel is in danger of capsizing if the engines are cut. Sitting dead in the water, the hull will be pushed by the giant rollers, and the swaying will increase," said the Captain with true fear in his eyes.

"Captain, if it sinks, that's a good thing. We can't let this vessel get one meter closer to the USA, and that means at any cost."

The Captain's face was puzzled. "All of that over a drug shipment?" he asked, his eyelids closing as he passed out.

Bull closed the linen closet door, and both men initially lost their footing as the ship whipsawed with a strong listing motion. Like a twisting pendulum, it was rising and falling from front to back at the same time as swaying strongly from side to side.

They grabbed the doorframe and peered down the companionway. All was clear, and they quickly made their way to the service stair entrance and wound their way down the stairs.

At the fifth floor, above the engine room, they opened a fireproof door and entered the noisy main engine gallery, standing on a steel walkway with railings that vibrated from the engines. They could look down and see the entire engine room, which was all open for the remaining five floors like a huge atrium. Fully electronic, there was a soundproof glass enclosure on the floor in the middle of the four engines with a large black man reading a National Geographic while leaning back in a reclining chair mounted on castors with his back to the engines. His legs were up on the control panel, and he wasn't watching the black-and-white monitors, which showed various areas of the engine room.

"See it?" asked Tank, pointing out the large yellow knob on a pipe at the center of the space between the four engines.

The roar of the engines was deafening.

"Hey, you!" came a muted shout from behind.

Another door had opened down the walkway, and four men were now approaching Tank and Bull, who were backing up.

The men were spitting out a vile white liquid onto the steel walls and gangway.

Tank looked at the wall and saw an emergency fire hose hanging for quick access and a large red knob.

Grabbing the hose loops and tossing them to the floor with one hand, he turned the knob wide open with the other, sending a massive jet of water onto the four men.

"What pigs! Nobody spits in my clean engine room," shouted Tank, who struggled to hold the hose, which twisted like a huge live snake.

The jet stream of water knocked the men to the smooth steel gangway and forced them back, and they tumbled as the water was funneled against the inner wall and a twelve-inch raised solid lower portion of the railing, then through an opening in the railing to a ladder, flushing them out to fall forty feet to the deck below, killing them.

Tank reached over and closed the valve, and the hose went limp.

"Another nasty example of poor safety practices. Whoever washed these decks should have posted signs warning others that there was work underway," said Tank.

Peering below, they could see that the man reading the magazine in the control room hadn't noticed a thing.

"Okay," said Tank, "I think I'll use the same ladder; worked well enough for them. Be back in a minute," he motioned to Bull.

Tank slid his feet and hands down the sides of the ladder as swiftly as a new recruit fireman and then crouched his body close to the giant hot engines to avoid being detected, as he made his way over to the yellow valve.

He was standing right next to the engine control room enclosure with roof-to-floor glass, with the man on the chair sitting only a meter away, facing the other direction. Tank was so close he could read the print in the article, which was about the jungle.

Tank pulled back a safety lock switch and turned the valve, which was exactly as Captain Manoa described, releasing the water into the main fuel tank.

He crept along the same route back to the ladder. Pausing at the base, he looked back to see the man standing in the control room with his jaw open, pointing at Tank, who quickly crawled up the ladder.

At the top he met Bull and stretched his mouth closer to his ear. "I think he saw me."

"Me too," replied Bull, with his mouth to Tank's ear.

The African man had now exited the control room and was wearing large headphones.

Bull reached into his shirt and pulled out a handful of grenades and pulled the pins and tossed them down toward the man.

Within seconds, the grenades exploded, and the concussions were barely audible against the engine room din.

The man fell like a sack of potatoes, and Tank looked at Bull and said, "We best be leaving, unless you want to stay and face all those angry passengers when their cruise is interrupted."

"Okay. I don't like the service on this crummy barge anyway. And I hope you haven't forgotten that we can't leave without the Captain, and that means going back up the five flights on stairs."

"Let's find an elevator," replied Tank.

They left the engine room to find the adjoining companionway eerily silent.

"How long until the water hits those engines and they blow?" asked Bull, noticing the massive German MTU diesels hadn't missed a beat despite the grenades.

"Very soon."

"By the way, have you figured out how we are going to get off this tub?" asked Bull. "I hope you are not thinking of waiting until the vessel slows and then dropping a lifeboat."

"I had thought of it, but being sprayed with AK-47 machine gun fire as we board the boats won't exactly help our chances of surviving."

They were creeping along the companionway, moving forward so they would be below the bridge.

"Why are we going forward first? Why don't we go up to the bridge level and then make our way forward?"

"Because most ships have a crew or Captain's elevator, which typically blocks busy passenger levels from access. I would rather see if there is one than chance moving up near the Plaza deck. There may be dozens of men in that area now, taking advantage of the free food, as the Captain said," replied Tank.

There was a small sign that read, "Service Elevator," with an arrow pointing down a small side aisle leading away from the main companionway toward the ship's side.

They could feel the ship's sway and huge up and down motion as they approached the bow.

Seeing the door, Tank pressed the button, and the doors parted.

They entered a tiny service elevator with a plain interior. After Bull entered, both men were squeezed tightly like sardines.

Tank pressed the button marked "Bridge," as Captain Manoa had done for ten years.

A light flashed: "Elevator Deactivated, Ship's Motion Excessive."

"Just our luck," said Tank.

"The service on this barge just keeps getting worse," replied Bull.

They left the elevator on the same floor as the doors opened. Peering to the right, they saw a sign that read, "Bridge Stairs."

"Thank God there's some logic at work here. Hopefully the stairs will take us to the same place," whispered Tank.

Both men entered the stairway and walked up the flights to a door one level above the Plaza level. They opened the door, and Tank leaned out and motioned to Bull to follow.

They dashed across the aisle to the room where they had left the Captain, who was awake and lying in the linen.

"Ready to leave the ship?" asked Tank.

"Have you figured out how to get off?" asked the Captain.

"I am just putting the finishing touches on my plan," said Tank, rubbing his jaw.

"Ah, at least now he has a plan. We are making progress," said Bull.

The ship was rocked by a massive explosion from deep in the bowels, and alarms bells started ringing on the deserted bridge, the sound echoing down the companionway.

"Well, someone has kicked this nest of hornets," said Tank, as men poured into view from doors down the companionway.

One man shouted, pointing at them, and they started running up the aisle toward Tank, Bull, and Captain Manoa.

Bull reached into his vest and pulled out three grenades, throwing them toward the men, and they ducked back into the service stairs and ran down them, with Tank carrying Captain Manoa in his arms.

They heard three explosions in quick succession above them, as the door from the hall to the service stairs was blasted in toward the stairs.

The ship rocked as the second main engine exploded from the water in the fuel, and a new whooping alarm sounded, accompanied by flashing red lights.

"That's the Abandon Ship alarm. The engine room must be a total loss," said Captain Manoa weakly.

"By the way, Tank, can you let me in on your secret escape plan off this tub?" asked Bull.

"Will this way take us to the bow?" asked Tank, looking at the Captain and completely ignoring Bull.

The Captain, barely conscious, said, "Yes, that will take you to the bow."

"How far?" asked Tank.

The Captain looked puzzled and replied, "What do you mean?"

Tank looked and said, "I want to go right to the bow."

"Yes, that will take you there," replied the Captain.

Tank exited the stairs and opened a door onto the lowest level companionway on the ship, which was deserted.

They started walking forward, the ship's wild motion making it difficult to stay on their feet as they clutched the railings.

The ship shuddered as a massive explosion ripped through the remaining two engines simultaneously, stopping all mechanical motion. All vibrations stopped. The lights went dim, and then the emergency lights activated dimly on their low battery power. The only sound was the alarms.

Without forward propulsion to help stabilize the ship, it was now adrift and swaying madly from side to side and up and down in a corkscrew motion.

The Captain, in Bull's arms, had a look of fright in his eyes.

"We get the message, Captain, we are about to disembark," said Tank softly.

"Can you tell us why we are heading to the bow? There are no life rafts, lifeboats, or even lifejackets up there, right, Captain?" asked Bull, with concern in his voice.

"There's nothing in the bow but death," moaned the Captain.

Tank ignored them as they made their way forward along the companionway, clutching the railings to stay on their feet as the ship listed wildly from side to side, and they could feel their feet fall out from under them as the bow plunged into the troughs of the huge rollers.

A door ahead read, "Anchor Room," and Tank grabbed the handle and pulled.

A torrent of salt water surged over the raised deck lip and past their legs down the companionway, as they stood staring into the three-deck-high gallery.

They stepped up over the lip and stood staring at the piles of rope and chain, with the strong smell of dank sea air.

Water suddenly burst past the anchor chains from the opening through the hull and washed down to the floor, which was already ankle deep.

In the center were two massive winches with huge chains wrapped around them that stretched to the open holes in the bow, on the port and starboard sides, from which the anchors hung just beneath, on the outside.

Tank braced himself and walked over to an anchor hole, the water sloshing around his legs and threatening to throw him to the steel deck, crashing against the massive chains.

Waiting for the pause between seawater surges when the bow plunged into the troughs, he stuck out his head and peered back toward the stern along the 800-foot length of the ship and saw it corkscrewing and rolling, with the water surging above the lower tourist cabin porthole windows as it never had in the ship's life.

He crawled back and over to a massive coil of cotton spring line. He took the end and wrapped it around the winch, expertly tying three nautical knots that would not come loose even with the Empire State Building hanging on the rope.

Captain Manoa nodded in respect from his position in Bull's arms. He had never seen a man tie such an impressive knot so quickly in all his years at sea. In his weakened state, he wondered what such a knot would be for.

Tank walked over to Bull and wrapped the line around Bull and Captain Manoa so that they were joined together and could not be separated. Grabbing three Styrofoam line floaters—used to ensure boaters did not come between the ship and the land and be crushed when the ship was anchored close to shore and would move with the winds and tides—he tied the markers to Bull, so that they hung on his front, ensuring his airways stayed above water even if he was unconscious.

"See, I even found you guys life jackets. It's time to get wet. Bull, I am going to feed the line so you descend slowly, using the winch friction to help me. The ship is still moving forward, and that motion is going to take you to the stern in no time.

"You are on the lee side. The wind is hitting the bow on the other side, so you won't be blown in under the bow. In fact, if we time your fall right, the huge bow wave will carry you away from harm. When you hit the water, swim away at least fifty feet. This tub has smooth hull sides and shouldn't be a problem, but then again, I have never swam next to a rolling cruise ship, so let's not take any chances.

"Okay, go." Tank pushed them toward the opening.

Bull had been going through various scenarios for them to escape and could not come up with another plan and was speechless as he maneuvered the Captain gently through the opening.

The Captain was too weak to object.

Both men placed all their faith in Kurt Tank, a man who had never let a person down.

Tank waited for the pause between incoming roller wash through the anchor hole and lowered them around the anchor, gripping the rope with all his might as the 450-pound load stressed the rope with each sway, swinging them below like a pendulum, threatening to smash against the hull. The powerless ship had slowed and most of its motions were from side to side.

Tank watched as they gently entered the water and drifted away toward the stern, with the white line floaters trailing a meter behind. He pulled his head back into the anchor room and searched the walls, as the water sloshed around his calves, stinging the one with the arrow wound, which was still raw.

He opened a locker and grabbed what looked like a plastic medical kit and a rusty slot screwdriver and knife, pushing them into his vest and zipping it up to his neck.

Looking over many types of lines, he turned away, clutching one, and crawled to the anchor opening. He pushed his head out, paused, and then, crouching into a ball, thrust his body headfirst into the water far below, striking the surface and plunging ten feet into a massive roller. Tank felt a surge of water push him away from the ship, as the bow's deflection of the wave when it plunged worked just as he had described to Bull.

His head broke the surface twenty feet farther from the ship than where he had entered the water to see thick, black smoke billowing from the smokestack and rear glass portholes, which had cracked from the heat of the inferno in the engine room. The entire rear third of the ship was shrouded in smoke.

Without any experienced seamen on board, nobody had firefighting skills or knew any safety procedures.

The ship's automatic fire suppression system had initially activated, and water was pouring from the upper deck, but later, with the ongoing explosions and fires, generator power was lost, and the batteries had given out, shutting down the water pumps and leaving the fire to burn freely.

High above, on the bridge and the outer bridge deck, there were dozens of men in lifejackets, looking up at the sky. They had tried launching a lifeboat on the other side, filled to the forty-person capacity. It had flipped with the rolling ship, and those who weren't killed outright were floating and being attacked by sharks.

Those up in the ship were afraid of being eaten alive by sharks and wouldn't try to launch a lifeboat again and were awaiting a helicopter rescue from their SOS beacon, which would never come. Early in the ship's takeover, the leader had sabotaged all emergency beacons in case any crew member came to his senses and wanted off the ship, and only he knew they didn't work.

An Olympic-level swimmer, Tank's legs kicked with urgency until they burned with pain, and then he bodysurfed, the rollers carrying him to the stern within minutes, where he shouted to Bull, "Think I should get aboard a sinking ship?"

Floating up and down with the waves, Bull said, "I've been waiting for the next part of your plan. You got the rope length exactly right; we are being kept right at the stern. Not bad, considering it's stretching eight hundred feet to the front—plus, these sea conditions."

Captain Manoa's eyes were open, but he was too weak to speak.

Tank clutched Bull's back and the Styrofoam floater to stabilize himself and reached into his vest to bring out what looked like a white medical kit that he had grabbed in the anchor room.

Opening it, he pulled out a line-shooting handgun, used to shoot light ropes across to shore or another ship, which were then used to carry across heavier lines and ultimately supplies or even people.

Up on the ship, the fire had rapidly spread and now engulfed every level, and the windows had shattered, and there were flames licking out and upward forty feet toward the sky.

The lifeboats were flaming hulks, with gobs of molten fiberglass spitting out, falling to the ocean below. Four of the lifeboats had burned so that the anchor points where the hoist cables attached broke free, and the lifeboats tumbled to the water and were floating infernos among the men, who were treading water, petrified of the shark attacks, which had already started to claim victims.

With smoke engulfing most of the ship and the crew frantic to avoid being burned alive or eaten alive by sharks, nobody was paying any attention to the rear.

Aiming up at the ship's stern, Tank pulled the trigger and the gun fired, carrying a lightweight line up and draping over the drone's propeller hub and falling back down to the sea.

The open decks of the rear of the ship had nothing flammable but the smoke was intense. Occasionally, between the wind gusts, Tank could make out the rear deck as the smoke cleared for a second or two. When the stern crashed down, the water shot out in a jet, making his job almost impossible.

Tank gripped the two lines draping down to the water from around the drone's propeller hub, and with each forty-foot up-

and-down motion of the ship, he clenched his hands to ratchet himself higher.

Within minutes, the black smoke was searing his eyes as he shimmied up the final portion of the line and jumped across the railing next to the drone.

All was silent, except the fire alarm bells, which clanged in the distance, running on batteries that were almost dead.

Water was sloshing across the deck, coming from the companionway inside the door. The water was sourced at the fire suppression system, which had doused the vessel with water before the pumps stopped. Steam was rising from the hot steel walls and doors, which had raging infernos behind them.

Crawling across the deck through the smoke to a dim red mark, Tank fumbled and grabbed the small hammer attached with a cable and smashed the window and reached in, clutching the fire axe.

He turned his back to the drone fuselage and raised the axe as high as he could, bringing it down in one mighty blow, then another, then a third, which shattered the carbon fiber wing that was pinned most tightly to the deck, and the drone dropped on one side.

He cut the first rope wrapped around the propeller hub, securing the drone to the railing and tossed the axe aside and crawled over the railing.

Tank wrapped his arms around the propeller, hanging over the water below and upside down, and then he pulled on the tail with his body weight, pushing with his legs up against the railing and his head down toward the ocean below, as the drone inched over the railing.

The tail slid lower and lower, dragging the remaining wing tip out from its pinned location.

Then Tank and the drone fell together to the sea below, crashing into the water and narrowly avoiding being crushed by the stern as it plunged down.

All was silent, as the shark-infested South Atlantic Ocean swallowed man and machine.

Bull looked over as Tank and the drone had briefly become visible from the smoke and then disappeared beneath the waves.

Preoccupied with keeping Captain Manoa's head above water and looking out for the dorsal fins of sharks—a few of which he had noticed as they floated to the stern—Bull felt shock and dread as his friend was swallowed beneath the waves and feared for his own life and the Captain's.

A roller with a large whitecap surged across them, dousing the Captain and rousing him from his stupor, as he spat out the salt water and said, "The ship is finished, and it looks like the sharks will have their way with me, as before. You guys call this a rescue?"

Bull was silent and staring into the distance with his back to the ship, dazed, as the massive rollers pulled against the line, tying them to the bow anchor winch eight hundred feet away.

Behind him, he heard a loud splashing sound.

He thought the ship may have capsized, or that it was a roller with a surging whitecap that had broached.

Turning his head, he saw the drone's remaining twenty-three-foot wing rise up vertically to its full height and then flop down on the water, lifting out in places as the waves swept across its length and created eddies underneath. At the wing root, the drone was floating upright on two giant inflatable pontoons, with Tank lying across the fuselage with his head resting on closed arms on the bulbous snout with the sensors inside.

"Want a lift?" he shouted, grinning.

Bull started swimming over to the drone and soon was alongside Tank.

"I thought you were a goner," said Bull.

"So did I. I guess all that smoke affected the water sensors and delayed the automatic inflation of the pontoons," said Tank.

Bull reached up, and they both secured the Captain to the driest part of the drone.

Tank fiddled with the drone's laptop keypad.

"What are you trying to do?" asked Bull.

"I am trying to get the engine to start, but it looks like we are out of luck," said Tank.

"Well, we were lucky it worked with the Beriev, but I guess these drones aren't built Russian tough."

"I guess not," said Tank, as he tossed the keyboard into the water. He placed his hand on his jaw and started rubbing.

"What are you thinking?" asked Bull.

They were both casting their eyes toward the ship, with black smoke and red flames billowing from every portion and a massive list having developed.

Some had taken refuge at the highest point, in the Matterhorn swimming pool, only to find the hot deck plates had heated the water to scalding temperatures, forcing them to jump out into the flames and smoke or be boiled alive.

Men were screaming from the top decks and some were jumping clear of the structure and falling to the ocean below. There were now too many shark dorsal fins to count.

"I am thinking you should release your line and let us drift away from the ship," said Tank.

"That won't help our chances of being rescued when help comes. I assume somebody, somewhere will eventually notice an 800-foot cruise ship missing soon, or somebody's satellite will notice all this smoke," replied Bull.

"Maybe, but that ship is going to death plunge soon, and then there will be even more of a shark feeding frenzy. I don't think these pontoons will stand much of a chance against shark bites, at least if I recall my shark information," said Tank.

"What shark information?" asked Bull.

"Jaws 3," replied Tank.

"The drone motor is dead. If we release the rope, we are still going to simply drift with the ship anyway, and we will still be around for the shark feeding frenzy."

"We will have one advantage. If we cut that line that goes to the anchor room, I can use it for something," said Tank.

"Use it for what?" replied Bull, who noticed the Captain opening his eyes, momentarily interested in the answer.

Tank was already gone, swimming as fast as he could, fifty feet from the drone. He reached into his vest and produced the rusty knife, cutting the line.

The drone with Bull and the Captain started to drift immediately, and Tank swam with powerful strokes and was winded when he pulled himself up onto the fuselage.

Nervously, he looked back to check if any sharks had followed.

"Looks like we have some fans," shouted Bull, as they all looked toward the ship and could see a large group of crewmen swimming toward them with dozens of dorsal fins following.

"My idea won't work with any more than the three of us," said Tank.

"Good to hear. With that mob and the sharks following them, we won't last ten minutes," replied Bull.

Tank quickly tied an expert lasso and moved out along the wing and then jammed the lasso into the gap between the wing flap and the wing, near the tip. He wrapped the rope around the wing tip several times to make sure it wouldn't come out.

Next, he took out his rusty screwdriver and moved around so he could reach the drone's smooth belly and pried open the parachute compartment, flooding it with water.

The three white chutes burst out from their tight packing and pulled themselves like sea anchors behind the fast drifting drone, until all three were side by side, connected to the drone by hundred-foot-long white shock cords, and drifting away.

Tank gathered the cords and wrapped them around the drone's bulbous snout and then tied the separate line from the wingtip to the parachute's three lines, which he had gathered as one, halfway along their length.

"Okay, we now have three spinnakers pulling on the bow with a control line and mast. Good enough? Now it's your turn," said Tank, tossing the line to the wing tip to Bull.

"Pass him to me," said Tank, as Bull passed the Captain to Tank, who held him securely above the crashing waves rolling over the drone.

Bull dove into the water with a mighty splash, with the line around his waist. After swimming twenty feet from the drone, he loosened the line and held it in his hand. With each surge from the rollers, he pulled harder, his rhino legs kicking with all their might.

Tank adjusted his position to keep the Captain secure, as the drone's fuselage rolled over onto its side.

The remaining wing was now vertical and serving as a mast, and as soon as the parachutes were pulled up from the water into the wind, they each billowed to their full size and rose. The drone was quickly swept away in the fifty-knot wind, leaving the crewmen who had come to within ten feet frantically shouting, as their last hope of life was lost.

Tank had secured the Captain, and he was resting comfortably on the wing side fuselage, which was completely clear of the water.

The drone skimmed along at forty knots, with the sunken pontoon inflated under the water, acting as a bulbous hydrofoil wing, and the smooth aerodynamic fuselage providing little water drag. Tank used his hand on the vertical tail rudder flap to steer the unusual craft, holding the propeller with his other hand to keep himself in place, which was difficult as the parachutes pulled so strongly they occasionally pulled the drone almost vertical, leaving them all scrambling to hang on.

"Which way, Skipper?" called Bull, who had a huge smile on his face.

"Whichever way the wind blows," said Tank, with great relief.

"Aren't these easterlies coming across from Gambia?" said Bull.

"Right you are," said Tank.

Tank looked across to the Captain who had awoken with fear at the drone's violent motions to view the most unorthodox sailing craft he had ever seen, which looked like it would sink at any moment.

"Where will we land, Captain?"

The weary Captain looked back toward the flaming ship in the distance, then in the direction of the wind, and drifted back into the dark comfort of unconsciousness.

CHAPTER FORTY-ONE

The Good Times Express had vanished from sight hours ago, the blazing flames and black smoke stopping suddenly as the ship finally capsized and sank, leaving the remaining survivors to their grisly fate.

The drone surged along with the high winds, surfing the giant rollers as the three billowing parachutes served as excellent spinnaker sails.

The breaking whitecaps washed over Tank and Bull, keeping them sharp, as they struggled to control the ungainly craft, as one miscalculation could flip it.

Tank watched the massive waves and adjusted the vertical tail mounted stabilizer used as a rudder to keep them from flipping as they crested the rollers and descended into the troughs, over and over.

Tank and Bull felt their muscles burn with pain as the hours unfolded. Exhaustion was not far behind, as the exertion of holding themselves in place and working the improvised sailing drone took its toll, with blood seeping from skin worn raw.

Tank looked over at Bull's hand wrapped in the rope, which was red with dripping blood, and then looked to his own hand also dripping blood and thought of his calf wound from the arrow shot at him on the Amazon, which had been wet with blood the entire time since.

Both men knew that if they flipped the drone as it surfed the waves, the sharks would be upon them before they could right it again.

The waves were growing more massive, and it took all their strength and skill to keep the ungainly craft upright.

"I think larger waves means we are getting closer to land," Tank shouted to Bull, who was having more trouble keeping the wing upright.

"I hope so; I am barely making it here," replied Bull, who was shifting his eyes between the wing, the drone, and the waves ahead.

The giant waves surrounded them, and their only focus was to stay alive, as the drone surfed up one roller, only to speed down the next.

"How about I lower the wing a little and slow this thing down? I don't have the strength to hold it," shouted Bull.

"If you lower the wing, it will be less vertical and will be heavier for you. Plus, you are going to change the drag of the drone, because you will be rolling it over in the water, and I don't know if this rudder arrangement will still work. With the parachutes dragging us, we may cause the wing and tail to veer into the water, dragging us down like a sub doing a crash dive. Let's keep it the way it is," shouted Tank.

"I can't. I am too weak," Bull protested, as his hand lost its grip from the rope, cutting his tendons.

The wing dropped down, causing the drone to turn sharply to the right and the underwater pontoon to rise, so the drone sat flat on the water on both pontoons.

Both men crawled up onto the fuselage near the Captain and stretched out to rest their muscles.

Occasionally a wave washed over them, but for now the craft was stable.

Tank looked in the direction of the wind in front of the parachutes and could see gray mountains along the shore, with giant colored birds flying back and forth along the land.

The sun beat down on them mercilessly, as the swells lifted and dropped the drone, and they drifted into unconsciousness, joining the Captain, and unaware of the circling dorsal fins that surrounded them.

CHAPTER FORTY-TWO

In his delirium, Tank saw a colored dune buggy and heard the clatter of an ancient air-cooled Volkswagen engine and saw camels walking along a crest on a sand dune and chattering voices. He vaguely thought he was in the middle of a dream and wondered how the dream would turn out.

"Welcome to the Raffles Beach Resort and Hotel. How do you feel?" said a cheerful voice in a Portuguese accent.

Tank looked in front of him to see a gentleman with a friendly face.

"Where am I?" wondered Tank, ignoring the question and looking around at the luxurious king-sized bed and white linens.

"At the Raffles Hotel," repeated the man, looking to a shy young female assistant to his side, both dressed in their professional-looking hotel uniform sport coats and slacks.

"And where is that?" inquired Tank, who started drinking from a bottle of water held to his lips by a third person, dressed all in white. His eyes scanned the room and out the window he could see swaying palm trees and the ocean.

The memories flooded back.

"Where are the others?" asked Tank.

"The large man is in the room next door. The smaller man was taken to hospital."

"You are in Natal, Brazil. How did you end up on our beach?" asked Nicolaus Bordon, the hotel manager.

"How long have I been here?" asked Tank, who Bordon was growing frustrated with.

"You have been in our hotel for seven hours. You were found on our beach this morning, lashed to some sort of recreational craft I am not familiar with. We thought you had come from one of the nearby resorts and went out too far and had problems. However, we have checked with the local hotels and no guests are missing. We also checked with the Coast Guard, and they have had no reports of missing or lost people. These waters are rife with bull sharks, and you were all bleeding. You are lucky to be alive.

"I was hoping you could help clear up the mystery," said Bordon, with more than a little curiosity.

BLACK V

Tank looked down at his hands and saw that they were professionally bandaged and then felt down his leg and could feel a tight dressing around his calf.

"A doctor was here earlier and bandaged you—your big friend as well. Other than being dehydrated, he thought you were not in too bad of shape and could recover here. Since we could find no identification with you, I suppose a lack of health care insurance may have guided his decision somewhat. He left this intern to monitor you and keep you drinking liquids," said Bordon.

The young intern spoke to Bordon in Portuguese.

"She just reminded me that the doctor wanted to know if those are pacemakers on both your necks. They buzz every once in a while. Your hearts appear very strong, she says."

Tank felt his neck. His head was clearing, and he placed his third water bottle down, moving his legs over to the side and pulling his sheets back, to see he had on a hospital gown.

The intern blushed.

He pulled himself to his feet and walked over to the windows to see a large pool three floors below and dozens of guests loitering around. The hotel was hung on a low bluff and the land and facilities positioned on descending levels that ended on the beach below. Looking further down, he could see the drone next to a beach cabana, with the parachutes alongside in a pile.

Bordon was standing next to Tank.

"There have been a lot of people looking at that sailboat, or ultralight, or whatever it is. It looks damaged; what happened?" asked Bordon.

Tanks mind raced, and he thought back to the Good Times Express.

The crewmen may not have sent a distress signal. Perhaps the man Bull sat on in the radio room was the only one who knew how to operate the sabotaged radio system. Tank remembered the crewmen, screaming, swimming toward the drone as the wind caught the three parachutes and they slipped away.

"We even had a guy in a helicopter come by and land," said Bordon.

"What kind of helicopter?" asked Tank.

"A small black one. A big menacing man at the controls. He looked injured. I suppose he was scanning the Coast Guard radio. I don't know how else he could have known about you. He asked one of our staff a lot of questions while they were dragging your boat up the beach to secure it. Just as suddenly as he had appeared, he fired up the engine and off he went."

Tank's eyes watched as young men flew by with parasails, using the steady forty-knot winds to fly the sails like planes.

They were dropping down to the beach and picking up tourists to take them for rides.

Two camels came down a sand dune toward the flat beach, being led by the owner, with two chubby pink ladies giggling atop the creatures.

Tank heard a familiar sound and looked down the beach to see brightly colored dune buggies and their noisy air-cooled Volkswagen engines.

"How long ago was this?" asked Tank.

"Not long after we had taken you up from the beach, a few hours ago," said Bordon.

"He knows we are here?" asked Tank.

"I imagine so. After all, you did arrive right on our beach, and we have signs posted there so that our guests don't lose their way among the various hotels."

Tank switched modes and demanded, "Where are my clothes?"

Bordon was shocked and replied, "What was left of the clothes you were wearing was disposed of. We hope you approve of these; it's all we have."

The young woman with Bordon pulled a hanger from the closet and laid the hotel uniform out for Tank.

The young intern started protesting to Bordon in Portuguese and waving her arms.

Bordon looked at Tank and said, "I am reminded that the doctor made us promise to let you rest until tomorrow. He had planned to come back to check on you. Apparently your blood pressure was poor, and those hand and leg wounds are still oozing blood. The intern here feels quite strongly about it. She will look bad if you leave so soon."

The intern was making a call on her cellphone and looked to Bordon and spoke rapidly in Portuguese.

"At least let her track down the doctor and tell him your plans," said Bordon.

Tank was busily pulling on the clothes the hotel had supplied. He had drunk liters of water and eaten a good amount too. His blood pressure would have improved, and even if not, it would still be far healthier to get moving.

"Where is the hospital?" asked Tank.

Bordon looked confused. "Just up the hill—a big white building."

"Which room is my big friend in?" Tank asked.

Bordon pointed to the room next door, and Tank ran out the door, rushing down the hall with Bordon running behind.

"Wait. I have to open the door for you," Bordon said, running after him.

Tank heard the sound of a helicopter, as Bordon fumbled with the door pass.

Entering the room, Tank yelled at the top of his voice, "Okay! Rest time's over; let's go."

Bull opened his eyes, stunned, and rolled over, crushing the mattress with his bulk, and stood up on his rhino legs.

"Hey, what should I wear?" asked Bull, clutching the white bed sheet.

Bordon entered the room and said with some embarrassment, "I am sorry, we couldn't find anything suitable for your friend to wear. Due to his…dimensions, we are still trying to figure out how to clothe him."

Screams could be heard as the helicopters engine slowed.

Bordon raced to the window and looked stunned. "That is the man who was asking questions on the beach this morning, but now he has a friend with him, and they have guns. Who are you anyway, and who are they?" asked Bordon, staring at the black chopper that had landed next to the pool, sending guests running in all directions.

A simple act of kindness taking in marooned sailors now had his guests smack in the middle of some sort of commando or terrorist raid, and there was no telling who the bad guys were.

Bull stood clutching his bed sheet, trying to make a Roman toga out of it.

Tank ran next to Bordon and saw the familiar black Robertson 44 and two ominous figures in all black with dark sunglasses, running toward the hotel with AK-47s.

Tank ran back to Bull and grabbed his arm, giving him a strong shove toward the door.

"Okay, the holiday's over. Thanks for the hospitality; we'll be sure to recommend you," shouted Tank hurriedly.

Both men ran with difficulty, as they were still weak from their high-seas drama. They jogged down the hall and up the short flight of stairs to the hotel foyer.

As they raced across the foyer, Bull reached down to a buffet cart and pulled the entire contents into a basket formed in his toga, shocking bystanders with his lack of modesty.

They ran out the front entrance and saw a white Volkswagen Kombi hotel courtesy van with the hotel's pirate ship logo on the sides, which had just dropped off new hotel guests.

Tank raced around the front to the driver's door, and Bull dove in the open sliding passenger side door, landing with a crash on a black vinyl bench seat meant to hold three.

"Just our luck!" yelled Bull, surveying the 1960s-design vehicle which normally had the engine of the Beetle and thus was very slow. "They'll catch us on foot with this hippie van."

Tank fumbled with the key, and the engine roared to life amidst the shouts of the driver, who had paused inside the foyer only long enough to collect his tip and now stood not knowing what to do.

He jammed the loose, wobbly shifter into first gear and smashed the accelerator to the floor, as the engine screamed from the rear.

Tank released the clutch, and the Volkswagen surged ahead and was thirty feet down the driveway when the sound of the machine guns could be heard from behind.

The rear window and then the windshield exploded in the hail of bullets as the Volkswagen leaned, and the tires squealed as it came out of the paved driveway onto the cobblestone street of Natal's tiny luxury hotel district, which sloped toward the ocean.

"Hey, we made it. You better take it easy; this thing's gonna blow," said Bull, as Tank kept the engine wide open, and the tall narrow bus leaned around tight corners as alarmed tourists ran to get out of the way.

"The Captain isn't safe," said Tank, who was frantically turning the antiquated black manual steering wheel through the cobblestoned streets of the European-like oceanside city and finally saw the hospital at the top of the hill as Bordon had described.

The Volkswagen bus screamed down the palm tree-lined one-way street leading to the hospital. To avoid driving around to the parking lot on the curved driveway, Tank aggressively turned the wheel, sending the bus flying up over the high cement curb onto the meridian, cutting trenches through the soil and flowers, and then bumping down to the asphalt on the other side directly to the hospital entrance doors with the large admissions sign.

Tank stomped the brake pedal into the floor, and the bus screeched to a halt right in front of a "No Noise" sign, written in English and Portuguese.

"Watch our ride, garçon," said Tank, flinging open the thin door and looking back to see Bull's mouth so full of buns from the snack tray at the hotel he could only grunt.

Tank ran into the hospital and met an English-speaking woman at the admissions desk.

"Could you please tell me which room my Uncle Manoa is in?"

The lady looked at her computer screen. "Manoa? Oh, the doctor will be pleased to meet you; we have a lot of questions about that patient," she said, picking up the telephone.

"Which room, please?" he repeated rather patiently, considering.

"Room 55, top floor. The doctor is anxious to speak to you."

Tank was already gone, brushing by two people leaving the elevator. The doors closed, and he tensed himself as it slowly rose to the fifth floor, running out the doors to a small room, with windows facing the beach two kilometers away.

BLACK V

Tank saw a black speck in the distance, rising from beyond the hill that descended down to the beach and the hotel.

"You again!" said Captain Manoa, who looked much better, with IV drips attached and resting in a clean bed.

Tank brushed the nurse aside, who raced to a phone. He leaned over and picked up the Captain, and the IV lines pulled out harmlessly.

"Put me down. I am good here. My wife is coming. Leave me alone."

"You're not safe," said Tank, who was towing the Captain down the hall.

"Why, I haven't done anything, and I don't know anything. I am not a part of your CIA drug war," said the Captain.

"I know that, but they don't know that, and they will kill you if you stay here. And we aren't CIA," said Tank.

"Who will kill me?" said the Captain. "The ship sank, and there are no survivors. Nobody here even knows the ship was off the Brazilian coast in the first place or that it had been seized by bandits. The ship's owners don't answer any calls, and these people here think I am crazy and the whole story is due to me being delusional. They keep asking me which hotel I am staying at, and they think your drone, which we washed up on the beach with, is some kind of millionaire's Hobie Cat."

They left the elevator, and Tank tensed as he heard a familiar sound. They felt the warm hundred-degree air as they left the air-conditioned hospital. Tank saw that Bull had heard the approaching Robertson 44 and had moved to the driver's position and had the side door open and the engine running.

Tank pushed the Captain across the black vinyl back seat where Bull had been sitting and closed the sliding door and then jumped in the front seat.

The helicopter landed directly in front of them and its doors were opening, as Bull gunned the throttle and steered the Volkswagen in a tight circle and left the way they came.

"Where to now, boss?" asked Bull as they sped away, and Tank looked back through the smashed window to see the ominous figures let loose a hail of bullets that failed to strike the van and then run back toward the helicopter.

"We need something a bit faster than this to get away from these guys. Without any firepower, all we can do is run at this point. It seems our toys never made it to the beach."

"Where's the nearest airport?" asked Tank, craning his neck back toward Captain Manoa, who pointed to the nearby Natal International Airport.

Bull kept the pedal floored as they weaved through traffic to arrive at the crowded airport.

The three got out and looked up to see the helicopter landing a short distance away, causing confusion among the airport personnel.

Three men approached, and with a nod from Tank, two of them assumed the Captain.

Giant had been tracking them and assumed a bit of assistance might be needed.

"Where are they taking me…" said the Captain.

"To a place where you and your family will be safe. I will see you soon."

The third man ushered Tank and Bull to an unmarked door looking like a service entrance, located under a concrete staircase.

They entered to find a high-tech electronics room with sit-down consoles and helmets that looked like the ones jet fighter pilots wore, with eye shields and displays on the inside.

The man quietly provided the simple instructions before disappearing.

"Let me guess: these guys are friends of Giant's?" asked Bull.

"Correct," confirmed Tank, as they slid down and donned the helmets to be transported 8,000 kilometers away…arriving in the White House to a meeting with the President.

CHAPTER FORTY-THREE

In the basement of the White House Situation Room, National Security Advisor Taggert sat with his head in his hands and then stood as the terse-faced President entered the room with several key assistants trailing, calling out urgent questions.

A capable man, with a military-style pig shave, Taggert had an earnest and honest manner that had earned him respect and trust in a Washington where those commodities were in short supply.

The President was under pressure that would have tested a man half his age, with dozens of aides, governmental department heads, and politicians waiting to see him each waking hour, while several phones calls were kept holding.

The entire White House had the atmosphere of a military command center under heavy bombardment.

The President felt a small degree of calm as he saw Taggert. At least he would be getting information he could trust, which was often not the case.

Standing up wearily and still wearing yesterday's rumpled clothes, Taggert held a large package of papers in his hands. He was tired, having spent the previous night reading the papers, over and over, and taking them from their binders to copy. It was large enough to have normally warranted its own briefcase, but Taggert clutched them like he had grabbed them unexpectedly while running from a house fire.

"Mr. President, it's good to see you, sir," said Taggert, sounding exhausted. He sat down and rested the papers in front of him on the large table.

"Tell me some good news," said the President amidst the din with a warm half-smile, glancing up at the screens which had on ongoing stream of news stories depicting the media's theme, that the various vehicular crashes, suicides, and other mini-catastrophes were connected and were probably man–caused. The media offered the usual sprinkling of end-of-times type perspective, with book authors offering their two bits' worth, including alien theories. That there could possibly be any good news in such a grim scenario was the humor highlight of the day and lasted only a second.

"Well," began Taggert, with only the briefest hint of a smile to acknowledge the President's attempt at humor, "there is good news, but not much, as I have just discovered, and I'll leave that for the end."

"Okay, shoot," said the President, who sat down on a sofa opposite Taggert and hunched over his knees in earnest attention, as the background noise of the roof faded to each man, staring intently at each other.

"Two days ago, we directed those in attendance at the second meeting at the Alternate Command Site to order all agencies within their general authority to spare no expense at taking all measures thought necessary to deter and prevent the continued supply of the tainted neurotoxin product from reaching the citizenry through cocaine, or any other means. Since that time, we have run into the usual problems, but also some unexpected ones," said Taggert in even tones, glancing around to see who was within earshot.

"So what are the unexpected problems?" asked the President.

"As we discussed in the meeting days ago, the United States has citizens of widely varied cultural and religious background, and to my knowledge, there has only been a small scattering of examples where that stood in the way of those same immigrants from standing behind the flag of the USA and doing their part."

"Of course," replied the President. "One only has to look at World War One or World War Two to see that there was representation from all backgrounds in the armed forces."

"So can you tell me what the problem is?" asked the President, who gave a cold glance to the throngs hovering for his attention only paces away.

"Well, sir," replied Taggert, who had developed a bead of sweat across his brow, "all leaders present at our earlier meeting have reported that there is a form of bureaucratic inertia working against us here that can only be described as sabotage from within."

"From within? Taggert, I don't know if you are being tactful or what, but you are going to have to lay it out for me more quickly," said the President, a slow fury building.

"Sir, we have found that orders have been given across all affected agencies but that there has been almost zero compliance in the field. There have even been a few problems in the CIA, FBI, and the military, although not many. Critical emails have disappeared. Personnel that were spoken to and whom were given orders verbally claim they don't recall the conversations. Others who will acknowledge receiving the orders disagree with the orders and are claiming those orders do not comply with new legislation on the books or even their constitutional rights to act against their conscience. As a result, the orders have in effect been nullified initially, and the staff are reformulating responses, quoting obvious obligations under emergency measures as per employment contracts and even military law. That has taken a lot of time, involving human resource personnel and government lawyers."

"What possible effect could that have on the laying out of these master directives at the field level? I don't see how it is possible that a few examples could have frozen the entire implementation of emergency measures," said the President, who had never heard of such disobedience in sixty years of public life.

"Why don't you simply issue new master directives to sideline all problematic staff temporarily, until such time as the human resource people have formulated new directives? After the crisis or at a later time, you can fire them for disobeying orders. In fact, you can fire them now and find just cause later," said the President, waving his arms in frustration.

"Sir, excuse me for saying, but these are not a few isolated examples. We are talking about tens of thousands of people across federal, state, and county levels. Health officials, sheriffs, judges, mayors, Coast Guard officials—the list is endless," Taggert said, standing and pointing his thumb over his opposite shoulder at the imaginary disobedient employees.

"Tens of thousands can't be right, but even so, there are millions of employees in the entire government apparatus," replied the President, causing a politician walking by to pause and look over, then continue on. A gaggle of impatient people waiting to talk to the President hovered closer, with crises that they could not solve.

Taggert was nearing total exhaustion and rallied his strength, and his throat was starting to sound raspy and weak.

"Sir, thousands of employees are refusing to comply with our emergency directives for a variety of reasons, all seemingly legal but actually in the final analysis bogus, and the result is that the fast track measures to stop this crisis have been halted," said Taggert, who was pointing to the screens, which depicted the stories of accidents.

"What in God's name is behind all this? How could thousands of people be refusing to work at the same time? Surely there does not exist such an efficient interconnected communication system to coordinate such an action," said the President, who was clearly exasperated.

"It would not even be possible for such an action to occur without a central control."

"Who is the central control?" asked the President.

Suddenly the "whoop, whoop, whoop" of the emergency siren was heard, indicating a final stage emergency, such as a bomb scare.

The PA system announced, "This is not a drill. Please evacuate the building immediately."

Secret Service personnel rushed toward them, and Taggert and the President were ushered away to a safe holding location, complete with a doctor, medical assistant, and eight military officers forming a perimeter guard.

CHAPTER FORTY-FOUR

After several minutes, the all-clear was given, and they walked back to the center and resumed their conversation

"A small minority of Muslims, who are intent on bringing down the USA. We have traced a company called Excel Electronics, which is controlled by a Saudi Arabian national. From the information supplied by the FBI and CIA to my source, this company has been the bid winner for the supply and service contracts for the electronic voting machines used in all elections in the USA for the past ten years or so at state, federal, and county level.

"We have been running an investigation to confirm if there is evidence of pro-Muslim policy positions in voting patterns and committee work by these election-winning individuals, and it appears at this early stage to be the case, and it is blatant. There are perhaps hundreds or even thousands of elected officials that have their jobs through voting fraud. The voting machines were probably altered—like at an amusement park or gambling casino—to produce a pre-determined outcome, so that however weak the candidate or their campaign was, they still won the election. It could be that the candidates did not even know that they had won by these illicit means."

Taggert appeared like a weary soldier, explaining a conspiracy that was like a spider web.

"Excel Electronics is the single largest user of the Federal Green Card system in the entire country and has brought in thousands of employees under the program. Because those Saudis or Iranians were not being processed for citizenship applications, they were not investigated thoroughly and have been running loose doing whatever they want for years."

"This is madness. Can you substantiate this?"

"Before last night, no. In fact, I had no idea of virtually ninety-nine percent of what I am telling you," replied Taggert, "but last night I reviewed the papers in this package, and I am still in shock at the big picture it not only presents but factually supports.

"Sir, there are upwards of twenty million undocumented people of Mexican background that are in the USA illegally."

"I am well aware."

"The problem is that the exact same federal, state, and county agencies responsible for that mess have been incompetently admitting Muslims in general from dozens of countries, for years."

"You are saying we have undocumented or poorly documented Muslims. I agree. We also have undocumented and poorly documented Buddhists and British and those from the Philippines and Christians and people from every background and religion on earth. So what?" said the President.

"There is no other group that is as aggressive at pursuing its own self-serving agenda as Muslims," said Taggert. "We know that there are tens of thousands of passively extremist Muslims, in at least thirty countries worldwide, who are actively and openly trying to establish Islamic states, to convert or remake the countries of which they are new citizens to be totally Muslim, including of course a very strict application of Sharia Law.

"In other words, they are trying to accomplish the exact same thing that the so-called Muslim extremists are trying to accomplish with open conflict, suicide bombers, and the like."

"What do you mean, passively extremist?"

"I mean, there are many who are law-abiding on the surface, but deep within them, they have a core of their Muslim faith that inspires them to resist the efforts to save the USA, rather to sort of destroy the country from within, or let's say in this case, allow it to be destroyed."

"Well, why on earth would they want to do that?" asked the President.

Finally, an aide literally pulled the President aside for a moment and whispered something in his ear.

The President shouted in a voice so that all who were waiting for him could be heard, "Folks, please give us a few more minutes."

Taggert continued, "Because they hate the West generally, and although they are benefitting from the life and opportunities the USA has given them, they still have a core portion of themselves that hates our country and will participate in destroying it if given the chance. Of course, I do not mean physically destroy, which is the agenda of other Muslims, but rather to erode the historic institutions and identity and to advocate for the installation of Islamic replacements. Certainly, for example, they dislike any reference to Christian holidays, in order to create a vacancy that will be later filled with Muslim alternatives."

A light went off in the President's mind.

"And this is their chance to make a move. They are creating a so-called law and order crisis, which will create a situation that

Sharia Law will be sold as the solution to. Well, that's rich," said the President, rocked at the implications.

"Yes, sir. We will be taking all actions we can as fast as we can with these problems, but it is going to take time, and we don't have time."

"I can see that," said the President, looking at the large screens and the various disasters from around the country.

Taggert continued with the onslaught of information.

"I hate to tell you, but we have received word from an undercover FBI agent in Miami that the main infusion of the neurotoxin drug agent is still to come. It will be fifteen hundred times the amount in circulation now. By using criminal distribution channels, they are utilizing methods that our agencies have already been unable to close for decades. We have strong suspicions that a large load is destined for our shores within hours, and there is nothing we can do to stop it or subsequent shipments at this point."

"I have heard that the shipments are sourced in South America," said the President.

"Correct, sir."

"Well, let's take them out," said the President, who was starting to slump at the enormity of the crisis. He felt like President Theodore Roosevelt in the minutes after learning the Japanese had bombed Pearl Harbor.

"Easier said than done," interjected Ferret.

Taggert ignored him. "From an undercover FBI agent in Miami, we believe the shipments are coming from deep in the Amazon Basin and may involve the territories of up to eight nations. It seems there is strong internal resistance to assist us in these countries, a problem we are working on, and there is another problem we are having. We have very few people down in the deep jungle, and those we do have, are mid-level bureaucratic types, none who could assist us with this type of operation. It is likely that these tainted drugs will be sourced at a huge mega complex with hundreds of crooks and guns protecting it."

"We've taken out drug operations in the past," said the President.

Ferret looked over at the President. "Not like this. We can't even find it with our best satellites. It not only is probably extremely well hidden, which means we may not be able to find it in perfect conditions, but it's the monsoon season, which means that the jungle floor is masked from most satellite detection due to the massive and rain-sodden, low-hanging clouds and the mist from the pelting rain bouncing from the jungle floor. Any life forms that may show up periodically are not quickly discernible from the thousands of animals' body heat signatures.

"We have no effective ground operatives. There are few roads in that area, and as I mentioned, trying to work above board with these countries is a whole 'nother kettle of fish. Most decisions are made with consideration that they will be leaked at some point, and therefore have to be justifiable to the people, or they will be used as political fodder by the opposing party or even by enemies within the same government. You might as well forget enlisting these countries, at least in the short term."

Taggert chimed in, "I should also mention that the Saudi Arabian government, while to our knowledge not a part of this current crisis directly, has been funding Islamic groups around the world for years, to the tune of a hundred billion or more."

"Okay," said the President, throwing up his arms, "now you want me to worry about a major source of our oil imports? If they don't seem to be involved, then why mention them?"

"I said not involved directly. They are not in Amazonia growing the toxic cocaine themselves. But, as to general involvement, they are involved up to their ears," corrected Taggert. "As this report documents beyond the shadow of a doubt, they have created fertile soil, if you will, for these weeds to grow. In other words, the pro-Muslim sentiment is kept vibrant by the Saudis.

"The Saudis, and by that I mean the ruling Saudi royal family, are of the most violent, intolerant, and crudely puritanical Wahhabis sect of Islam, which is closest to the original teachings of the Prophet Muhammad himself. By its nature, the adherents of this sect hate not only the Christians of traditional American culture, but also Jews, Hindus, atheists, and most surprising, the other Muslims comprising Shiite, Sufi, and Sunnis, who to at least some degree, are more moderate, but to the Wahhabis sect are practicing a form of Islam so watered down that it motivates the Wahhabis to kill them along with the others.

"I should add that it is technically true to say, according to the scholars I have consulted, that this Wahhabis interpretation of Islam is the most accurate. For this reason, they are impossible to reason with, since they fall back on the written Qur'ān to support their actions, and they are ultimately behind almost one hundred percent of worldwide terrorism."

"Muslims who want to destroy other Muslims? What next?" said the President. "Well, at least they got the equal opportunity part of our beliefs right. Seems these guys hate everybody," he said, trying to inject a little humor into the troubling conversation.

Taggert attempted a weak smile, out of respect. "Unfortunately," he continued, "these extremist Islamists are mixed among other Muslims in our country because our immigration or work visas and other government forms do not ask for information about the specific details of their religion, due to our laws."

"You mean our freedoms," interjected the President, once again seeing the irony that the Constitutional guarantees of freedoms and rights and justice that made the country the hope for millions in the world were being used to destroy the country.

"Our immigration and travel documents require disclosure of criminal charges, no matter how minor, disregarding that many times people are wrongly accused or can't afford a proper defense," said Taggert.

"Yet we aren't asking Islamists if they belong to a sect that openly advocates violent killings and the destruction of the country to which they are requesting to visit or immigrate to. Well, I'll be a monkey's uncle," finished the President.

"As I said at the beginning, I have two bits of good news for you, sir."

"Shoot," said the President.

"I am sorry, I can't tell you much more than that the agency has their two best people working on it."

"The same people that we are not allowed to know anything about. From an agency that doesn't exist. When you say you have bad news, you aren't kidding. Please try your best to get a progress report about the two operatives who are trying to solve our problem. Of course, give them anything they need without requirement for any formal approval; we are in no position to quibble."

"No promises about their progress; they work with no oversight whatsoever. I am not sure if this reputed agency exists or to whom in our government it reports. As to resources, they have never requested any, at least to my knowledge," said Taggert.

"Understood," said the President.

Rising slowly from his chair, exhausted, the President looked like he had aged ten years since sitting down.

He looked over to Taggert, and asked one final question, "I know we have tens of thousands of listening devices and agents in this country and that all agencies are tasked to protect the USA. Keep your ears tuned through computer screens, and directly, for key words and phrases that would signal the existence of such a vast and destructive conspiracy. How did we miss it?"

"It appears at this point that meetings took place at hundreds of Islamic mosques across the country, which we are not allowed to monitor or even send undercover agents into due to Constitutional limitations. We can assume that the Imam, or minister of the mosque, would have known of the meetings and entire operation in at least some instances. The communications between individuals seem to have been by satellite phones with a very high-level inscription mechanism that makes eavesdropping, or for that matter, the existence of the calls completely insulated from our best listening and sensing equipment," said Taggert.

"Excel Electronics developed and supplied the equipment in house, as there is nothing even approaching this technology available anywhere on the world military or spy equipment markets."

"How is it possible that they can have better equipment than the best we have and that we never knew about it?" asked the President, now standing over Taggert, who remained seated.

CHAPTER FORTY-FIVE

Taggert pondered the President's question.

"Since they are a private company, our access to their internal records is limited," he said with a partial shrug.

"Think of it as a very big family business. There is, I believe, only one shareholder—this Samir Hussan character—and other than his accountant and the little guy in the anonymous booth at the IRS who processes their taxes, nobody else knows a thing about this company, including its many divisions or branches, which have various brand names which adds to the confusion. We can assume, given their massive and rapid start-up years ago without issuing shares on any stock market, that they have almost unlimited access to funding, technology, and key technical personnel from a range of Middle Eastern states. As they have been supplying the government with the voting machines for years, they had already passed a basic evaluation, such as a criminal check of staff.

"But, as their key staff were already Iranian or Saudi nationals, we could probably not have known if Attila the Hun was working there. We can assume the money for the communications equipment, which it appears is central to their actions against us, was paid for by the US taxpayer through tax credits, government grants, and the like."

"How on earth did we get to this position?" asked the President. "You have enough information about this problem's origins in those papers in front of you to write ten books. Why haven't my predecessors and other leaders acted on this years ago? It doesn't take a genius to see these issues and that altogether they pose a grave threat to our country."

"As I said earlier, I didn't know of ninety-nine percent of this myself, nor did the FBI, the CIA, or any other agency to my knowledge, and as National Security Advisor, it's my job to know and of course to tell you and other leaders. I was just briefed last night," said Taggert.

"Most of this information would have been impossible to assemble without warrants. It's been assembled piece by piece by piece, over a period of years, using Senatorial Authority in a low-profile, behind-the-scenes investigation. Only when viewed together is the picture obvious, and that only became possible days ago."

"So who carried out this investigation?" asked the President.

"One man: Senator Frank Oster."

As Taggert rose and walked toward the door, the President's mind was numbed. The problems were simply too many in number to absorb.

Only a miracle could save the USA as they had known it.

CHAPTER FORTY-SIX

Senator Oster sat in the back of the limousine, slumped in exhaustion.

The death of his son, the national crisis, and the nights spent having his trusted adviser organize the results of his years-long secret investigation into the Muslim assault on the USA had all taken a toll. Now in his seventies, although he was still tall and lean, he didn't have the endurance of his younger years, when as a newly elected Senator, he wanted to change the world overnight and had the energy to do it.

It had been hard to keep the astonishing results secret, as he travelled and gathered the information that now painted a true picture that the West had been under a massive and well-organized assault for decades, which was now reaching its peak of intensity.

Revealing all he knew while answering the National Security Advisor's shocked questions for four hours earlier in the day had left him spent.

The car pulled up to the same Washington brick townhouse he had used for five decades. The modest but comfortable residence provided at no cost for Senators, which he had noticed in a tourist brochure, was over 150 years old.

The car door opened and his trusted chauffer walked ahead of him to open the door. The chauffeur would change duties to be a de facto security guard until relieved in a half hour by a Secret Service guard. The National Security Advisor had arranged the security detail with one phone call, minutes after the Senator had started explaining the explosive contents of the package he had handed him.

They both entered and turned on the lights.

Oster gasped at the mess. The entire residence had been trashed, with furniture torn apart, clothes pulled from the closet, and even the cupboards ripped from the walls. Somebody had been looking for something.

"Sir, we need to leave here immediately. Grab what you need and let's go," said the driver, who knew they were at risk.

The Senator paused. He had never bothered to use computers, so there were no discs or other electronic devices to be concerned about. He hardly even used a cellphone, although he was required to carry one around. He had always found that if someone wanted to reach him, they could.

He pulled it from his pocket and could see the words, "4 messages."

He walked over and saw that his twenty-year-old home answering machine also had four messages. Much easier to operate for his old fingers than the tiny buttons of his government-issued cellphone, he had found.

He pressed the Play button and heard, "Senator, this is Julie. The office has been burglarized, and your home too. I hope you are okay. Please call when you get the chance."

The Senator felt his years catching up with him, as the feeling of being hunted came over him.

"Sir, we have to get out of here, it's not safe. *Now*," implored his driver, who was standing next to him and had heard the message.

He grabbed the Senator's arm and pulled him toward the door.

As they walked to the car, a black Mercedes pulled up on the opposite side of the street, with two large men inside.

"Okay, Senator, let's run," said the driver, who had received security training years ago, after applying for the driver position.

He pushed the Senator the short distance remaining into the limo and slammed the door, running around to the front left door and jumping inside.

He glanced over at the Mercedes, just as the car's engine was gunned and it was coming at them with blinding headlights. In seconds it had crossed the street, and there was a loud crash as the front driver's side fender was struck. The limo lurched upward from the impact and then settled down again.

Senator Oster had been asked to change limousines years ago, but the 1976 Cadillac limousine was the last of its breed, with refined square headlights, a 500-cubic-inch motor and comfortable ride that no car had matched since. He had even offered to spend his own personal money to maintain it, before the Fleet Manager had relented and allowed him to keep it at taxpayers' expense. Even the Cadillac Club featured the car on its website.

The 7,000-pound Cadillac shrugged off the collision with the Mercedes like a water buffalo twitching from a gnat bite.

The driver gunned the American V8 and the rear wheels squealed in a burnout like a muscle car. The Mercedes, with the safety crumple zone pushed in and brushing the front tires, was left to frantically follow, the gunman leaning out with his handgun, taking shots at the limo, which struck the USA Government Issue bulletproof glass harmlessly.

"Where are you headed?" asked the Senator, who craned his neck around to look through the small back window at the pursuing Mercedes.

"I don't know. Haven't had a chance to think that far ahead, Senator," said the driver, who kept the collector's item Cadillac's throttle pushed to the floor as it careened through the streets at ninety miles per hour.

"Well, why not head over to the White House? Surely they won't follow us there," said the Senator.

"Okay, the White House it is," said the driver.

The limo came up to a busy intersection and had to slow, as the light was red and there were already cars crossing.

Seconds later, the Mercedes smashed into the rear at fifty miles per hour, and the limo lurched out into traffic, pushing aside a small Toyota.

The limo's rear trunk was smashed in, and the fuel tank burst, leaving a trail of gasoline behind.

The driver smashed the gas pedal to the floor and the massive V8 easily spun the rear tires, leaving blue clouds and the smell of rubber as it left two long black strips on the road as it left the scene.

A hail of bullets immediately followed, as the gunmen in the Mercedes recovered from the collision long enough to lean out and train their guns on the limo.

Again, the giant American vehicle easily absorbed the bullets.

Minutes later, they pulled up to the White House security gate, and the guard walked out of the booth and surveyed the damage to the familiar Cadillac.

"Is that you back there, Senator?" said the guard, who waved them ahead, as another guard noticed the black Mercedes roaring up the driveway with a man with a gun hanging out the passenger side window.

The second guard immediately reached over and pressed a button, and the forked driveway steel tire shredders rose up like giant rakes.

The Mercedes hit the forks, and the wheels were torn from the car, sending sparks flying as the metal suspension ground along the driveway, igniting the trail of gas the Cadillac had left behind it.

The Mercedes was now surrounded by a ring of fire, and the two gunmen were inside screaming for help as the interior grew hot, and they could not escape since opening the windows or doors would only allow the flames in and speed their deaths.

In the trunk, the temperature rose within seconds, and the fuel tank exploded, which in turn caused the massive detonation of the other guns and ammunition that were the tools of their trade.

The Cadillac had been allowed to drive into the inner White House driveway, and Oster was quickly surrounded by a ring of

Secret Service men, two of whom stood ready with fire extinguishers in case the fire at the Mercedes moved along the gas trail on the driveway to the Cadillac.

Within moments, another Secret Service agent had used a water hose to clear the fuel trail.

Senator Oster stood watching the spectacle, and for a moment, tried to absorb the action and catch his breath.

His driver, who had been at his side for thirty years, said, "Senator, that old Cadillac saved your life."

"Stick with it until you know where they are taking it. You have my direct orders that it is to be rebuilt to original specifications, not scrapped," said Oster.

The driver nodded.

CHAPTER FORTY-SEVEN

Coming from above was a familiar voice, "Well, Frank, it's been too long. I didn't think you'd come over this quickly," said President Vance Virtue, looking down from the White House balcony, where he stood in a housecoat and holding a glass of fine whiskey, neat.

"Nor I," said the Senator. "We were just looking for a safe place to run to."

"Please escort the Senator upstairs to see me," the President directed the Secret Service.

Senator Oster followed the Secret Service men and recognized that many of them had been working the White House detail for many years. There was a comfort that came with being in the White House. There was a feeling of safety and warmth and honesty.

President Virtue was there to greet the Senator as he walked off the elevator to the second floor.

He thrust out his hand, and firmly shook the Senator's hand. At ninety-one, President Virtue was the oldest serving President in history and still stood tall and erect and passed all fitness tests with flying colors.

"Frank, of all the people I know right now, you are the one I most want to see. Again, please accept my condolences about your son."

"Thank you, Mr. President."

"Oh, humbug on this Mr. President stuff. Please call me Vance, or not at all."

A white coated house staff member entered with a tray of coffee and small cakes.

"Frank, I have been scanning through the dossier you gave to Security Advisor Taggert and am still in shock."

"I can understand that, Mr. President," said Oster.

"I mean, it's absolutely diabolical."

"Sir, every additional minute I spent ferreting out this information shocked me more than the last. I spent a lot of time at the Suitland, Maryland National Archives.

"You mean that place with underground vaults measuring twenty acres?" said the President.

"The same," said Oster.

"I've been meaning to have a look at that place myself but haven't found the time," said the President.

"I also travelled to several countries and must admit I used my Senatorial clout and experience to gain access under dubious pretenses. It took three years," said Oster.

"Why didn't you alert us with your early findings?" asked the President.

"Because this is a war, and it's not like any war this nation has fought. I realized the enemy has poisoned the interior of our nation, right down to the core. There are so many rotten apples in the basket, if you will pardon the phrase, that I couldn't risk revealing my preliminary conclusions until I was absolutely certain and had irrefutable proof. Otherwise, my activities might have been shut down, and whatever I had found out, whitewashed or handed over to the CIA or FBI to be put in a file somewhere and forgotten about," said Oster.

"So, this file is, without any doubt, factual. There is no exaggeration whatsoever?" probed the President, staring at Oster from under his half-rimmed reading glasses.

"I will place my reputation on it," said the Senator, who had an unequalled reputation for honesty and had had a scandal-free career.

"I started in Washington as an aide in the 1930s. Did you know that? In those days this was a marsh and without air conditioning. Good Lord was it hot in summer," said the President.

"We met about ten years later. And yes, all of Washington knows about your early days in this town; it's usually a part of your speeches," said the Senator with a smile.

"Frank, I must admit, I am a little dumbfounded. The only thing I have done since learning of this has been to cancel the Saudi Arabian delegation for tomorrow. I feel so betrayed I can't even bring myself to face them. They come through here so often, I am sure they won't be too concerned."

"That's a great start, Mr. President," said Oster.

The President walked over. "Every time I go into that situation room, it's worse. Every law enforcement agency in the country is working overtime. The jailhouses and courts are jammed. All the nation's labs are swamped with blood tests for those with jobs requiring drug screening. That means that every important job—the ship pilots, the train engineers, the pilots, and twenty others—are sidelining their people due to flunked tests, we believe sourced primarily from the spiked food or drinking supply, and that has ground commercial activity to a halt. That group, plus the recreational drug users, are all having this hyperactive reaction that renders them fit only for the hospital or the jail, at least until they have been administered something to sedate them.

"In essence, this entire country is paralyzed, and paychecks and tax revenues will be stalled. If we don't act soon, there will be calls for a new government. We have to act. Deferring action to the official agencies in charge, when they themselves are affected, is getting stale quick, and the public knows it."

Oster looked up from the couch where he had been sitting. "The problem is, how do you solve a problem when you don't know who you can trust?"

The President pointed to a report on his desk. "They tell me that 300,000 federal, state, and county employees are not following our orders, some by blatantly refusing, citing every harebrained excuse in the book, and most by dragging their feet and acting dumb. Some of them have already retained lawyers, if you can believe it, and have involved these high-priced Muslim support agencies that are a nest of trouble. Between them and those with the reaction to the drug and who require legal representation to defend themselves from actions for the damage they have caused, and a hundred other related types of cases, I bet every lawyer in the country is busy."

Both aged warriors walked out the glass doors and watched as the last of the fire trucks and tow trucks took away the charred wreck of the Mercedes with the two ghastly corpses inside, loading it and the Cadillac limousine onto flat deck trucks to be taken to the crime lab for analysis.

CHAPTER FORTY-EIGHT

Tank and Bull were suddenly in the White House.

More correctly, all the sights and sounds delivered through their headsets made it seem they were there. But they were still in the little electronics bunker room at the Natal, Brazil airport.

The President waved Tank and Bull into the Oval Office from a side chamber. More correctly, he waved over the motorized, gyroscope-balanced, basketball-sized white ball with a flat screen monitor at the top of a telescopic steel rod with Tank and Bull's face on them.

"Thank you for attending," said the President, looking at their flat monitor faces. "I am not sure how the message got conveyed to you, but I am glad you are here no matter the form. I want you to sit in on a little presentation I've arranged."

Tank said, "Thank you, Mr. President," as the electronic balance balls rotated the screen to face the door.

Quietly, two videographers entered the room and set up dual cameras and microphones with backdrop and lighting.

"I have never stopped thinking about our troubles with Islamists... Of course, it's in the news every day, even aside from this massive Islamic Sharia Law debacle, which the press will likely blame on a tiny group of extremists.

"But I have been confused, and I think a good many Americans are confused too. Bombings and murder of our honored military and, of course, the Twin Towers. Group abductions, rape, beheadings, and terror across Africa and the Middle East. Conflict and tension across the South Pacific. Threats by official Islamists to raise the Islamic flag over the White House and eliminate Israel. The Europeans, who have welcomed them with open arms for decades and now find themselves with an enemy within, with bombings and Muslims self-declaring hundreds of Sharia Law zones which are illegal, as much anti-Semitism as there was in the thirties before the Holocaust, strapping bombs on youngsters..."

The President walked to the balcony, scanning out over the historic grounds. He was pondering Taggert's information from Oster's report, which had been causing a festering rag to build, hour by hour.

"...And yet, we hear this nonstop refrain that Islam is a religion of peace. That's a circle I have never been able to square. If we renamed Islam the Nazi Religion, we would have long since outlawed it. But the world remains apprehensive about what to do because of this confounded confusion. And now, they very nearly steal the country from under our noses and may yet succeed, and the Islamists and our own Liberals and even a good many American Jews are still talking this crap that Islam is a religion of peace?"

The two opposite streams of information continued to race through the President's mind.

The millions of wonderful Muslim families peacefully living in the United States who were more gracious and honest than most others, and the toxic teachings of their Islamic religion, both in the books themselves and through the Imams in the mosques.

Two totally opposite descriptions for the same idea: Islam.

Were the President's mind a computer, it would have entered a self-destroying loop of contradictory facts and had a total meltdown.

But the President was a man.

He stood up and lifted his arms high in the air in frustration. He drew his hands down as if pleading with the small group for an answer that would allow him to act.

"I still don't know what to decide," said the President suddenly, bringing his fist down a little too hard on an ancient lamp table gifted by Abraham Lincoln, collapsing it.

"That may not have been very presidential; I am sorry," he said, only partly regaining his composer, as an orderly appeared out of nowhere and picked up the pieces for repair.

"I appreciate your information," said the President, scanning the small group. "In a few minutes, I will receive my final lesson on this Islam issue."

A knock came from the door to the outer office.

In stuck the head of his secretary. "Mr. President, your guest is here."

She opened the door wider and stood aside, and in came a tall, thin man with glasses, looking very much the university professor he was, with a plaid English coat, Sherlock Holmes style hat, wool pants, and soft-topped, brown leather shoes.

"Ah, you must be Dr. Truetell."

The President walked over and extended a handshake, and Truetell hesitantly shook his hand.

Truetell could hardly believe the circumstances, having arrived in his modest old Ford Escort. He glanced over to the flat screen faces of Tank and Bull.

Security Advisor Taggart, who had slipped in the back of the room, reached over to shake his hand and then sat back down in a tufted French colonial chair with a clipboard and pen in his hands.

Senator Oster nodded to Truetell as if they knew each other.

"Okay, sir, please proceed, and don't hold anything back," said the President, motioning for Truetell to stand in front of the white screen.

The lights turned on, and the videographers started recording.

Dr. Truetell rubbed his chin and then took off his coat, looking down at the floor, as if unsure of where to begin.

"Mr. President, you have asked me to, as you said, give you the no holds barred truth about Islam without regard for political considerations… And that's what I am going to do."

He stared at the video cameras. "My name is Dr. Edmund Truetell. I have been asked to help our country. At the end of the presentation, there will be contact information for the hundreds of books, websites, and individuals documenting what I will say.

"I will start by saying that I do not, nor do I think others should, bear malice toward Muslims generally, and my entire purpose is to help Americans, including Muslims, by communicating to them— and to all who will listen around the world—the harm in Islam.

"I will say at the beginning that Islam, the religion of Islam, self-identifies as being at war with the United States and with the entire non-Islamic world, for that matter, because they—we—are not Islamic.

"It is my conclusion, then, that Islam is absolutely not a religion of peace. The following comments I will make will be in support of this conclusion. I must emphasize that while the following is my opinion, I believe in all my heart it is the factual truth, and I believe my credentials and the years I have spent verifying that information will withstand alternate opinions on these same facts and conclusions. These facts I will inform you of have been on my website, in my books, and contained in my student lectures and debates for years, and I have not received a single factually supported contrary written or verbal conclusion as to my interpretations and conclusions, although I have been criticized personally."

Truetell took a deep breath. He paused, as if waiting for the perfect words to continue with. He started again slowly, as if retelling the story caused some degree of pain. Having repeated the message for years to small groups of interested students and having sold a few books, he was completely invisible on the national or international stage.

All that was about to change with his patriotic agreement with the President, signed in the outer office, completely assigning all usage rights to the United States of America. The White House team would produce a finished product true to form in the hours ahead, with the Presidential Seal and a short intro by the President.

His past life was over. The audience would soon be in the hundreds of millions, as the presentation was translated into almost all known languages and distributed in all electronic and other formats to Americans and then worldwide, for free.

The current calamity caused by the Islamists, in combination with Truetell's confirming message, would be the foundation for the President's actions in the hours and days ahead.

Truetell would receive a security detail for the rest of his life. If the threats became unmanageable, the FBI would supply him with a new identity.

Truetell spoke in a down-to-earth, conversational, believable manner. His voice had a rich authentic tone belying his thin frame.

"I was raised a Muslim in Kenya. I was told to recite Islamic verses and never to ask questions. It is against Islam to question, and kids like me were beaten if we asked questions or pursued our own investigations. In my opinion, many Muslims simply do not know enough about key aspects of their own religion and do not know enough about the world at large to make independent evaluations about certain points about their own religion."

A calm started to descend over the President, as if there wold be no more searching for answers. The distant, muted din of the White House was heard beyond the walls.

"This leaves many vulnerable to the toxic teachings of their religion's leaders and, of course, to the social pressures of their family and friends to conform. So we must have sympathy for the vast majority of Muslims that are caught in this tragic bind, we really must…"

Truetell glanced down at his notes, and stretched his back, inhaling deeply.

"Blame can be firmly laid on specific Islamic leaders and teachers who know the truth and proclaim it to be followed. They know that the truthful teachings of Islam include key elements that can only be accurately described as…" Truetell paused to find the perfect words, "…critically problematic. It is only our luck that eighty percent of American Muslims do not know of, or at least, believe in these particular teachings, at least for now."

The President had sat his lanky frame down in his green, leather-tufted executive chair on castors and swiveled it so that his brogues could rest on the desk top.

"Okay, so what are the problematic aspects of Islam from your learned perspective?"

"Well…" said the professor, with obvious apprehension.

"Please be forthright, as we discussed on the phone. I need outside confirmation of some of what I have been hearing internally over the last few hours. That's why you're here."

Truetell began again, "Islamic teachings comprise earlier and later, with earlier being Mohammad's time at Mecca, which were mostly peaceful, and later when he was asked to leave and travelled to Medina, when the teaching became more violent.

"I should mention before I forget, that over the ten years in Mecca, while peaceful, only a handful of followers resulted, perhaps 140.

"Over the next ten years or so, after Medina, the entire region was Islamized through violence, by the sword. Of course, when you have gangs of so-called believers robbing, beheading, and raping victims, followed by the threat of death if you renounce Islam after converting, it tends to speed up the growth of any movement," said Truetell with an unconvincing smile.

"The problem is, teachings over the two periods are interspersed with each other in the Islamic texts. So we have people saying the peaceful elements are the ones that comprise Islam, and that is the reason we hear that so often."

"Well, do they?"

"Unfortunately, no. The teachings are very clear that the later teachings, from Medina, are to be followed if conflicting with the more peaceful Islamic instructions, and, as I said, they are the ones that are truly violent. I am really sad to tell you this, as sad as I was over the years that I spent studying this to confirm it—but it is without question the truth.

"By the way, and this is important, Islam is not to be changed, ever. The following points were never recanted and are as valid today as they were hundreds of years ago, should any

Islamist tell you otherwise. As I said, most Islamists do not know the problematic teachings, or if they do, do not follow them. Many are peaceful and do good works."

"Carry on."

Two white-clothed kitchen servers came in with rolling tables, one with quartered sandwiches with the crust trimmed off and the other with a variety of pastries and tea, coffee, and bottles of water.

Bull's monitor screen panned over, as he sat hungrily in Natal, frustrated at the modern way to attend a meeting.

Truetell's tone changed. He felt his cautious preambles had gone too far. He had had enough of apologizing for Islamists.

"I want to make clear that there is no such thing as an Islamic so-called extremist. This term, intentionally in my view, causes people to think that there is a tiny group of Islamists that do not follow Islam correctly and that is why they do the terrible things they do. In truth, there are only Islamists who follow a faith that advocates these things, and there are some who do them and others who don't, or at least, don't yet. Personally, I feel that the horrific international Islamic violence and rape we hear about, as bad as it is, is equal to the insidious attempts to convert the USA and the West to Islam, because these attempts, if successful, will lead to more blatant and truthful Islam teachings eventually, as Islam steamrolls across the entire planet unopposed and settles into the truthful teachings without fear of reprisal."

"So what does Islam instruct its followers?" asked the President in a soft voice, respectful of the video production process.

"First, all Islamists consider non-Islamists to be 'demitudes' or 'kefirs,' which are derogatory terms meant to imply a distinct second class of personhood; in truth, they refer to excrement. Of these, the Jew is considered worst. According to Islam, these groups are to be variously allowed to convert to Islam or to pay a toll. However, if they refuse, they can be enslaved, raped, killed by beheadings, tortured, and so on…

"To be clear, this means that all non-Muslims, including all of us in this room, are second class to Muslims and they live a second class life in most Islamic countries. For example, in Islamic Sharia Law, a non-Muslim cannot even testify in court about a crime he or she saw; they simply have no standing."

Truetell's eyes gazed across the room as he recollected facts from memory.

"Today, as in centuries past, across Africa and the Middle East, we see Islamists applying these teachings, which are to employ raiding parties to loot, capture, or behead non-Muslims and to gather female rape slaves. While these appear the actions of the most evil, demented criminals, they are actually following detailed Islamic faith instructions on how to rape woman, repetitively, indefinitely, as captives. Before I forget, wives can be legally beaten and raped and can essentially be held captive by not allowing them to leave the house except at certain times and in certain conditions."

Truetell glanced at the small audience, with the President slowly shaking his head in his hands in disbelief.

"They are considered to have half the intelligence of men. If a woman is raped, it takes four Muslim men to witness it before a perpetrator can be charged in a Sharia Law court for the crime. If a woman witnessed the rape, she would not be recognized in the Islamic court."

Truetell shuffled the small collection of papers on the table in front of him, as if confirming the facts already embedded in his memory.

"Last, Islam has a tenant called 'fatwa,' where an Islamic official can simply declare that a person be killed, for a wide range of reasons, all of which are related to that person doing something offensive to Islam. From that declaration forward, the person becomes targeted by thousands of Muslims across the planet."

Truetell, recalling the many killed by Islam over the centuries, pointed his index finger for emphasis. "This, and all of these points, are not some ancient forgotten practices; this goes on today, frequently.

BLACK V

"In other words, Islam kills its critics."

CHAPTER FORTY-NINE

Tank and Bull sat transfixed at their consoles in Natal.

The President was silent, Taggert was taking notes, and Senator Oster was exchanging glances with the President, knowing that the presentation confirmed their earlier conversation about the Sharia Law crisis in the USA.

"Muslims worship a god they call 'Allah,'" Truetell continued.

"More than half of Americans and probably the same number of other Westerners think that Allah and God—as in, the God mentioned on US currency when it says 'In God We Trust,' and associated with Christmas, and which has been integral to all Western civilization and the Russians and their neighbors too—are the same entity. However, this is propaganda, an intentional lie. Without question or debate, it has been known by respected academics the world over in many accredited published works over the last two hundred years, that Allah was one of several pagan entities worshipped before Muhammad, in fact, being referred to as a sun god at the time. Islam teaches that Allah, one of ninety-nine names given him, is called 'The Greatest Deceiver.' I should add, as an aside, that the bibles of Christians and the Old Testament Jewish portion refer to Satan as 'The King of Lies,' so there really could not be a more blatant differentiation between the two… one God being the way of the truth and the life and the other God described as a liar when required.

"It's important to mention that Islam teaches that Jesus, who was prophesized in the old Jewish Bible—called the Torah—and who died on the cross in the Christian Bible and faith, was actually Judas with his face made to look like Jesus by Allah while the actual Jesus lived on for years after. Of course, that a God would engage in this type of trickery for no apparent reason is never explained…

"Islam, then, strikes a sword through the entirety of the Christian religion and therefore, in turn, these religions are akin to opposites, and the attempts to talk about them as if related just because the Koran mentions overlapping Bible facts and history available when it was written—and most likely copied— are shocking at their base to anyone with a modicum of knowledge about these things."

Truetell reached down for a bottle of water near his notes and took a drink. He glanced around the room, and then continued.

"I was surprised when at a young age I confirmed the Islamic teaching of Taqiyya, or, to lie to advance Islam, if other means fail, when Islamists are in a position of perceived vulnerability, which could easily mean always. And that an Islamist is to misrepresent his faith in Islam or the extent of it, while internally fully retaining that faith.

"For example, a US President who was a Muslim could lie and say he was not, while he actually was. This would be in keeping with the accurate teaching of Islam. He could even be advancing Islam within the United States by deconstructing our Western culture, causing direct or indirect harm to the USA, and that would be fully in keeping with Islam. You see, an Islamist is to never cease vying for the conversion of his host country, and the world, to Islam.

"That's why appeasement or the introduction of measures to satisfy Islamists so that they will live peacefully among their new countrymen, such as by introducing holidays, changes to school curriculum, employment laws or any other, will never work. To an Islamist, any appeasement to their demands is not considered satisfactory. They know that their only goal is a complete collapse of their host country's current culture and replacing it with Islam. When we appease them, they consider us stupid. They view it as them outwitting us as they continue their battle to conquer our culture and replace it with theirs.

"Islam is self-declared as the only true religion and its goal is to dominate and ultimately eliminate the others. They will never stop—if allowed—until this happens. In fact, Islam teaches that an Islamist is to destroy the house, or destroy the country, of his host or home country by that country's own hand—in other words, by using the country's laws and citizens against itself. Of course, these tenets pose extreme problems with American citizenship. I should add that that is also true for the entire West, all the countries with whom we share a similar culture and heritage.

"In essence, they instruct the Islamist to undertake activities that appear seditious toward treason under the US Constitution, at least as I understand it when I read it, and the constitutions of most Western countries. If a person confirms they are an active and loyal Islamist who believes in undertaking every tenet, they have by definition pledged to destroy the USA as we know it.

"Thankfully, as I said, most Muslims do not know the undertakings of their own religion and if they do, would never act on it. But given the toxicity of these teachings, a tiny minority poses an extreme danger in and of themselves as this Sharia Law attempt proves, and, as for the majority of Muslims, there is the danger that a charismatic leader at the right time and in the right conditions in our history may cause them to newly endorse these violent teachings, in reaction to some real or perceived injustice or for some reason difficult to envision at this point.

"We see from history that a very advanced and frankly wonderful country, Germany, under Adolf Hitler, adopted occultist teachings and practices, transforming the nation almost overnight into a murderous beast both to other countries and its own citizens, and while there were crimes, it is nonetheless true that this was done lawfully using the democratic process. As I see it, the faith of Islam, as written, contains certain teachings that are every bit as toxic as the Nazis, with whom key Islamists were involved with prior to and during the Second World War.

"We see examples of lying and of forms of jihad generally, to promote or advance Islam, right in front of us, even at the state level. Islamic Iran incorporates the concept of jihad right in its constitution, something its neighbor Israel is acutely aware of. In other words, the constitution of Iran states clearly that the goal and obligation of Iran is to destroy non-Muslims—starting with Israel.

"Saudi Arabia, a harsh Islamic country, officially claims to have no Religious Administration component to its government. But without question, they do, and it is the most powerful segment, controlling most aspects of life for Saudis. Plus, they have spent one hundred billion dollars promoting this Islamic sect worldwide, including to the USA, to build mosques and Islamic schools with curriculum that blatantly teaches the things I am saying."

Truetell briefly removed his glasses and wiped the sweat from his face with the white hanky that had been neatly protruding from his pocket. He stretched both arms in front.

CHAPTER FIFTY

The small audience exchanged glances, while the President awkwardly glanced at the flat monitors, unsure if the faces were actual or phony to conceal identifies.

Having returned from visiting the latrines and eating a bite of food, Truetell continued.

"Many things can be involved in the Islamification of our Western societies. For example, the publishers of Christian Bibles have altered crucial parts about Christ to make the religion more acceptable to Muslims, after years of pressure from Muslims. And Muslims are now allowed to pray in Washington Cathedral, a Christian Church. Public school curriculums in California have been altered to allow the teaching of Islam under the auspices of group architecture tours and food selections in schools, and universities have been changed to be Islam-acceptable. In fact, Duke University, right here on

American soil, announced it would have its bell tower send out the Muslim prayer tone each day, and New York proclaimed Islamic school holidays.

"We hear proposals to form a new religion called Chrislam. Of course, as I said, in that Islam denies Jesus was who He said He was, and instead says that Allah—who they say is the only God and who I confirm is different from the Christian and Jewish God—altered the face of Judas to make him look like Jesus, this is preposterous in and of itself. There are petitions to install Sharia Law in the USA, aside from this brazen attempt uncovered hours ago, and court pleadings have incorporated Sharia-based arguments, in which at least one judge accepted, which will now poison who knows how many others with precedent setting."

Sweat beads had formed across Truetell's face.

"In the UK, Islamic Sharia Law has been incorporated into the civil law code across 150 counties, so that, for example, Muslim women in the UK are suppressed in the same fashion as in their home countries. Plus, the UK Islamic schools are carrying on as if they too were in their home countries, teaching all the same things that run contrary to British life and with the schoolgirls forced to sit in the back of the class. Some Islamists would gladly turn back the clock of Western advancements and equality a thousand years if we let them.

"Of course, we hear from some Muslims that the ten Christian Crusades of eight hundred years ago, which were defensive acts to right the Islamic conquests of Christians and Jewish lands four hundred years earlier, are justification for their barbarity today. The Crusades included limited examples of Christians doing things unapproved by the Church and Christians at the time and which were not part of the Christian faith whatsoever. The Islamists know it's nonsense, but they say it because they know most media and consumers of media are not fully educated on the these matters and therefore won't call them out on these lies. So, as I have discovered to be usual, they, meaning some Islamic spokespersons, feed this misinformation into the debate and get away with it.

"And it's global. Your predecessor and his Madam Secretary of State were instrumental in supporting a UN motion by fifty-seven Islamic countries to declare criticizing religion—Islam of course—illegal. Obviously, such a UN declaration was and is preposterous and supports the idea that some Islamists are relentless in their pursuit of world domination.

"It is very obvious to me that such a proposal—that it become unlawful to criticize Islam—is the most blatant example of Islam cowing the world that I am aware of. It's like a group comprised of marauders terrorizing a town trying to have the town pass a law that people of the town cannot criticize the same group. It's so outrageous it's difficult even to fathom it."

"What are the pastors from the other religions saying about all this?" asked the President gravely.

"The Christians are the only ones saying much of anything, but that's from the radio and TV shows, or the website and books. As to the thousands of everyday church pastors, hardly a peep. Ninety percent of them say nothing about this from the pulpit or in the community. I understand that a good many of them are simply not equipped to deal with such a massive conspiratorial mosaic of lies and are flummoxed as to what to do, given the politically correct society we have, where you can hardly say anything, true or not, or in the public interest or not, without somebody complaining. Sadly, as I have discovered personally, there has been an absence of courage in speaking out against it, even when all of this is brought to their attention."

Truetell walked over to the tray and grabbed a bottle of water, twisting off the cap and gulping down the entire contents in seconds.

The videographers continued filming; they would clean up the footage with their editing later.

The President got up and walked over to the window. "Who is behind all this?"

Truetell walked back to in front of the screen.

"The Saudis, rich Middle Eastern citizens, the Gulf States, some of the 1.5 billion worldwide Muslims—these are the ones bankrolling it. As for the people doing the violence, it's wrong to think these are poor and misguided people. A high percentage of them are from middle or upper class families and are well educated—as were many of the 9/11 hijackers."

"So, they accept our money for their oil and then spend the same money to undermine our society," said the President in a somber tone.

Truetell nodded in agreement with the President.

"The Islamists have a strategy that is working very well so far. First, they complain in the media about so-called Islamophobia and keep repeating the lie that Islam is a religion of peace, blaming what they call extremists and saying that critics, like me, have not correctly interpreted Islam due to translation problems, all of which is to throw everybody—by which I mean the average American citizen—off guard or at least confuse them such as they tire of the subject.

"Next, they aggressively advance Islam throughout our society and the West generally. If anybody calls them out, they wrongly use hate laws to conscript our own taxpayer-funded police, or in some countries bodies called Human Rights Councils, to silence and prevent the truth tellers from trying to help their fellow citizens. That it is obvious that the information is in the public interest seems a logic that public officials are oblivious to.

"For example," Truetell held up a New York Times newspaper, "here is a front page story article from days ago. The reporter is quoting an Islamic Imam who says, in response to the mass slaying of innocents by Islamists in France, that Islam is a religion of peace.

"These guys are using a technique from Joseph Goebbels, Hitler's university-educated Minister of Propaganda, who said that if you tell a lie often enough, people think it's the truth. They're peddling this 'Islam is a religion of peace' stuff around the world to distance themselves from the very insanity that key aspects of their Islam appears to all to be the root cause of.

"You are right to be incensed, Mr. President; I have been waiting for a leader to finally click, in their mind, as to what these guys are up to."

"Here's one from the UK," said Truetell, holding up another article. "A hopeful politician offering his services to his fellow man during an election, talking to a group on the street, quotes Sir Winston Churchill's dire observation about Islam, quoted directly from Churchill's 1899 book, The River Wars. I am younger than you, Mr. President, but even I know that Churchill, who was knighted by the Queen for his heroics as Prime Minister during the Second World War against Nazi Germany, is one of the world's most storied and respected people, named Britain's most stand-out military figure of the twentieth century."

"So what happened to this new politician quoting a respected British giant?" asked the President.

"He was arrested and faces charges. Apparently a woman on the street reported him, and he was hauled before a judge for failing to stop talking about things offensive to Muslims, even though what he was saying was true and was a quote from a respected giant of Britain and was clearly in the public interest.

"The blatant irony appears not to have dawned on the editor of this story, being that Churchill was himself ostracized for warning of Hitler's plans for the six years prior to World War Two, which after being proven true by Germany's invasion of Poland, his critics proclaimed him Prime Minister. Many have said since, that had Britain and the world heeded Churchill's warnings during the thirties and confronted Hitler, World War Two may have been averted.

"Seems history really does repeat itself," said a somber Truetell.

He continued on with examples in current events. "And there's a courageous politician in Holland who has had a death threat issued against him by Muslims because of what he truthfully says about Islam, and the Dutch must pay for a team of bodyguards to travel with him. Meanwhile, there are thousands of Islamic enclaves throughout Europe where the Islamic residents have illegally proclaimed Sharia Law and where firefighters, ambulance workers, and police are pelted with rocks.

"As for the Jews, whom the Islamists hate with a vengeance, there is now widespread violent anti-Semitism across Europe similar to what was seen in the 1930s run-up to World War Two. A Jew who goes out in public in obvious Jewish garb will be assailed immediately by Islamists. Jews are being told to move out of newly Islamic areas, where they have lived for decades, and to hide their faith if they fear for their lives."

Truetell picked up a book from among the notes spread before him.

"In fact, Mein Kampf, Hitler's anti-Jewish madman diatribe, is a respected bestseller in the Middle East to this day. The Koran denigrates Jews even more than Hitler's book, so it's easy to see why they hate Jews."

"You couldn't make this stuff up. Has the world gone nuts?" replied an incredulous President.

"It gets worse. Before the current crisis, we have had the same types of things going on across the USA. For example, the Dearborn police have stopped peaceful and truthful speeches of law-abiding American taxpayers, rather than arrest the Islamists who are pelting them with rocks and bricks and clearly intimidating them. The police side with the lawbreakers.

"Mr. President, this is a war. This Sharia Law attempt was just a salvo; they won't stop. They will just say, as they have been, that this was just a tiny group of extremists. The rest of the activities will continue, and they have to continue, because that is what Islam instructs them to do, to never stop until the country is converted to Islam and all other religions are crushed.

"I have read of the hundreds of billions being spent each year in Western countries by police, spy agencies, border control, and the military, not to mention the preoccupation of politicians' time. Every dime of that money has been diverted away from other urgent needs, such as for hospitals and food stamps, by Islamists. In this way, you could say that Islamists control the American budget and the budgets of every non-Islamic country.

"When you consider that hard-earned taxpayers' money could be spent on the betterment of society, on food programs for the poor, on solving crimes, you can see that the West is being bled to death, even aside from the recent brazen Sharia Law attempt, and it's been going on for years. It's all part of a plot to attack us in multiple ways, to weaken us, until we are on our knees. And it's working."

The Oval Office was silent, and all sat stunned at the final truth.

Truetell was finished and looked emotionally drained.

The work was done.

All left the room, except for Tank and Bull, or at least, their electronic robot selves.

It was just as well, as the President had already reached his conclusions and was thinking to the days ahead, to a solution that would put a permanent stop to this new war, this brazen abuse of USA and Western hospitality, for this generation and for the generations to come.

CHAPTER FIFTY-ONE

"Since you are here, at least in a manner of speaking, can you offer any advice?" asked the President, looking at Tank's monitor.

"Having reviewed a little about your powers," said Tank, "I would suggest you enact, by Executive Order, the Federal Emergency Management Agency, which allows you to bypass all normal regulations and remove any employee from their job who does not follow the directives exactly."

"Okay, Mr. Tank, we have discussed that already. But that doesn't solve the problem of how to run the country with hundreds of thousands of key employees removed from their posts and no time to train new ones."

"Am I correct in assuming these problematic employees have been on the job for ten years or less?" inquired Tank.

"From Oster's investigations, a lot less than ten years in most cases," said the President.

"Remove the most key personnel first, and only when you have located the person who had the job before them, put them back in their old job," said Tank.

"You mean, you want us to call up all the retirees and have them come back to work?" the President asked for clarification.

"That solves the training problem, sir. Most are probably bored with going on cruises and playing golf anyway, and you may find the response is better than you hoped," said Tank.

"Right you are. Certainly any cruises you are involved with. Even if we get half to come back, that will be enough," said the President. "And after the crisis, how do we keep the bad eggs out of their jobs?"

"By Executive Order. That can be ongoing. You can hire new people according to new employment regulations that the Federal Government can draft. Because these matters go to the heart of the nation's security, you can bypass the regulations and impose the Constitution for legitimacy," said Tank.

The President called in his closest staff and began giving them directives to accomplish what Tank had laid out. As a veteran power broker, he had his hands on the levers of power, and after one hour, the next days' sweeping administrative orders were dictated and would be put into place, leaving the country astonished that the President had suddenly acted so decisively and wisely. "You think he is doubtful of our story?" asked Bull.

"Nope," said Tank. "This guy's been around, and there are probably few things that surprise him."

Just then the President walked in and said, "Well, I can say that for the first time in days, I feel good. It looks like all your ideas will pass muster. There is light ahead. I don't know how to thank you, Mr. Tank."

"You know how, Mr. President," said Tank.

"Yes. I will invoke Executive Privilege and everything about your friend here and any associates, now and in the future, are to remain highly classified, which means they won't be accessed for at least fifty years."

Tank's monitor nodded and said, "Agreed. Now, we have to get back to work to stop the next seven shipments."

The screens went blank, and the meeting was over.

CHAPTER FIFTY-TWO

Tank and Bull removed their headsets and rose from the consoles. After putting on the fresh clothes that had been laid out for them, they called Giant.

The dark sinister voice answered, "Where have you been? Have you not noticed the buzzers?"

"So much to tell, so little time," said Tank.

"The main shipment is at the bottom of the South Atlantic."

"What about the rest?"

"That is the second part of our plan," said Tank, with no idea how they were going to track down and stop the seven additional shipments that the undercover police in Miami had learned from drug dealers were on their way to the USA.

"We will keep you posted," said Tank, as he tossed down the phone.

Bull looked over. "And how, might I ask, are we going to do that?" he asked.

"First things first," replied Tank, as they exited the through the service door back into the throngs of the Natal airport.

CHAPTER FIFTY-THREE

"What comes next?" said Bull.

"I am not quite sure about that yet," said Tank, rubbing his chin.

"What's there not to be sure about?" asked Bull.

"Let's start with the short list. There's nothing to be sure about," replied Tank. "It may well be that there are seven similarly hidden vessels of a design we are still not sure of. This time, they are all in different countries."

"Sure, but the President now has a plan," said Bull. "Or weren't you listening at the meeting we just had with him?"

"I suggested to the President how to deal with the problems he has been having here on American soil, and the solutions should work. But they should have been done days ago. And if seven additional shipments hit the USA of the size being carried on the Good Times Express as this so-called undercover cop has reported to the National Security people, this country may be sunk yet," said Tank.

"What does that mean to us?" said Bull.

"We need a ride back to Manaus."

CHAPTER FIFTY-FOUR

Arriving in Manaus two hours later in a small plane they had hired, Tank felt apprehensive as they descended into the pelting rains, unsure of their next steps to stop the drug shipments.

They attracted no attention as they exited the small craft and covered their faces from the rain, walking toward the arrivals section.

Flagging a cab, they jumped in and were soon at Admiral Oliveira's command headquarters.

They were ushered past the security checkpoint, and the Admiral met them with a warm handshake and ushered them upstairs.

The fourth floor dining room overlooked the monsoons on the Amazon, which now spread thirty kilometers across to the other side.

Bull dove into the menu and kept the chefs busy.

The Admiral was appreciative, offering his congratulations on sinking the cocaine ship.

"Admiral, it will be difficult to shut down the remaining shipments," said Tank.

"But, Mr. Tank, surely there is a chance. After all, you were able to track and sink the last shipment, also within hours," said the Admiral.

"That was a bit different. We had a bit of luck on our side."

"I would say you had skill, intelligence, and daring on your side, from what I have heard, and those are still with you. If you need help from the Brazilian government, I will arrange it."

"Sir, this next shipment is spread among seven vessels," said Tank, "which are each located in different countries, all within the Amazon Basin."

"How can you know that?" asked the Admiral.

"The bragging drug dealer has included the information as part of his sales pitch…to an American undercover police officer," replied Tank.

"But surely it is not that difficult to locate the vessels with satellites and then to track and destroy them," said the Admiral.

"There are few helpful assets in South America of the US or, for that matter, any other government. The Amazon Basin is even worse. There are almost no assets, period. And by assets I am including personnel. There are almost no roads, and the heavy rainfall at this time of year interferes with the best satellites we or any other country has," said Tank.

"And these drug people don't use vessels," he imparted. "At least, no vessels I am familiar with."

"I don't follow you," said the Admiral.

"We located the ship we sunk by following the trail of a vessel unlike any we have known," said Tank. "It doesn't show up on radar or satellite sensors in this jungle. It's fast and crosses land and water with equal ease and can submerge."

"Surely you must be mistaken. I have been a seaman for many years, and no such vessel exists, military or civilian," said the Admiral.

"And, I forgot to mention, it's 1500 feet long," said Tank.

The Admiral motioned the waiter for his third glass of Johnny Walker and gulped it all down.

"Five hundred meters? Mr. Tank, perhaps the jungle has affected you…"

"It's affected me, all right, and my friend here too," said Tank, motioning to Bull, who was hungrily eating with the manners of a starving man and keeping the waiter busy making trips to the kitchen for more.

"We have reason to believe the seven other vessels are of the same technology. As you can see, it involved a bit of luck to track the first shipment, but considering the many difficulties, it will take a miracle to track all seven of the next, thus my contact with you to ask for your assistance," said Tank.

The Admiral nodded his head and looked out the panoramic windows at the swollen thirty-kilometer-wide Amazon River and the pelting rains.

"We have only a handful of government workers in the entire basin, due to budgetary constraints. They are environmental officers, to guard against deforestation and illegal hunting. Of course, this military base guards our sovereignty, but the militia numbers are small, since we have had peace with our neighbors for decades," said the Admiral.

"As you are aware, we do have scientists in the region who undertake both biology and archeology studies, such as my daughter, but I hope you would agree that these people would not be of any assistance. And the citizens that live here are scattered and speak over a thousand different languages, as they are mostly indigenous tribespeople. Many still wear their traditional dress, and they travel only a short distance around their original territories. Only a few years ago, a tribe was discovered that had never been in contact with modern people before. As far as they were concerned, up until meeting the Brazilian logger that discovered them, it was still 2,000 BC.

"Mr. Tank, I am sorry I cannot help you. I will give it some thought, but for now, I think it best you go to the quarters we have provided and have a rest; you are exhausted."

Tank and Bull stood up and followed the waiter to two side-by-side rooms that were used for important visitors.

"Thank you for your time and hospitality, Admiral," said Tank, shaking his hand and entering the room allocated for him.

CHAPTER FIFTY-FIVE

Tank awoke, and noticed he felt a little disoriented. His clothes had been removed and he was in bed.

There was a knock on the door.

He rose and opened it.

"Mr. Tank, how do you feel? You and your friend had contracted classic dengue fever and we had to let it run its course."

"How long have I been sleeping?"

"You have been mostly unconscious for five days. We had our medical team monitoring you."

Tank ran his hands through his hair, as his mind raced to catch up.

"If you feel well enough, can you come with me? We have been busy with our ideas…" said the Admiral, motioning toward a meeting room.

They walked to a meeting room with a gigantic, colored map on the wall, which showed the entire Amazon Basin in great detail.

"As you can see, there are few roads and only a handful of airfields in Amazonia," said the Admiral.

"I have lived in it and flown over it at low altitude," said Tank. "I would agree it probably has the least infrastructure of any place on earth, except for the polar regions. But we talked about this over dinner."

"I know we did, but I am simply confirming to you that I have given it thought from the perspective of a person with decades of experience, and I agree with your analysis. There is one option, and I have confirmed they will help us. It may sound like not such a good idea, but I have given it consideration and believe it's your only option," said the Admiral.

"I am all ears," said Tank, rubbing his eyes.

"The only relatively contiguous network throughout Amazonia that exists is that of the church groups," said the Admiral.

"Church groups? Don't you think involving them would be a little inappropriate? These are deadly killers. A few scattered churches with the young missionary type pastors are hardly what we need."

"I thought the same but have had a change of opinion after talking to several of them who have bases here in Manaus. In fact, there are thousands of tiny churches of all denominations throughout the basin, and most have US citizens as benefactors. I hadn't thought of it, but most have fast shallow draft motorized boats and shortwave radios.

"And the tribal family members are motivated to help us search the secret trails and canals. They have already started, in fact, while you were sleeping. We have instructed our scattered science outposts to tune their radios to receive the short-range messages, in a basic code, for relay to us here. It is a coordinated effort," said the Admiral.

"Apparently, the biggest victims of these Muslim terrorists, at least so far, have been the people of Amazonia themselves. There has been a crisis for months, perhaps years. Thousands of their sons have simply disappeared, and with the news of the toxic drug attack on the United States and the disgusting side effects of spitting which my daughter confirmed, they now finally have hope to find their sons and release them from this evil grip. We never had direct knowledge of this because Brazil chooses to have a hands-off approach with its natives, to avoid the poor results over the centuries in other countries. As such, we have relatively poor channels of communications with them to begin with, and in this case, due to the nature of their sons' disappearances and the rumors of their activities and drug use, many families were apprehensive in case it led ultimately to their sons' arrests, so they kept quiet, which played into the Islamists' hands."

"I haven't mentioned the spitting, at least not that I recall," said Tank, rubbing his head.

"You never mentioned any spitting, that's true," said the Admiral.

"I did," said a voice from the hallway.

Dr. Oliveira walked in dressed in a white pantsuit and sat down.

"Those natives that abducted me never stopped spitting or drinking that rancid orange juice the whole time I was with them. That kind of disgusting behavior is not to be forgotten," she said with a frown.

"And now I find out that you and your big friend are far from scientists," she said with a note of triumph.

Tank's heart melted as the voluptuous Dr. Oliveira continued.

"No wonder you are so annoying, Mr. Tank," she said. "I didn't know I was working with secret agents."

"We aren't secret agents," said Tank.

"Well, whatever you are, I think we can help you, if the information my father told me is correct."

The Admiral looked at Tank. "I am sorry; I couldn't keep her locked up forever after the jungle rescue, and she hasn't stopped asking questions about you since. I made her pledge a pact of secrecy about you two."

"Don't worry, Mr. Tank, your secret is safe with me. In fact, I thought that to repay you for rescuing me, I could help you in some small way," said Dr. Oliveira.

"It seems," said Tank, "that I do better work when I am sleeping."

"But one last thing…" he added. "When the villagers find the vessels, what will they do next?"

"They are not looking for the vessels," said Dr. Oliveira.

"Then what are they looking for?"

"They are looking for the supply of the rancid orange juice."

"What good will that do?" wondered Tank.

"The strong addiction is what is causing the enslavement of the natives, which are the foundation of the entire operation," said Dr. Oliveira. "I watched the natives closely while held by them, and they never stop drinking that juice, and its immediate effects were obvious, as they started acting—how you say—wacko."

"Okay, so what are you going to do about it?" said Tank.

"We are neutralizing the juice and returning sanity to the natives—after their withdrawal, of course," said Dr. Oliveira.

"I am sorry to tell you, but first you would have to analyze the drug additive itself to have any hope of developing a neutralizing agent," said Tank.

"As you said while we were marooned in the green dome, the Germans are very proficient at everything they do," said Dr. Oliveira.

"Well, keep in mind, I was trying to feed you some decades-old schnitzel," said Tank.

"So what are we discussing all this for?" he inquired.

"Mr. Tank, remember the leather satchel you gave to me, from the unfortunate pilot in the stainless steel capsule?" said Dr. Oliveira.

"Yes. I hope you didn't lose it; I am sure it will be a perfect complement for a museum display with the aircraft remains. A tragic story, all told," said Tank.

"The pilot had the flight plans and typical travel documents inside her flight jacket. Inside the leather satchel was the complete chemical breakdown of the toxic agent, including not only the original formula but manufacturing methods to cheaply make both it and, fortunately, the antidote as well. There was also a handwritten note, which I will discuss with you later," said Dr. Oliveira.

"We have many pharmaceutical companies operating in Manaus to take advantage of the tax-free incentives, and one of them, a German one, was able to translate the instructions and produce a batch of antidote within half an hour. It almost seemed as though the chemist was familiar with the formula," said the Admiral.

Tank looked over, perplexed.

"We now have hundreds of liters in hand and thousands of liters in production. We are delivering it in parachute drops by our government's entire fleet of low flying Dehaviland Buffalo STOL cargo planes, throughout the entire Amazon basin region," added the Admiral, with some pride.

Dr. Oliveira added, "It is in kits with the antidote in all forms."

"All forms?" said Tank.

"Juice, pills, nasal spray, and more. Of course, we had a police sketch artist quickly concoct simple universal instructions, photocopied and included for whoever came across the airdropped caches," said Dr. Oliveira.

An assistant poked his head into the room and spoke some words in Portuguese.

"It appears the antidote is already working. There is word that the first native that drank it was so relieved to be out of the grip of the juice he cried with joy. Word spread, and they were all in such misery they wanted the antidote and gave up their arms without a shot being fired. Having worked for years in the grip of the drug, he knew the entire network, showing exactly where these additional seven vessels you mentioned are located and even drew a map showing the terminal where the rancid orange juice was delivered from Florida by tanker and the kegs near each drug supply vessel from which the natives were encouraged to drink all the spiked orange juice they wanted. Of course, it had a stimulating effect and caused them to work much faster and to go for days without concern for food or sleep, and many have died as a result.

"Venezuela has already seized the tanker, which apparently had been used to transfer smaller trial batches of the drug into the USA through Florida, for months, under the cover of the orange juice cargo pickups. The other countries have agreed to go to where the natives direct them and seize the vessels. They will airdrop the antidote over the vessels first to neutralize all or most of the resistance. Once they heard that the US government was not a part of this operation, they were happy to participate."

Tank looked up at the map and then smiled and looked over at the Admiral.

"Well, it seems you have done a fantastic job over the hours of my sleep and have had a fair bit of luck on your side, as did I in my efforts," he told the Admiral.

He walked over to the window and gazed out at the pelting rains across the massive expanse of the Amazon.

"What are you rubbing your chin for, Mr. Tank?"

"The resources available to these Islamists are seemingly limitless. Just considering what I am aware of, they are able to exceed the capabilities of a small country. With your daughter's and your own gracious help, it appears we have thwarted the worst of this particular attack before it landed in the US. The chaos currently ongoing will take some years to fully work its way through the system as the administration implements the plan I discussed with the President, but..." Tank trailed off.

"But what, Mr. Tank?" said the Admiral.

"I am very worried that we did not pull out the root," said Tank.

"I am sorry, Mr. Tank—the root?" said the Admiral.

Dr. Oliveira quickly translated into Portuguese for her father.

"I see, you are not comfortable that our Brazilian security forces will find and destroy the main mysterious delivery vehicle you mentioned, the one you say stretches 1500 feet," said the Admiral.

"No disrespect, sir, but no, I am not comfortable at all," said Tank, who roused Bull from his sleep.

They both started walking toward the door to get some fresh air outside on the covered walkways and gather their thoughts.

Tank's mind could not let rest the unknown image of the 1500-foot mystery vessel that the natives would not be able to find, since it was no longer in its jungle base.

CHAPTER FIFTY-SIX

"I forgot to mention, Mr. Tank," said the Admiral, joining them outside.

"I ordered the staff at the Amazon Surveillance System headquarters in Brasilia to be focused on the corridor you mentioned and to tune the sensors to the attributes of this mystery vessel you speak about, and when they ran various scanning parameters of their data through the computers, they found they already have something. Near where you told us the vessel entered the South Atlantic Amazon River estuary, we have many sensors, and they noticed an inexplicable spike in temperature, which simply could not have been due to natural phenomena. Because the temperature spike affected forty sensors, we were able to determine speed and direction. Apparently, they confirmed it was travelling at over four hundred knots and that it arched southward as it emerged from the jungle and neared the South Atlantic."

"How would they determine that?" asked Tank.

"About one kilometer from the ocean, the north side sensors went cold and the south side lit up disproportionately more—that told the technicians that run the operation that the entire vessel passed over the sensors. One more thing: they told me something interesting about the size," said the Admiral, with a smirk. "Five hundred meters."

Tank looked at Bull with a smile and said, "So the great whale lives."

Bull shot back a glance and said with defiance, "Not for long."

CHAPTER FIFTY-SEVEN

"Can you loan me a plane to finish the job?" asked Tank, looking at the Admiral.

The Admiral nodded, and the three of them boarded a Jeep for a quick ride to the airport.

"I am going to let you use the fastest plane we have, with the least entanglements. This is a military jet, but the military has no interest in it anymore because it has been donated to a museum of which I am the director," said the Admiral, pointing toward the new hangar.

"Wow, an Aermacchi. What is it, early sixties?" asked Tank.

"It's an Embraer AT-26 Xavante, our own made in Brazil, license-built version. This one was parked just three years ago, and has been kept in flight-ready status," said the Admiral with pride.

He continued to assure them, "I just had it up a week ago, before the rains. It's in good condition, the tanks are full, and it's got a 1500-kilometer range. The radio is tuned to my headquarters' radio channel where I will be the in-between for any information you may need from the ASS people in Brasilia. Now that we have a confirmed sighting within Brazil, the cat's out of the bag, and I can involve more Brazilian resources. We will be sure to keep you two anonymous, of course."

Tank surveyed the aircraft, a two seat non-afterburner single engine jet trainer good for eight hundred kilometers per hour. He was aware that they performed so well that many countries used them in active combat in a light ground attack role.

He shoved Bull toward the jet impatiently. "Okay, every minute we waste gives us less chance to catch them."

At the touch of a button, the large clear canopy rose to reveal two tandem seats. Tank jumped in the front and Bull squeezed in the rear.

Within minutes, the Bristol Siddeley Viper 9 turbojet was lit and Tank had, as usual, pinned the throttle to the stops. The jet started rolling forward, as the Admiral intercepted an alarmed security guard running toward them. He explained that Tank and Bull were heritage jet aircraft experts who were assisting with the preservation of the jet so that its museum internment would be enhanced.

Tank and Bull were soon pinned to their seats as the jet trainer accelerated down the vacant runway and rose into the sky while rain pelted the canopy.

"What's the plan? Just track him down to confirm it does exist and get a bearing so he's not lost forever?" asked Bull.

"I certainly hope we can do more than that," said Tank.

"How? This thing was a trainer; it has no operational weapons, and we never thought to pick up some armaments from the cache over near Noddins' trailer," said Bull, sounding frustrated.

"I haven't thought that far ahead yet," replied Tank, who was concentrating on mentally triangulating the mystery ship's current direction and speed so that the 1500 kilometers' worth of fuel they had would take them to an intercept point, hundreds of kilometers down the Brazilian coast from where the vessel entered the South Atlantic Ocean.

"Let's catch them first."

The ancient Xavante flew remarkably well, as good as or better than any new similar aircraft Tank had flown. He had the throttle pegged and the jet was absolutely quiet and stable as it swept across the skies at its 800-kilometer-per-hour maximum speed.

"So, what do your calculations tell you?" inquired Bull.

"If he maintains a speed of four hundred kilometers per hour, we will intercept near Natal."

"Great, I've heard lots about the crêpe and shrimp specials. I'm getting hungry already. Those rolls I grabbed from the cart at the Raphael Hotel were stale."

"A day like every other, you mean," came the reply.

"We have alerted the entire coastal and interior patrol forces as to search parameters, and it looks like your target is still heading south at four hundred kilometers per hour. How is the plane performing?" crackled the radio voice of Admiral Oliveira.

Tank picked up the antiquated microphone, and pressed the transmit button.

"Like a dream," he responded. "It looks like we will be able to intercept at Natal. Do you agree?"

"Your calculations are correct, if they maintain current speed and heading. We have dozens of people now on the lookout for the strange craft," said the Admiral. "In fact, we just had a report it's fifty kilometers north of Natal now."

"Roger," replied Tank, who nosed the Xavante into a steep dive, causing both him and Bull to clutch the grab handles as the plane hurtled downward, breaking the speed of sound.

Tank reached across the cockpit and pulled the handle to deploy the single drag brake, which flipped up, and both men immediately felt a pull from the rear.

They glanced down as they descended into the muted sunshine and misty ocean off Natal's coast, and Tank swung the nose north and gunned the throttles toward the mystery vessel. They peered ahead and could see nothing but the mist kicked up from the African winds buffeting the area, looking for all the world like a London fog.

"Do you see that?" asked Tank.

Bull pulled against his harness and looked over Tank's shoulder to see a massive white storm approaching from the north.

Tank saw the storm grow larger within seconds and could just make out the bizarre sight of the nose of the behemoth ekronoplan, which had four sets of twelve giant jet engines apiece, perched up on racks above the top of the fuselage, poking up from within the white storm. It looked like a prehistoric monster of some sort, not an aircraft.

"Only the Ruskies could have developed a tub like that."

Seconds later, the combined 1200-kilometer speeds caused the ekronoplan to blast by in a blur.

Bull said in shock, "I am seeing, but I am not believing what I'm seeing."

"If it was built by men, it can be destroyed by men," replied Tank.

BLACK V

He pulled on the stick and pushed the rudder pedals, and the jet responded with a sharp high-speed turn, almost knocking them out from the g-forces, and soon they were southbound again, hot on the trail of the ekranoplan.

Ahead they could only see a massive white moving mist, as the downward pressure of the ekranoplan's lifting body design forced thousands of gallons of salt water to be compressed into mist and deflected up hundreds of meters, effectively shrouding the vessel behind the moving white mist.

"There's a familiar smell," said Bull.

"Probably fifties era jet engines stolen from a warehouse in Ukraine," said Tank as he pulled back on the stick, and the jet rose to clear the trail of scent from the engines that followed the ekranoplan, mixing with the mist.

Inside, Carlos walked over to the Hussan brothers and said, "It looks like we have somebody who wants to meet us."

He pointed to a large screen which showed the military markings of the Xavante as it loitered above and behind the ekranoplan.

Gran Hussan sneered and said, "How has the military caught on to us? I thought we are invisible to radar."

Carlos barked an order, and within seconds, the camera had panned in for a close-up of Tank and Bull.

"It's not the military," he said, as Tank and the much larger Bull could be seen in the cockpit through the vestiges of white mist.

"Those men again!" came a shout from a side cabin, as two men walked in.

"You recognize them?" asked Gran Hussan.

"Those men have been chasing me for days!"

They realized he was fully capable of killing them and— in the same breath—would be hard to destroy.

The others on the bridge, who were not aware of the details of the long pursuit, were perplexed.

Carlos walked over to Gran and said, "You know them?"

"These are the field biologists from Manaus, you fool!" as he recalled the idiotic assurance Carlos had given him in the lead-up to the launch, that all would be well.

Gran walked over to a side cabinet and pulled out a gun and walked over to Carlos and shot him in the face, sending blood spewing onto the bridge floor.

He motioned to two bridge personnel to remove the body.

"What's that?" said Tank, as he saw what looked like a body tumbling across the back of the ekranoplan.

"Guess he wants more speed and is dumping excess weight," said Bull.

They were chasing a demon-possessed criminal who had left a trail of death and destruction wherever he went and who would return to destroy the United States with absolute assurance and no conscience whatsoever.

"Okay, enough of this follow-the-leader stuff," said Tank with renewed anger.

He pushed the throttles to wide open, and the ancient British engine screamed in protest and thrust the plane alongside the ekranoplan, where it was enshrouded in streams of the white mist blinding Tank and Bull and where violent shocks buffeted the old jet, forcing Tank to peel away and follow several hundred meters to the side.

"Wow, those shocks almost tore off the wings. Must be pockets of compressed air from the underbelly coming up the sides, like sonic grenade explosions. Makes wind shear a walk in the park," he said, referring to the sometimes lethal shocks a smaller plane experiences when approaching an airport behind a larger plane and encountering the compressed wake.

Tank glanced over in the distance and thought he saw the strange, tall manservant standing looking at them through the bridge windows, but it was just a glimpse, and then the white mist closed the opening.

Tank maneuvered, pulled back on the throttle, and allowed the mist-shrouded vessel to pull ahead and then banked over so that he was directly behind, and then he pulled ahead and flew directly over the ekranoplan, lowering the landing gear.

"Without weapons, I guess we have to do this the old-fashioned way," said Tank.

"What does that mean, hand-to-hand combat?" asked Bull.

Suddenly, Tank cut the engine and pushed the control stick forward, nosing the jet directly down to the back of the ekranoplan, between the third and last bank of engines.

Like landing on a high-speed aircraft carrier, the jet touched down and rolled a short distance across the vast back of the ekranoplan facing the wind and came to a stop, with Tank applying the brake.

The wind rushed around the cockpit canopy, buffeting the aircraft as they sat.

"What's the plan?" asked Bull.

"I needed time to think without using up our gas reserves," replied Tank.

"What's there to think about? We have no weapons, and if we blow the canopy, we will be sucked out of the plane, so forget about trying to walk around and cause damage," said Bull.

"I know all that. But I wanted a minute to think about our next move. Done," said Tank.

With that, he opened the self-start duct, and the turbine could be heard spinning from the 400-kilometer-per-hour wind the same as it would, had it stalled when airborne.

Tank pushed open the throttle, and soon the jet lit and the thrust pushed them forward a few feet, and then they lifted off and were once again looking at the mist-shrouded ekranoplan from a distance.

Tank banked the plane over and centered it directly in front of the twelve most forward engines, mounted in a row up on a single pylon over the windows of the bridge.

"What's the idea; do you want us to get sucked in to the engines?" asked Bull with concern.

"Something like that," came the confident reply.

Suddenly the jet surged up and forward as the two wing-mounted drop tanks had been released, sending them down to bounce off of the ekranoplan's massive back and up, to be immediately sucked into the two innermost of the front bank of engines.

The highly explosive fuel vapor in the empty tanks caused a massive explosion, and shrapnel was sucked into the engines on either side of the pylon, which protruded up from the top of the fuselage. The weight of the five engines on each side overstressed the weakened internal bracing, causing both banks of engines to fall down against the top of the bridge. Broken fuel lines erupted into a massive fireball, destroying the remaining engines.

The airborne, flaming debris field from the destruction of the front twelve engines bounced off the fuselage and was in turn sucked into all twelve engines of the second bank, and Tank and Bull watched in awe as the process was repeated with domino precision to wipe out the third and fourth pods.

A huge plume of black smoke trailed the stricken behemoth, which sank down to sea level, surging along the water on the air cushioned between its rubber skirts as it lost speed, sending vast jet streams of water out from the sides.

"Look ahead," said Tank.

Bull craned his neck over and could see the Portuguese-built fifteenth century Three Wise Men Forte looming up in the distance, its fifteen-foot thick stone walls perched on the shifting sands that left it surrounded by water at high tide.

"A high-tech fortress that's stood for centuries. I think the walls of the fort should hold up, don't worry," replied Bull.

On the bridge of the ekranoplan, the Islamic gangsters looked around in stunned disbelief as alarm bells rang and crew members ran around in circles to control the experimental vessel which was still moving at over 250 knots.

It was hopeless, as not a single engine remained, and the only thing that kept them from dying of toxic smoke inhalation was the crisp wind that continued to sweep the smoke away before it could enter the interior air intakes.

They approached at high speed, striking the sharp corners of the Christmas star-shaped walls of the forte, which drove through the aluminum structure of the ekranoplan like a hot knife through butter.

The 1500-foot-long vessel broke apart in a shamble of parts that littered the high tide ocean surrounding the fort.

Crew members who were tossed into the sea alive tried to make it to the shore or the fort, but were attacked and eaten alive by the area's dense population of bull sharks.

The vessel's shroud of mist and the background white mist blown up from the ocean by the strong winds ensured that not one person onshore had seen a thing.

By the time the mist had blown past, the remains of the vessel had already sank into the ocean and disappeared.

Tank dropped the landing gear and pulled up on the stick while gunning the throttle so the jet was riding partially on the thrust of the engine, allowing a slow sixty knot speed, as he and Bull looked down to see the carnage.

"High risk occupation, the drug business is," said Tank.

"When you say you are going to think of something, you aren't kidding, are you?" said Bull.

"It came to me at the last minute," said Tank with a laugh.

The radio squawked, and Tank heard the Admiral say, "Have you found them?"

"Found what?" said Tank into the microphone.

"The UFO, the 1500-foot vessel, whatever you call it—did you catch them?"

"I don't see any 1500-foot vessel, do you?" Tank said to Bull.

"Nope, not a thing," Bull played along.

"Admiral, I guess we must have been imagining things because no 1500-foot vessel exists," said Tank.

"What are you talking about?" squawked a reply.

"We are at the coordinates and can't see a thing," said Tank.

"What do you want us to do to help you?" came the Admiral's reply.

"Nothing. We're tired and hungry for a huge plate of shrimp in hot white cream sauce, wrapped in crêpes, and Natal has such a dish at a lovely spot, as I recall," said Tank.

"Of course, but what about the 1500-foot vessel?"

"Three Wise Men might know more," said Tank, exhausted, and whose memory of the first difficulties with the drone seemed like an eternity ago.

The aged jet had only fumes left in the tanks, and Tank retracted the landing gear and banked over to Natal International Airport.

"Hey, shouldn't you get him to arrange landing clearance for this crate? Remember, it's in full military colors and will cause quite a stir if we land it dressed in Australian outback gear."

"You've got a point," said Tank.

"Even if I tell the Admiral that it would take longer for him to arrange than we have fuel left, and we would still be taken to a holding area, and there would be inevitable press exposure."

"So what does all that mean?" asked Bull.

"It means a Caipirinha at the Lagoon of Artituba," came the reply.

"Gibberish to me," said Bull decidedly.

"And a relaxing place to have a drink for both of us. Don't you think we've earned it?" asked Tank, as he maneuvered the jet slow and low above an area with a thick ring of palm trees surrounding a ten-acre white sand dune with a large lagoon in the center.

With a pop, the engine ran out of fuel, and they could only hear the sound of rushing air, as they descended toward the dune.

Tank expertly controlled the vintage jet and gently sat it down for a belly landing on the soft smooth sand with gear retracted, where it slid to a stop alongside the blue water of the lagoon without so much as a scratch.

He pressed the button and the huge Plexiglas canopy rose, allowing the fresh Natal air in.

"What now?" asked Bull.

"I am going to have a swim in the best freshwater lagoon in the southern hemisphere, then enjoy the best shrimp crêpe entrée money can buy and then drink the most refreshing and powerful drink in the world."

"I thought you don't drink," said Bull, as they pulled themselves out of the cockpit and trudged the short distance to the cool water of the lagoon.

"So did I," said Tank, falling into the cool waters.

CHAPTER FIFTY-EIGHT

Tank arrived in Oakland on a commercial flight on a brisk sunny day and took a cab over to Jack London Square.

He was satisfied. He felt good inside. He had done something significant for people, and the effects were everywhere. The world might someday know of his contribution, but he was hopeful that they never would because he did not want praise or adulation of any kind; in fact, it was against his beliefs.

As the cab approached the harbor, they passed multiple Secret Service checkpoints, finally arriving at the gangplank where he was ushered aboard the newly refurbished and rechristened USS Pontomac.

Admiring the varnished teak and brass of the former high-society boat, he sat down on the 1930s tufted green leather chair in the main salon, the entire boat looking like it had been lost in a time warp.

"Well, it's nice to see you again, this time in person," said the President, walking from the front compartment past a brass lamp toward Tank.

"Yes sir, and it couldn't have been a nicer day," said Tank, as he scanned the San Francisco harbor.

"Well, what did you think of my efforts?" asked the President, who looked tense.

The country was stabilized, and thousands of government employees had been arrested.

The Islamic video made in the Oval Office as well as other electronic communications that had been released, representing the finished product of which Dr. Truetell's presentation was central, was news the world over.

Hundreds of millions had been produced in all formats and all known languages and supplied free around the world. Thousands of information booths with the video's information in various forms had opened across America. They had signs over top proclaiming "Love and Truth" and had attracted small protests, as expected.

It had sparked debate about the accuracy of the content, which could not be assailed. The Muslims were criticizing it, but the world, armed with the truth from the presentation, was refuting those criticisms.

Many Muslims, appalled at the video, were leaving Islam.

The world was pausing, and it looked like politicians that did not agree were dropping in popularity, and the entire world was cheering desperately-needed American moral greatness and leadership.

"I thought the video was excellent. Accurate, while polite and compassionate toward Muslims."

"I am glad you think so; we took great effort to make it inoffensive," said the President.

"Of course, a great many have been offended nonetheless."

"So I've heard," said Tank.

"The world is aflame with Muslims calling for my death. They have activated every tool possible—lawsuits, UN motions, protests in the streets. Talk of the video and me being a bad guy have replaced talk of the Sharia Law attack on the USA. They truly are masters of propaganda–or, in truth, masters of lies. But you know what they say, don't you?" said the President.

"Those who stand silent in the face of evil have let it be known they agree with it. And that is simply not the American way and never was."

An orderly came out with a small tray with sandwiches and coffee.

"And of the other measures I proposed?"

"Commonsensical, no more, no less," said Tank. "Having all potential immigrants screened for application success according to a process now weighted toward common values—that is, that they have sufficient common values of the country they are applying to move to. Having all visitors to the USA from countries with significant Islamic populations undertake much more extensive screening. Having mosques and other Islamic meeting places in the USA suspended from constitutional protections on privacy, to allow monitoring. Having Muslims specify, before entering as visitors or applying to immigrate to the USA, that they disavow the Islamic tenants that promote values contrary to the constitution of the United States.

"You have also disclosed that as part of an extra security ramp up that hopefully will never be needed, you reserve the right to have some of them wear monitoring devices, and have also set aside land for the building of holding camps for some of them, similar to what Australia has been doing with general migrants for years," said Tank.

"But Islam Island doesn't sound like a great place to visit," he added laughingly.

"Islam Island was never our name. That's the name the press has dubbed it," replied the President with a smirk.

"I don't see a problem with any of it. After all, we are at war, as we were with Japan and Germany when their ancestral citizens were put in concentration camps in the USA during World War Two. You've been honest, compassionate, and most importantly, firm," said Tank.

Minutes later, the Potomac's two original Winton Model 6 diesels started, belching black smoke from the center exhaust stack, which disappeared in the breeze. The ropes were cast off, the three brass propellers set in motion, and the vessel eased into the choppy waters of the San Francisco harbor.

Tank watched as two black Secret Service helicopters hovered in the near distance, while four black Secret Service speedboats accompanied them, two hundred meters in front of the bow, and two the same distance hanging off the stern.

The Potomac's sharp bow and narrow hull cut the waves, ensuring a smooth ride, as they cruised north up the coast, enjoying the view from the main salon as they rolled gently to port and starboard.

"I want you to meet a friend," said the President, who stepped aside to allow Captain Manoa to walk past and shake Tank's hand.

"Thank you again for saving my life," said the Captain, a tear in his eye.

"When you requested we protect the Captain, I could think of no finer way. He's familiar with this type of vessel. Can you believe it's the same basic design as the boats plying the

Amazon? And this way I can assign him and his family twenty-four-hour protection," said the President.

"Thanks," said Tank.

Tank looked toward the low hills on the San Francisco shoreline and then windward to the north, where small whitecaps were now forming in the breeze, which was picking up strength.

He peered to the west, which was featureless, and then to the south, with the wind at his back.

Across the south was the foggy mist of a typical sea view on a blustery day.

Captain Manoa came back from the bridge. "Mr. President, I have just been radioed that the weather conditions are deteriorating. We are turning around and heading back to our berth."

"Well, that's a shame," said the President. "I am really enjoying the cruise."

Tank turned around and saw that the two Secret Service speedboats that were in front to the north had swung around and were now in a line with the other two, so that four Secret Service boats now formed a line to the south of the Potomac.

Looking up, he saw that a fixed-wing C-130 gunship had arrived in the airspace and was circling along with the two Secret Service helicopters.

BLACK V

The President and Tank looked up as the Potomac's smokestack belched thick black smoke from the engines being raced at full throttle.

"Wonder what's got them all in a fluster?" the President asked Tank.

"There's some sort of threat, sir. Not sure what," surmised Tank.

Suddenly they heard an ominous roar and looked to the south to see a white squall spread across the horizon.

"Is that a noise I hear?" said the President, pointing to the squall and not able to tell if the noise was from the various aircraft and boats around the Potomac.

The roar became loader, but it was coming from nowhere in particular, and Tank and the President looked on in curiosity.

Suddenly the C-130 banked sharply, and the four turboprop engines could be heard increasing to full throttle.

The plane was racing to the south, toward the white squall.

Seconds later, smoke could be seen coming from the gunship's Gatling guns that hung from the side, and missiles could be seen launching toward the white squall.

Tank raced to the bridge and looked at Captain Manoa. "What is going on?"

"It's a Level 1 threat," said Manoa. "According to the Secret Service procedures, it's the highest threat level."

The roar was growing intense, and Tank looked to the south to see the same massive white squall that he had last seen off the coast of Natal.

The mist was approaching at breakneck speed and would soon be on top of them.

The gunship circled with guns firing, and one secret service helicopter was hovering, allowing the agents to fire their machine guns at the mist.

The four Secret Service speedboats had divided.

One raced to the Potomac to pick up the President and take him to safety, while the other three drove at full speed on a collision course to the white squall in an attempt to slow it down.

Another roar could be heard, this time coming from the north.

Two B-52 Superfortresses from Strategic Air Command had been on patrol only miles away. With target confirmation having been radioed from the C-130 crew, they greenlit the release of two cruise missiles.

After a straight run south for the minimum of two miles required for pre-launch, the missiles were programmed and dropped from the bomb bays, folding out their wings and proceeding at wave top level to the white squall.

The missiles disappeared into the squall, and then there was a massive white explosion followed by a mushroom cloud.

The B-52s flew straight over the Potomac with their eight engines shrieking seemingly a hand's reach away, before simultaneously banking sharply to the north and gaining altitude.

The C-130 emerged out of the mist, barely hanging in the air with two engines knocked out, along with the Secret Service helicopter trailing smoke and making an emergency ditch into the ocean.

Seconds later, the three speedboats came into view, all stalled and sinking.

The Captain came back to the salon. "I have been radioed that the threat level is reduced; whatever was behind that mist has been destroyed."

The President emerged and said, "Mr. Tank, I have been given the all-clear, but there's bound to be hordes of press back at our berth in the harbor. Can we drop you somewhere else?"

Tank glanced south and noticed that a Coast Guard helicopter was arriving to assist the downed Secret Service copter and speedboats. The remaining speedboat would hover near the Potomac for the remainder of the trip.

"Can I borrow one of your lapstrake rowboats?"

Captain Manoa slowed the Potomac.

With the help of two Secret Service agents, they pulled the canvas cover off one of the vintage varnished open lifeboats, and swung the davit so that it hung over the ocean.

Tank stretched across the open water to the boat and braced himself as it was lowered to the water. He reached, uncoupling the hooks from the eyeholes in the bow and stern, and the boat floated free, slowly drifting apart from the Potomac.

The President looked down. "Mr. Tank, can we count on your help again?"

"With a guarantee of anonymity and independence?"

"Of course."

"Anytime," said Tank with a wave and a smile.

Tank untied the long oars and placed them in the open top brass mounts, sitting on the solid teak seat.

He started to row and noticed the boat moved easily, allowing him to make good time.

As he rowed toward land, he saw dozens of boats going in the other direction.

Amidst the activity, none notice or cared about a modest white rowboat going in the opposite direction.

He decided to make land near Fisherman's Wharf, where he could blend into the crowd.

CHAPTER FIFTY-NINE

Bull was sitting back, relaxing in the enclosed aerial tram car, enjoying the spectacular view of Santiago, with his arm around an attractive young woman.

"Sorry for the interruption, Chinchilla," he said with a smile, while stroking her red hair.

"It's okay; you are a big, strong man and have important things to do. My father was a big important man like you—I understand," she replied.

Bull gazed into the distance, reliving the last few days, and a smile broke over his face.

"What are you smiling at, honey?" said Chinchilla. "Are you thinking about past days?"

"No," Bull replied, still smiling, rubbing his hand over his newly installed subcutaneous buzzer. "I am thinking about the days to come."

CHAPTER SIXTY

JANUARY 1944
OVER GERMANY

Hanna Fitch was impressed. She had expected the massive Amerikabomber to be ponderous, but it had accelerated down the runway like the nimble rocket planes she had test flown.

The six Jumo jet engines thrust the plane up from Hermann Goering's Karin Hall effortlessly, and the special rear facing periscope showed nothing but black.

In the distance through the cockpit windows, she could see the glow of fires and explosions as Berlin was being shattered with the bombs of the vast airborne armada of British Handley Page Halifax's dropping their lethal cargo.

Wing Commander Falk scanned his sharp eyes below and could see only black.

Suddenly he noticed something in the corner of his eye.

He squinted and was shocked by the bizarre glimpse of a huge, black, V-shaped craft, without any fuselage or tail, barely visible against the orange glow of the Berlin firestorms below, rising up to the same altitude as the Mustang.

"What the heck," uttered a shocked Falk. "Mustangs, are you seeing this?" his voice crackled over the radio.

In the night sky, shadows and ground glow from the burning buildings and bomb explosions played tricks on the eye, and it was hard to pick out a sleek, black object.

Suddenly, the huge black Horten Amerikabomber rose like a vast shadow to within two hundred feet of the Mustang, pausing briefly at the same altitude and then ascended to above and in front of the Mustangs.

The six Jumo jet engines exhaust outlets glowed like fireballs, and the pilots were initially confused and held their controls, stunned, as their minds raced to comprehend what it was they were seeing.

Within seconds, they got over their astonishment and realized this was a newfangled airplane.

"Attack, attack, let's get him!" shouted Falk over the airwaves.

The seven Mustang pilots pushed their throttles to the firewall and the Allison engines screamed, as they pulled back on the control sticks to gain altitude and take chase of the strange craft, following the bright orange glow of the six jet engines from behind.

"Enemy jet aircraft. Repeat, enemy jet aircraft," replied Falk, explaining the absence of propellers on the mystery craft.

In the span of a few seconds, the huge German aircraft had risen up to the same altitude and then passed them, rocketing ahead. The great Allison engines in the Mustangs had received their orders and were now reaching peak revolutions, stressing their motor mounts as they turned the blades of the propellers, trying to catch the huge, V-shaped aircraft.

"He's pulling ahead," shouted Black Menace, stating the obvious, as it was clear that the distance between the fighters and the Black V was growing greater.

"Drop tanks now!" yelled Falk, directing the pilots to release their long range auxiliary fuel tanks, which were mostly full of vapor now after the long flight from England.

Immediately, each pilot could feel his Mustang surge forward, with the aerodynamic drag and weight now both sharply reduced.

Commander Falk started to feel desperate. "Fire guns, fire guns."

Each Mustang had six machine guns mounted in the wings, and they all shook violently as the tracer bullets left white trails up toward the Amerikabomber.

The hail of thousands of bullets appeared to have no effect.

As they were reaching the 41,900-foot design altitude limit of the Mustang, pulling back on the control stick to raise the front of the aircraft to aim at the target was difficult. The controls were mushy, and the Mustangs threatened to stall or lose lift in the thin, high-altitude air and fall into an uncontrolled spin. Firing the guns had caused a loss of airspeed, and the aircraft fell further behind.

Their bullets were going to waste, having no effect.

"Cease fire, cease fire," Falk shouted over the airwaves.

Hanna Fitch peered through the rear-facing periscope to see the source of the wave of tracer bullets. A few had struck the aircraft, causing no apparent damage. Looking back and down through the periscope at the source of the bullets, she could see they were Mustangs, profiled against the burning Berlin below. Normally the Mustangs would be a formidable foe and could have taken down most planes in the German fleet. But at this altitude, when other aircraft became difficult to control, the Amerikabomber was stable, and she had needed to alter her course only slightly to keep well out of harm's way.

She felt invincible in her advanced German craft and now thought confidently of the American Mustangs as pesky flies and nothing to worry about.

Suddenly the Amerikabomber shuddered and she could hear two muffled explosions. In desperation, while breaking off the attack, Smith had fired six unguided air-to-ground rockets at the giant black Horten.

"Yahoo, pay dirt!" Smith shouted into the microphone to his comrades, as he saw two missiles strike the huge Amerikabomber's engines, one to port and the other to starboard. The massive fireballs caused him to think it was unlikely the plane would survive.

"Boys, she's coming down," Falk shouted, as the nose on his Mustang shuddered and dropped in a full stall.

His mates were all thousands of feet below, looking up through their bulletproof clear bubble canopies at the action far above and saw the two flaming engines at the rear of the giant black wing.

Fitch was alarmed, but not paralyzed with fear, as the cool test pilot's nerves had been groomed over many years and hundreds of flights to be steady in the most difficult situations.

She scanned the instrument panel in the seconds after the explosion, and before she could act, she was amazed to find a display panel had automatically popped up from below and showed the outline of the massive Black V in luminescent green, with two flashing red lights superimposed at the position where the damaged port and starboard engines were located on the plane.

"What's this?" she said to herself, as she noticed the temperature gauges for the engines had climbed off the scale, which she knew meant she had to shut them down.

While simultaneously making corrections to the climb angle to compensate for the reduced power and searching for the fuel shutoff valves, she noticed flashing script on the special panel and was surprised to find it read, "Drop engines now! Pull red handles between seats."

It seemed the wily Horten brothers had her flying an aircraft that gave emergency instructions!

Fitch reached down between the cockpit seats and saw that six big red handles had risen from the floor.

She counted along the row of handles and gave a mighty pull on the proper two.

Immediately, she felt the plane surge as it was relieved of the 5,000-kilogram deadweight of the two lifeless engines.

Looking up, Falk saw the two engines suddenly drop from the plane, while still flaming from the missile explosions and assumed it had been mortally wounded and was disintegrating.

He continued to look up and was astonished to see the plane continue to climb, without any fires on board.

"What in heck?" said Smith. "Are any of you seeing this?" he said to his wingmates.

He heard no reply as one of the jettisoned engines from the massive Horten, tumbling in the night sky, struck his wing just beside the cockpit and severed it, leaving the plane spinning out of control.

Smith awoke from the concussion shock seconds later to find himself still strapped in the cockpit of a shattered wreck, falling down with the shriek of the night air rushing around his head.

He struggled to find the ejection seat lever, but could only feel a mass of tangled wires. His radio was dead, and the g-forces were almost making him unconscious.

His wingmates had been shocked to see the P-51 smashed by the engine but could do little as their Commander was lost, in a flat slow spin, falling toward the earth.

Watching the plane spin downward, with thoughts of better pinpointing landmarks for a rescue by the Allied underground, they allowed their own aircraft to descend dangerously low.

A small secret base, nestled in the forests of Berlin, had ten special BA 349s ready to be launched to protect Karin Hall, which the Mustangs were coming close to.

Sitting in their small planes facing upwards at the base of what looked like a small oil rig, each fighter's pilot was nervous, for good reason.

Expected to black out from the upward launch thrust, they would awaken to regain control of their aircraft as it hurtled upward toward enemy fighters or bombers. Each aircraft was armed with twenty-four unguided air-to-air rockets that would devastate their targets.

Like angry hornets, the BA 349s were launched, and they screamed upwards with rocket power into the night sky.

Two of the pilots failed to regain consciousness and take manual control of the jets, when the rocket launch automatic guidance system disengaged, and they spiraled to their deaths. But the remaining BA 349s flew up and past the Mustangs and then, after their engines cut out, glided down at high speed like hornets unleashing their total of 192 rockets at the hapless squadron, and the Mustangs were blown to tiny pieces, as seen by Commander Falk.

The Black V was flying smoothly, apparently none the worse for wear from all the recent drama.

A bomber that could outrun and outthink a squadron of the Allies' best fighters? she thought, still rather amazed.

She guessed Lieutenant Tank was being realistic when he said she could float down into Bathurst like an angel, Goering could have his artwork loaded, and they could be back in the air within hours.

Another panel silently appeared, this time from above.

The screen glowed with a red luminescence, and she could read, "Automatic pilot, enter destination, desired speed, and altitude."

Fitch easily punched in the coordinates for Bathurst, Gambia and to satisfy the impatience of her passenger, she punched in "maximum" for both speed and altitude.

As the Black V had passed 29,000 feet several minutes ago, she pressed a button and turned a control dial to feed a suitable oxygen mixture to combat the thin air, remembering the warning from the Hortens.

Hanna Fitch was amazed to find that the gigantic V-shaped aircraft was still climbing fast.

Designed for a massive bomb load, but with only Hermann Goering as the cargo, it was already passing 50,000 feet, and this with the loss of the two engines!

She noticed that she was starting to become drowsy and lethargic, as the condensation in the oxygen system began icing up, restricting the flow.

The subzero temperatures were far below that at which the system had been designed. In fact, the system had been cobbled together by the engineers on a test mule back at the aircraft factory, for design and evaluation purposes, when they received a last minute order to install it in the Amerikabomber.

Fitch needed to descend quickly to warmer temperatures for the system to thaw and hopefully stop malfunctioning and to more oxygen-rich atmospheric air so they could breathe without any requirement of the oxygen system in the first place.

Reaching in the direction where the auto pilot control panel came from—above and in front—she groped for a switch or lever to allow it to drop down.

The overhead panel was smoothly finished, and there was no button!

She pounded the panel with her fist, trying to find some form of access, but there was nothing where the automatic pilot system controls had been. She clawed at the oxygen controls, pounding them and trying to adjust them but they were stiff and frozen and would not move. She yanked at the throttles, trying to reduce the full throttle setting, but they couldn't be budged. Pushing the control stick forward, the aircraft reduced its climb slightly, but it took so much effort she soon grew exhausted, and the plane resumed its death ascent.

She was truly scared and frantic for the first time in her life. Her skills were of no value in a robotic aircraft. Her mind raced, as she was desperate to save her own life. Parachutes had not been discussed! If only she had spent a few more minutes talking with the Hortens.

She was growing cold as she saw the altimeter pass 70,000 feet. The heating system was finally unable to keep up, and the inside of the cockpit windows frosted over.

There was now only a trickle of oxygen coming into the cabin, and Hanna Fitch's eyelids grew heavy as she lost her battle to stay conscious.

With the robotic mechanism expertly guiding the aircraft, the foot and hand controls moved silently as the huge Black V aircraft rocketed south across the sky toward Gambia.

When nearing the Equator's warmer tropical temperatures, the frozen oxygen system thawed, but only the portion that served the rear compartment due to the routing of the supply hoses. Fresh oxygen began to flood the rear compartment.

Waking from his initially drugged and later oxygen-deprived slumber, Field Marshal Goering sat for a while, slightly stunned. Goering was growing agitated, as he seemed to be locked in a compartment without means of communicating.

"The head of the Luftwaffe stuck in the back of the latest German advanced aircraft, with no way out! Those Horten brothers will answer for this!" screamed Goering to himself in frustration.

He looked around the compartment.

The Horten brothers, in their zeal to dress the aircraft up with the latest gadgets and features to hopefully get a large production order, had included the provision of a passenger module that was fully self-contained and could be simply fitted into the bomb bay.

This prototype did not have the planned pilot door access to allow movement from the rear capsule to the cockpit, only a lower and upper hatch to the exterior.

"At least it has lights," muttered Goering, puzzled at where the light switch was, or light fixtures themselves for that matter.

The compartment had futuristic ambient lighting, which came from behind smooth ceiling panels.

He reached up to claw at the panel and found it was smooth and without seams.

Looking to the back of the compartment, he noticed a door marked "John" and then looked to the other side of the module and saw his luggage stacked high against the sides.

A smile came across his face. "Now that's a good idea," he said to himself.

He got up and walked back and opened one large suitcase, finding two hundred small vials of morphine and a separate pack of injection needles.

He sat down.

Using techniques he learned in a Geneva hospital in 1924 when introduced to morphine while hospitalized to heal the pain of a police gunshot to the groin suffered during the Beer Hall Putsch, he smoothly set up his dose and stabbed his thigh.

Almost immediately, a warm pleasant feeling spread over his body, and he was now happy despite his circumstances.

He had been a full-blown addict for twenty years, and when he was deprived of his morphine during a spell years after the Putsch, he had become a raving lunatic and had been taken in a straightjacket to an asylum.

The German public never knew the reason for his smiles and jokes, his flamboyant use of dress—which had similarities with the American showman Liberace years later—and his open indulgence in everything his money and power allowed him to obtain, despite the hardship and deprivation of those he lorded over.

Goering slouched and looked around with dazed eyes.

He opened two other suitcases and found the provisions with the iced pack of caviar and other snacks and tore open the package and greedily consumed enough food for several people in less than thirty minutes.

Goering started thinking about the Americabomber.

It was smooth riding and stable, it was warm, and he was impressed with the excellent construction of the plane. Having seen hundreds of different production and prototype aircraft from the various manufacturers during his time in the Red Baron's Flying Circus in 1917 and 1918, and while head of the Luftwaffe over the last eleven years, he had an eye for quality, although Tank did the actual detailed analysis of new designs.

His mind focused back on the present, and he grew frustrated and annoyed by his inability to contact the pilot up in the front.

"I am going to order one hundred of these. It's an excellent plane, but they must install a communication system!"

He smiled, thinking of the lovely Hanna Fitch flying up front. Looking at his watch, he expected they would land soon.

He thought of the rare artwork he was about to see in Gambia, to add to his collection of 1800 stolen pieces which adorned Karin Hall, the giant luxury complex that had been expanded so many times at German government expense that he had lost count.

Purchased as a hunting cabin, it now comprised a vast estate, which included a massive main house and dozens of lesser structures for his protective regiment, and for his amusement, a zoo complete with young tigers and other rare species and a massive electric train covering the entire attic.

Reaching over to sweep aside the empty containers of caviar that littered the floor, to clear space so he could have a nap, Goering's hand felt a soft spot on a side panel.

"What's this?" he said and tore the soft fabric liner back to reveal a detailed control panel complete with instructions.

In the rush to deliver the Amerikabomber prototype, somebody had not noticed that the soft felt interior liner, left to prevent damage, had not been removed, leaving no sign that the hard metal instruction and control panel was underneath.

"What have those Hortens got here?" he said, as he saw the independent temperature controls, gauges, and instructions about the medical kit and a survival kit with maps and compass.

He noticed the altitude: 70,000 feet.

"My God, with this machine we can win the war!" said Goering, still high on morphine but with enough years of aircraft experience to realize that the aircraft was game-changing.

~~Goering noticed a section that had a radio microp~~hone and volume settings for communication with the pilot.

With many years of flying experience, he fumbled with the simple control and asked, "Frau Fitch, when are we landing?" and paused for a reply.

He repeated the question, fiddling with the radio controls and adjusting his headset.

"Hello, hello, is a ghost flying this plane?" asked Goering, who was becoming concerned.

"Answer immediately; this is Reichsmarschall Goering. Why is your altitude excessive!" he demanded, and there was still no reply.

In his intoxicated state, Goering became confused and scared.

No pilot answering. Stuck in a compartment in a prototype plane over Lord knows what territory?

Goering's eyes looked over the control panel, and he noticed the words, "Capsule Ejection," with a nearby red handle.

He leaned over and could see tiny engraved pictographs showing the compartment he was in, as seen from the outside. It looked like it would become detached, the next picture showing parachutes deploying. The last picture showed inflatable pontoons supporting the capsule in the water.

"Is any of this stuff hooked up?" he said to himself.

As the control panel was hidden, it could mean it may have been hidden intentionally and was not actually hooked up and therefore not functional.

"Will I be dropped like a bomb?" Goering wondered, amused at the idea of his bulk being a bomb and landing and crushing enemies, like in a cartoon.

With childlike puzzlement, and without realizing the full potential impact of his actions, Goering pulled lightly to test the resistance of the red handle.

Suddenly he was thrown violently to the ceiling, as the entire metal compartment dropped from the aircraft like a huge bomb.

The Black V, free of thousands of pounds of weight, lunged upward and surged even faster on its robotic mission.

Without the sound of the jet engines, there was just the sound of the air rushing around the capsule as it plummeted.

Amazingly, it was stable as it plunged.

As he gathered himself, Goering felt blood running across his face from a cut on his scalp from striking the ceiling, and he crawled with difficulty over to the control panel.

He noticed two red lights blinking but could not hold steady enough to read them.

One read, "Automatic Parachute Deployment," and the other: "Automatic Rescue Beacon."

Seconds later, Goering felt a large jerk as parachutes were deployed by battery-powered altitude sensors controlling electric servos, and the entire capsule was now suspended beneath three large white parachutes.

After a long interval, he felt the hiss of compressed gas as the inflatable flotation pontoons were automatically activated and burst free of their protective covers and swelled on each side of the bottom of the capsule.

More time passed, and then there was a violent crash as the capsule landed in the South Atlantic Ocean, followed by the sound of waves splashing up against its sides.

He reached up, grasping the aluminum ladder, and turned a wheel beneath the hatch. He opened it and pushed and squeezed himself up to arise from the hatch.

Finally, he squeezed through and scanned the surrounding seas, which were gentle, and he felt the capsule rise and fall with the ocean swells. The air was warm and sweet and the morning sky was clear.

He glanced up, as he recalled the drama of his escape from the Black V and thought of the pilot, Hanna Fitch.

Would she realize he was gone and swoop down to confirm his location and dispatch for his rescue?

He squinted and thought he saw a faint condensation trail high in the sky.

He wasn't sure how long ago he had ejected from the plane, and with the rise and fall of the capsule in the swells, it was an effort to focus up into the sky, and he soon lost interest in the whereabouts of the plane.

Goering slumped on the capsule's top with his arms holding him up and scanned the sea.

The morphine was wearing off, and as his mind cleared, he was starting to feel insecure about his predicament.

He knew nothing about seafaring and had no idea where he was, which way the winds or currents would take the capsule, or whether any marine or aircraft traffic was in the area.

For that matter, he thought, as he glanced down at the inflated pontoons, he had no idea whether the capsule would float for any length of time.

The thought of spending his last minutes trying to avoid drowning, or being eaten by sharks, was not appealing to Germany's aristocratic second-in-command.

After a short time, he was surprised to see a large white froth on the surface fifty meters away, and was expecting a giant whale or other sea creature to appear but soon saw the gray shape of a submarine and was relieved that it was German.

Goering's normal confidence started to return.

He waved his arms in impatience as he saw the submarine crew fumble with a black inflatable boat with a gas outboard motor, commonly used for nighttime spy deliveries on enemy coasts, which began making their way toward the floating capsule.

Within minutes, they bumped up against the metallic capsule's soft rubber pontoons, and, using a tossed rope and three pointed blunt grapple hook to the capsule's exterior grab handles, a seaman shimmied up to the Field Marshal.

Hundreds of kilometers from shore and bobbing in the remote South Atlantic, they expected an appreciative greeting from the Field Marshal, who instead exclaimed, "Okay, you idiots, don't drown me, or the Führer will be upset and deal with you accordingly. Don't forget to grab my luggage inside," said Goering, using his reliable methods of threats and fear to get the results he wanted.

He was pulled up to his feet, still only in his silk shorts.

Three men worked to place a rope around Goering, and they lowered him to the capsule's pontoons and then transferred him over to their small black pitching inflatable boat.

Goering rolled over the soft sides and nearly swamped the boat.

Within minutes, they had lowered his clothes and luggage, and the outboard motor wailed at full throttle as the tiny boat made its way over to the U-boat, which waited in the swells with its conning tower gently swaying from side to side.

Goering was hoisted aboard to the sub's open deck with the help of several crew and greeted the Captain at the base of the conning tower with a question, "How did you find me so fast? Is Donitz getting more money for technology in his toy boats than I am in the Luftwaffe?"

Goering pulled on his pale blue uniform, helped by two crewmen.

Intimidated and embarrassed at the same time, the young Captain saluted with a "Heil Hitler," which Goering did not return or even acknowledge.

"We are at sea, Captain, what is your answer?" said Goering, who never considered the childlike salutes applicable to him but only to the low-level zombies in the Nazi party who had no brain of their own.

"Field Marshal, we were advised by the Goliath transmitter at Sub main dispatch," he explained. "They gave us your expected landing coordinates by Enigma Code, and our own radio picked up the message. Apparently that capsule has a very sophisticated rescue beacon, and you must have been flying at an extremely high altitude to account for the clear signal reception and long drop time."

"Those coordinates would not allow you to get that close. You surfaced almost right under me—explain," insisted

Goering, recalling his pilot navigation training from his WWI experience.

"Field Marshal, we were actually fifty kilometers away when we first received the rescue directives, but since we could only see a maximum of eight kilometers before the horizon starts to drop from view if standing on the conning tower platform, we decided to deploy our FA 330 Water Wagtail," he said, referring to the observation platform many subs were newly equipped with.

"With the pilot four hundred feet up in the auto gyro being towed by the sub with the cable at fifteen knots, he could see forty kilometers and spotted the capsule's three billowing white parachutes high in the sky, after only minutes of searching, communicating with us by radio, and reporting your distance and direction with his range finder.

"We cranked him down, put the Wagtail away, and then submerged to proceed at flank speed, finally pinpointing you by periscope. It's fortunate you came down well south of Bathurst, as you know it is the African cross-Atlantic air shipment point for the Allied planes and materials coming over from the seaplane base at Natal, Brazil. If you had landed in that area, we would probably already be under attack now," said the Captain.

"I guess Donitz has been receiving more than his share for training and technology," said Goering, who instantly interpreted the efficiency and professionalism as a threat and felt jealousy of his colleague U-Boat Commander Donitz.

Compliments and thanks were out of the question.

"How do you propose to get me back to Germany?" asked Goering, who had lost interest in his art acquisition prospects after his near-death experience and wanted to return to the comforts of his Karin Hall.

"Field Marshal, I have already contacted a Milch Cow Submarine Sea Plane Tender in this region. They will have a seaplane land on the water near us and pick you up soon, for an immediate flight to Germany," said the Captain.

"Okay then, show me to your cabin. I need to rest, and by the way, have your cook prepare me the best fare you can muster and send four portions to my cabin, along with your finest spirits," said Goering. "And have my bags brought immediately. And I almost forgot, sink that capsule!"

The crewman manning the machine guns on the conning tower saw the Captain look at them and nod, and they punched fifty rounds in the capsule along the water line.

The air from the pontoons hissed, and the holes in the capsule allowed the water to fill the insides, and it quickly sank, taking the three parachutes laying on the surface along with it.

As he followed the Captain up the conning tower ladder, Goering was pleased.

He would soon have some hot food and an injection of morphine and would be on his way back to Germany.

There would be no sightings of him in Gambia or reports of any kind finding their way back to Germany.

As he started to lower himself down the conning tower hatch, which thankfully was sized amply enough to allow his passage, he suddenly remembered the drama of less than two hours ago and looked up, scanning the sky, but the Black V was nowhere to be seen.

He paused and then proceeded down the ladder.

Hours later, a three-engine Blohm and Voss BV 138 flying boat landed, having homed in on the location of the sub floating on the surface by using its FUG 200 Hohentwiel Radar, and the Field Marshal and his luggage were loaded and soon he was in the air.

With diesel engines, the plane had extended range between refueling and could always use fuel scavenged from diesel boats encountered on the way if needed, and with three manned turrets with heavy machine guns, it could protect itself to a reasonable degree if they had Allied encounters.

"Why was I not picked up in a BV Ha 139?" Goering had asked, referring to the largest and most comfortable four-engine German seaplane, which had been in long distance service since the 1930s.

"Field Marshal, all BV Ha 139s were transferred from the South Atlantic mail run to the Baltic for mine sweeping," replied the Captain.

"Who ordered them to the Baltic?" demanded Goering.

"You did, Field Marshal," replied the Captain.

Goering offered no disagreement.

The flight home took three days, as the BV 138 flew at a fraction of the Black V's speed and also had far less range.

First they crossed the coast in front of Bathurst at wavetop altitude to avoid enemy planes, and then for most of the remainder flew at only a 200-foot altitude one hundred kilometers out from the coast.

Twice, they landed and were refueled by submarines that formed part of their emergency support arranged by Enigma coded transmission for the journey home.

Goering coped with the cramped and uncomfortable conditions by giving himself regular injections of morphine and sleeping for most of the journey.

For days and weeks after his arrival back in Germany, Goering expected to hear from Hanna Fitch and to find out what happened to the great Black V, if only to quell the protests of Walter and Reimer Horten and Fitch's family.

There had been no information of her or the aircraft's whereabouts from Gambia, or any other countries in Africa, or the world for that matter.

His recollection of the trip eventually became similar to recollecting a dream or drunken escapade.

From time to time, in the months after, Goering would be asked what happened to the Amerikabomber prototype, and he would always give the same answer: that the plane had developed mechanical difficulties, that he had tried valiantly to save Hanna Fitch at great danger to himself, that he had heroically parachuted out and landed in the sea, and that the plane must have crashed shortly afterward.

In the chaos of Germany near war's end, there were hundreds of planes that were lost and there was no time or interest to question or doubt Goering's story.

The people involved and the memories with them were lost to the sands of time.

BLACK V

JANUARY 1944
RURAL SPAIN

The Islamic soldiers thought they would be killed instantly but were surprised to see a black SS train surge out from behind a small forest, which had been the pilot's targets all along.

Almost immediately, the bullets exploded the locomotive's steam boiler, collapsing it in a shambles of wreckage on the tracks, being pushed along by the passenger car's momentum.

The P-38's twin engines shrieked, as the Forked Devils—as the Nazis called them—banked for another pass, this time concentrating on the passenger cars, ripping them to pieces.

The two pilots surveyed the smoldering train and flew off to find more targets of convenience.

Approaching from the nearby hill, the two Islamic soldiers decided to search the silent wreckage for food or whatever valuables they could carry.

After filling their sacks with food and water, they stripped off the watches and wallets of the twelve dead civilian passengers and were about to depart.

Across in a nearby field was an object reflecting the sunlight.

One of the soldiers walked over and glanced down.

A polished, locked briefcase lay in the grass, having been flung out of the train by the explosion. He smashed it open with a piece of steel from the wreckage.

Inside were hundreds of pages of detailed numbers and words, written in sequences, all on the highest quality paper, bound in sections.

These papers were obviously very important, although he had no idea what they could be.

"Who were the passengers? They must have been important, but certainly not military people. Perhaps scientists. Perhaps the papers were instructions to make a bomb," he wondered aloud.

He removed all the papers and stuffed them inside his tunic.

He would give them to his Imam back in his Islamic homeland; he would know what they were and what to do with them…

CHAPTER SIXTY-ONE

Tank tied the rowboat to the dock and melted into the crowds on Fisherman's Wharf, smelling the popcorn and seafood, comfortable that the Potomac's tender would be returned since the name was right on the stern.

Walking away from the crowds, Tank watched the numbers on the buildings and approached an old three rise, dating from just after the Second World War.

He pressed #9 on the entrance buzzer panel.

"Come on up, Mr. Tank," said a raspy voice.

Tank heard the buzzer indicate that the door could be pushed open and, smelling the musky aroma of an old wood residential building, bypassed the elevator that looked like it was installed later, and strode across the small foyer over to the staircase and seconds later was walking down the third floor hallway, hearing the creaks and snaps of the aged floor under his weight.

He knocked on the door.

"Come in," came the voice from behind.

Tank slowly opened the door and walked into a room that looked like a museum, filled with old black-and-white photos, many showing a dashing figure standing next to a plane.

One picture in particular caught Tank's attention, the biggest one.

"That was my favorite plane," said the voice.

"How did you know it was me at the door?" asked Tank.

"Well, when you get to be my age, you have few visitors. I kind of guessed it would be you."

"Nice to meet you," said the old man, who was wheelchair-bound and had a blanket over his lap, and stretched out a gnarled hand to clench Tank's.

"You said in the letter that you had a secret I would want to know about?"

"I think so. You know, even with the Veterans Department at my side, it was tough as nails to track you down. Nobody knew who you were. The Brazilians were no help. Finally, I took a wild guess and simply sent a letter to the President personally, who, bless his soul, took pity on me and got the letter to you somehow. No press clipping, worldwide, even mentioned you by name, only saying that witnesses called you the stranger who was involved, along with a big friend."

"Well, here I am. Can you tell me the secret?" asked Tank.

"I just wanted you to know that the plane you stumbled across in the jungle was there because of me."

"How so?" said Tank, intrigued.

"In the last weeks of the war, I was in a Mustang and shot out two engines from that thing. We must have distracted the pilot, and the two engines she dropped allowed the plane to be light enough to reach Brazil."

Tank sat, stunned.

"The whole squadron was lost. Except me, that is," the old man said with a smile.

"I survived in a German hospital with advanced equipment that saved my life. After the war, I married one of the lovely nurses and had a good life, despite not being able to walk. I have three daughters, two that live close by, and my wife passed just last year. The other daughter spent her life as a nurse and missionary's wife in Pakistan and returned not long ago to Washington. I think her last letter says she will be free of a few things soon, and she is coming to see me."

"Captain Falk, your efforts to combat the Nazis in 1944 helped defeat the enemies of America and the west today," said Tank, slightly stunned at his own words.

"In a strange roundabout way, I feel proud of that. My injuries were not for nothing. Nobody believed me when I talked about shooting that thing; it sounded too far out, and it has frustrated me to no end all my life," said Falk.

With long-open wounds finally healed and a heart at peace, Captain Falk stared out the window to the restored gray WWII Liberty Ship moored nearby, the beginning of a tear forming in his eye, as he thought of his lost mates.

Tank scanned the walls and tables, to a picture of the lost squadron, together in front of a Mustang, taken only days before the fateful mission over Berlin that helped result in the successful defeat of an attack on the west, eighty years later.

He sat on the aged couch and watched dust swirl into the sun coming through the window.

"How about you let me buy you dinner?" asked Tank.

"What are we having?" asked the old man, who normally ate the usual shut-in fare delivered by a local charity group.

"I noticed a British fish and chips shack around the corner," said Tank.

"I haven't had fish and chips since the war," said the old man with a scowl.

"Why?" asked Tank.

"That was the last meal I ate with my mates," answered the old man.

"But…" he replied, pausing, "I guess I have mourned them enough. Today I celebrate, for them and for me."

"Good," said Tank. "I love the way the Brits do fish and chips; there's none better."

He helped the old man put on his jacket and shoes and then rolled the wheelchair to the elevator and out to the sidewalk and over to the fish and chips shack.

Seated behind a raised glass windbreak and under a heater, they each had their fill of the fine battered cod, and Tank listened to stories about the war, about the effort, and about the sacrifice and loss.

He pondered how the defeat of the Nazis and the Cold War, while essential, had distracted the world from the real enemy, who was gaining ground each day and had declared war on the West too many times to count, for hundreds of years.

The Internet was rife with the butchery of rampant Muslims across the world.

Villages invaded, with little girls helplessly raped or killed right in front of their families. Hundreds of corpses being found with their heads cut off, sometimes with videos left behind of the act taking place with a blunt hand knife and the screaming victims struggling to survive. The lies and subterfuge and open declarations of intentions to convert the West to Islam.

"I pity you," said Captain Falk, who seemed to be reading Tank's mind.

"What?" said Tank.

"I read the news. One daughter works in the State Department and the other was a missionary. I know what you are up against, young fella."

"But World War Two…"

"Was tough. But compared to fighting a world of Islamists, whose holy book commands them to lie to you and to kill you…" said Falk, shaking his head.

"A friend of mine was just telling me the same thing."

"What does he do?" asked Falk.

"He's in mail delivery," said Tank, looking across the busy harbor to several Secret Service helicopters and boats near the tied-up Pontomac.

CHAPTER SIXTY-TWO

In a private room in the post-intensive care recovery ward of Washington's Memorial Hospital, a young woman was quietly reading a book.

The warm yellow glow of the sun shone in through the parted blinds, landing on the blanket that rested across her legs.

Tears were streaming down her face, and sobbing waves of grief came to the surface as they had over the last few days.

The electronic monitor started softly beeping, indicating the rubber medication bag had emptied the intravenous dose into her veins.

A tall, noble, gray-haired nurse entered the room and walked over with a replacement bag and reset the monitor.

"How are we doing?" asked the nurse in a soft, kind voice. She had been coming in to check on the patient from time to time.

"I am having difficulty adjusting to how you are treating me," said the young woman weakly.

"What do you mean, dear?" asked the nurse.

"You are treating me with more love than I have ever experienced in my entire life," said the woman.

"You deserve it, dear."

"I am still not clear…" said the young woman.

"When the paramedics arrived, they had difficulty finding your pulse because you had lost so much blood. They came within a whisker of losing you.

"But when we discovered your extensive scar tissue of healed past wounds, of a type typical of spousal abuse, and after investigating the home security system video records that indicated your husband fled after almost killing you, the story spread, and this entire hospital cares about you. Not only now, but your future too," said the soft-spoken nurse with a warm smile, taking her hand.

"I am sure my husband was only doing what was best for me…those injuries were my fault…I know of other girls with far worse, or even…" said the young woman.

The nurse paused, reflecting on the file she had read, dating back to when the young woman was a teenager.

Married off at twelve years old. Brother trained to hate from the age of seven, later dying as a suicide bomber. An old Saudi

Arabian, good friends of the nurse, had been invaluable in the investigation.

"Even death. Don't worry, I know. None of what has happened to you is your fault. What happened to you was the fault of others," said the nurse with some authority.

"But they were following the will of Allah, through his last prophet Muhammad," said the young woman, with a confused look on her face.

The woman pulled open her white tunic to reveal a cross.

"What do you think of the book?" asked the nurse.

"These people, I have experienced the same things they have."

"That's because that is a book full of the personal stories of Muslims who have converted to Christianity," said the nurse.

"Leaving Islam is punishable by death where I come from. I can't stop crying… Why am I crying?"

"Because the Lord is letting the years of hardship out and melting your heart with His truth."

"How do you know about such things?"

"I have been leading Muslims to Jesus Christ for forty years, my dear. I thought I was done after leaving Pakistan when my poor pastor husband's heart finally gave out from decades of harassment. Pakistan is a place where there are many misguided people being effected by evil. But the Lord had other ideas for me," said the nurse with a soft smile and love in her voice, as she reached over and brushed the girl's hair from her face.

"Why?" asked the girl.

"Because my God teaches me to love everybody, and the least more than the most. I love Muslims, and this is my calling. At least, that's what the hospital staff say," said the nurse, with a smile.

"Your calling?" said the girl.

"This is what I believe God intends for me to do with my life, or what remains of it," said the old woman, self-consciously moving her hand over her gray hair.

"There are others like me?" she asked.

"More than I can keep up with, at my age," said the nurse, with a nodding sigh.

"What will happen to me?" asked the girl.

"Oh, don't worry; your husband's schemes won't affect you. In fact, he's wanted for attempted murder, but it's like he's dropped off the face of the earth. They haven't a clue where he is, or your brother and his wife for that matter. All the money and properties and businesses have either disappeared or been seized by the government," said the nurse.

"My family in Saudi are all dead, and I have nothing."

"Fortunately, a good friend of yours will help out and has offered a place to stay, and, if you choose, you may even be able to help her in her work. If that is your choice."

"My choice?" asked the girl.

"I will get you more books written from experts in history and other topics, and you can talk to experts I know personally too. It's your choice what you decide," said the nurse.

"What should I choose?" asked the girl, who was fatigued and starting to close her eyes.

"Love and truth are always a good choice," replied the nurse, seeing that the girl was starting to nod off.

The nurse glanced up to see that there was still plenty of medication in the drip bag.

She rose wearily from the bedside and walked quietly from the room to the nurse's station, where she leaned over a counter and picked up a file, opening it and making an entry for the time and day.

Under "Progress," she jotted down, "Healing, and moving in the right direction."

Then, with a smile, she placed Sasha Hussan's file back on the counter and started walking in the direction of another patient the hospital had asked her to visit.

END

Coming Soon
KURT TANK SERIES II: Blood Fog

BRIAN ANDERSON, a descendant of Robinson Crusoe (Lord Alexander Selkirk), was ambitious from an early age with the largest paper route in Canada, which broke his bike in half.

After completing studies at the British Columbia Institute of Technology, Anderson founded a private corporation. With his innovations winning support from the prestigious National Research Council of Canada, Anderson built a new laboratory, and as Research Director, led a four-member team of PhDs to develop the world's leading product in its category, unique in all the world.

Today, Anderson chronicles the tales of his friend, Kurt Tank.

Made in the USA
Columbia, SC
27 August 2018